SHE IS LYING

ALSO BY CAROLINE CORCORAN

Through The Wall

The Baby Group

Five Days Missing

What Happened On Floor 34?

Tiny Daggers

The Next Woman

PRAISE FOR CAROLINE CORCORAN

'Razor-sharp writing and deliciously dark humour, Caroline Corcoran is my go-to author for psychological suspense.'

–Andrea Mara

'Perfect for fans of Lucy Foley – this twist-filled mystery brims with electrifying suspense, unforgettable characters, and a finale you'll never see coming.'

–John Marrs

'Hugely original and gripping.'

–Claire McGowan

'Utterly addictive – a tense and clever tale that had me racing through the pages.'

–Claire Ackroyd

'I devoured this original, twisty thriller in a day; tense and atmospheric with an unguessable conclusion!'

–Jackie Kabler

'Twisty and gripping, this original and tense mystery will keep you guessing right up to the end!'

–Jo Cunningham

'A twisty, compelling and fast-paced thriller that plays out on a wild, sun-soaked island. This one will have you gasping.'

–Lucy Roth

'So elegant and addictive. Beautifully written, completely compelling and I could not stop guessing. The twists took my breath away!'

–Daisy Buchanan

'*Tiny Daggers* is a twisty delight.'

–Alex Michaelides

'An absolutely essential book for everyone's summer reading list.'

–Katy Brent

'I loved this smart, glamorous, dark tale of toxic friendship, marred pasts, terrible choices, and nasty outcomes.'

–Niki Mackay

'I loved it . . . I didn't see the twists! It's brilliant.'

–Ruth Kelly

'*Tiny Daggers* is the perfect combo of holiday read and twisting thriller . . . Channelling some of the best female-led thrillers ever written, just when you think you've got the story figured, it totally blindsides you. Then does it again . . . '

–Francesca Brown, Books Editor at *Stylist*

'Caroline Corcoran's workplace thriller has more twists than a forkful of spaghetti!'

–*Fabulous magazine*

'A propulsive thriller.'

–*Stylist*

'Just when you think you know everything, it surprises you again. A cracking thriller!'

–Emma Curtis

'*What Happened On Floor 34?* blew me away. The perfect setting . . . brilliant pacing . . . and JAW-DROPPING twists! I wish I could read it for the first time again.'

–Nicola Rayner

'Gripping, dark and deliciously twisty, I was hooked!'

–Zoe Folbigg

'A twisty and claustrophobic story with characters you empathise with but can't quite trust. Trying to work out who was telling the truth in this heart-wrenching story kept me turning the pages – I loved it!'

–Mandy Byatt

'Thrilling, gripping and unputdownable.'

–Rachel McLean

'Such a pacey, absorbing read – with living, breathing characters and an amazing twist.'

–Rebecca Ley

'Atmospheric.'

–*Good Housekeeping*

'With its steady beat of tension, perfectly judged portrayal of the maternal guilt and the familiar sense of dread women tend to live with, this kept me turning pages throughout.'

–Harriet Walker

'Fast-paced, twisty and moving.'

–Vikki Patis

'A thought-provoking and utterly gripping story.'

–Nicola Rayner

'A fiendishly addictive read that you won't be able to put down.'

–*Heat*

'We couldn't put this thriller down.'

–*Bella*

'*The Baby Group* is one of the most gripping, mind-bending books I've read in years.'

–Lucy Vine

'[A] successful foray into *Girl on the Train* territory, replete with jealousy, stalking, gaslighting and control-freakery.'

–*The Guardian*

'A deliciously twisted thriller.'

–*Red*

'Some thrillers peter out, but this atmospheric read really ramps up the pace as it nears its chilling end.'

–*Good Housekeeping*

'Corcoran maintains suspense throughout and is brave enough not to opt for a fairytale ending.'

–*Daily Mail*

'A well-paced, insightful but ultimately twisted look at modern life.'

–*The Sun*

'The narrative flows effortlessly as the tension ramps up.'

–*My Weekly*

SHE IS LYING

CAROLINE CORCORAN

THOMAS & MERCER

This is a work of fiction. Names, characters, organizations, places, events, and incidents are either products of the author's imagination or are used fictitiously. Any resemblance to actual persons, living or dead, or actual events is purely coincidental.

Published by Thomas & Mercer, Seattle

www.apub.com

EU product safety contact:
Amazon Media EU S. à r.l.
38, avenue John F. Kennedy, L-1855 Luxembourg
amazonpublishing-gpsr@amazon.com

ISBN-13: 9781662528224
eISBN: 9781662528217

Cover design by Lewis Csizmazia
Cover image: © Pete Stuart © Olya94 © needmoremars © jean morrison © tbutron / Shutterstock; © Yolande de Kort / ArcAngel Images

To my sister

PROLOGUE

SAINT AURÉLIE, THE CARIBBEAN

In a few minutes, Junie Winter's idyll will become a horror movie.

It will start with an emergency.

Junie will know there's an emergency before anyone tells her there's an emergency because emergencies are like that. They scent the air. Sprawl themselves all over bodies and foreheads and the pitch of a voice. Etch themselves across the scene.

Right now, though, Junie is still in the dark, her final few seconds of ignorance spent lying on her front, dusty sand on damp skin, on Saint Aurélie's Parrot Island.

Parrot Island is not actually an island. It hasn't been since the seventies, when it was attached to the rest of Saint Aurélie by a man-made causeway. It's just a beach now.

Just a beach. No, that doesn't cut it.

Junie has been to quieter coves on this trip; less touristy beaches surrounded by lush greenery where you can see out as far as Martinique. But they came here for the reef. For the snorkelling.

Junie has been desperate to snorkel around that reef, teeming with its underwater marine life, since the start of the holiday.

A snorkel lies next to her right arm, discarded on her sunbed which is tucked under a large umbrella. Moments earlier, she had done it. She had been underwater in the warm bath of the Caribbean Sea grinning like a loon because she'd just swum past a starfish. Something that looked like Dory.

'Nine across,' she mutters to herself now, lying on her front with her feet up in the air, sand sticking to pale forearms and still on a high. 'Bloodiest battle of the American Civil War, ten letters.'

She bats away a mosquito. Her slim ankles are already 90 per cent bite.

'Gettysburg.' She answers herself and scratches her right ankle. Damn, it got her.

Then she sprawls over towards her black rucksack, grabs her phone out of it and squints. Bloody things. You can't see a word on them in this sunlight and yet almost everyone on this beach is trying, squinting closely at their devices, twisting and turning them, this way and that.

She even saw a baby earlier, lying on its side wrapped in a towel, squinting at Peppa Pig. Zombie bloody nation. Give her a puzzle book any day.

'Still no reply,' she says to her sister Ruby, who is on the sunbed next to her, as she finally tilts her phone into a position where the words are visible.

'Mmm,' Ruby says, eyes closed, as she digs her AirPods out and pops them in her ears. Junie would describe Ruby's ears in the brutal way only sisters can get away with, as belonging to a tiny elf. One of the only major differences between their three appearances.

Three lots of long, dark-blonde hair.

Three sets of spindly limbs.

Three tall women.

But the elf ears . . . the elf ears belong only to Ruby.

She's more toned than her sisters too, never going a day without running at least a 5K, whatever the skies are doing. Which is particularly impressive since they live in Scotland. The skies do a lot of things.

Junie tries their youngest sister, Poppy, again. As she waits for the call to connect, she stares into the distance at the deep V between Grand Simon and Petit Simon. The mountains were declared a UNESCO World Heritage Site a decade earlier. Another thing on the list of must-dos this holiday; Ruby is planning to run up and down them both in one go (Junie would argue that Ruby is insane).

'Still straight to voicemail,' she says, but her insane sister is closed off. Eyes shut, ears plugged.

Junie can tell that she's back in the world of the true crime podcast she's been consumed by for the last few days. Ruby and her true crime, honestly.

They've been on the island for ten days now. The three sisters, Ruby's fiancé Emlyn, their dad and his girlfriend Robin. All under the same roof in their holiday villa. Space was overdue.

Junie spent yesterday at the Saint Aurélie museum, learning about the island's indigenous history and the colonial conflicts. In her history-buff element and thinking about how the whole thing could inspire a play when she gets back home. Junie is an actor; she sees most things in life through a 'how would this work in the theatre' lens. Has wanted to try her hand at writing for a while.

While Junie was at the museum, Ruby and Emlyn went to the island's drive-in volcano and mud baths. Afterwards, they stayed at The Pike, the fanciest hotel on the island, lauded for its architecture – it had no fourth wall, so you can see across the Caribbean. It was a treat, booked for Emlyn's thirtieth birthday.

Then, this morning, Emlyn had dropped Ruby off to meet her sisters while he went to hike a nature trail on the other side of the island. Emlyn is not a fan of an afternoon's sunbathing. Or of Poppy. The feeling is mutual.

Ruby hasn't said much about it but it looks like they had a good time at The Pike: she turned up looking horrendously hungover. Junie glances to her right. God, she still does.

Junie puts her phone back into her bag. Where *is* Poppy? She wants to tell her about the snorkelling.

They had this meeting spot arranged by the lifeguard stand. Poppy had wanted to stay behind yesterday to finish the chapter she was working on, but she was definite about joining them to snorkel. Now though, here they are. Two hours after she'd said she would meet them. No message. No call.

Then again, is Junie surprised? Poppy's probably gone on an impromptu trip to an uninhabited island. Decided to swim naked with some dolphins. Trek to some distant part of the rainforest and wild camp, foraging for all her meals for a few days.

Poppy is . . . well, she's erratic. She has a habit of disappearing; going off-radar and finding some random project to throw herself into. It's one of the things that Emlyn – a man who likes control and order and sensible choices – finds irritating about her. It's also one of the reasons she finds him the most tedious man alive.

A beachball lands next to Junie's shin and she sits up, launches it into the air and volleys it back to the teenage girls who are playing in neon bikinis in the shallows.

'Thank you!' one of them yells, and Junie gives her a thumbs up. Props herself on her elbows and watches their game for a minute or two. While she's up, she checks her phone again.

'Huh,' she mutters with a frown even though Ruby is still lost to her, still not responding.

There *is* a message from Poppy, but it was sent yesterday. And it's been deleted. When Junie replies to it, her own message can't be delivered.

Weird.

But then something pops up to distract her.

Damn news alerts, stealing time from her when she's in paradise. Damn crappy attention span which can't just ignore it.

> Breaking news: double murder on the island of Saint Aurélie

Her phone knows where she is, of course. Don't they always?

A double murder, though. Whoa.

She clicks on the story.

There's a video which she watches with the sound off – unlike Ruby, she's got no headphones with her – of police arriving at the scene. A villa, which looks . . .

'No,' she mutters. 'No.'

No, it can't be Green Fig, the villa they're staying at in the south of the island. It can't be Green Fig, even if the thick grey cushions on the sunbeds look the same, and the ginger lilies that grow next to the table where they eat breakfast look the same, and the swimming pool looks the same and . . .

No. Rich people's Saint Aurélian villas probably all just look the same. (Jesus, isn't that depressing?)

So it's fine. It's fine.

But that's the last moment. That is the last moment that Junie Winter has a feeling of calm and contentment. Because when she looks up, there are two of them walking towards her. Police officers in short-sleeved white shirts, hats and smart black trousers.

She looks around.

'Bonjou!' one of them shouts from across the beach, the French Creole she hears all over the island, even if English is officially the national language. 'Hello!' the other yells, grim-faced.

She looks behind her. Are they talking to her? She remembers one of Poppy's favourite phrases: *Juno, it's not always about you.* That nickname that only Poppy calls her – has done ever since they watched the film *Juno* together, years ago now.

Junie shakes her head; gives herself a talking-to.

Still, there's no doubt that the officers are coming closer. No doubt that they are moving in her direction. Ruby notices it too now and takes her AirPods out, propping herself up on her elbows. Junie has no time to tell Ruby about the breaking news. How it looked very much like this – Christ – *double murder* had happened at their villa. The one where their dad is right now, packing his case to go on a world cruise tomorrow.

The one where Poppy – silent, off-radar Poppy who hasn't turned up where she was meant to today and isn't answering her phone – is barefoot in her pyjamas, writing.

Other people on the beach have seen the officers arrive and begun to wade out of the sea, to layer clothes on top of the swimwear which suddenly feels wildly inappropriate. They have stood up from sunbeds, hands on hips. Called their children to come closer.

The situation is confusing, ramshackle, a mixture of English, Creole, crisp white police shirts and bikinis and stern hats and bare bum cheeks and bafflement and speculation and inflatable beach balls still flying incongruously through the air, thrown by children who don't respect danger and panic while parents tell them off and pull them to their sides.

Junie looks around and a noise comes out of her mouth. A nervous laugh. She looks for a lone gunman or someone wielding a knife. Perhaps the double murder was the start; now whoever did that is terrorising the rest of the island. It's a safe place. But it's 2018; this stuff can happen anywhere.

Does she need to protect herself?

But no-one is holding a weapon. No-one is hurt, no-one is bleeding. No-one is running. In fact, many of them now stand still. Watching. Waiting.

The officers come closer and a dread rampages up her spine.

And it's then that Junie is sure. The police are not just walking in their direction. They are walking directly towards her and her sister.

She reaches over and grabs her towel. Pulls it around her and sits up. A swimsuit is not the right thing to be wearing when things get serious, and she wishes for trousers and socks. Something that would give her armour as the police officers move towards her and her sister faster now, as though they think she and Ruby might run. As though they will flee and must be stopped. As though they are about to be arrested or restrained.

Then Junie sees something else. Guns. The officers don't hold them in their hands but keep them in the sides of their belts. Their hands are on them though, poised. Ready.

And then one of the officers shouts, 'Stop!'

They think, because she has stood up to wrap her towel around herself, that she is trying to leave.

That nervous laugh flies out again.

Junie puts her arms up, away from her body, not a surrender exactly but something instinctive.

The towel drops.

Then, there is a hand on her arm, and the officers are on them and there is no doubt any more. This is about them. She has no idea why but somehow, this emergency is about Junie Winter and her sister Ruby.

PART ONE: JUNIE

HOTTER

'Ruby Winter? June Winter?'

The officer is heavyset, sweating and squat, a handlebar moustache running across his top lip and an Adam's apple that is distractingly prominent, almost dangling.

'Yes,' I say, speaking for me and Ruby as we stand barefoot and nearly naked in front of the police officers. My younger sister says nothing.

'This is Ruby. I'm Junie.' I formalise to my proper name. 'June.'

'I'm Superintendent Delice, of the Royal Saint Aurélie police force.' He nods to a woman next to him, taller than he is and fit. Toned arms, strong shoulders. 'This is Sergeant Henry.'

'What's happened?' I ask, sharp.

'Is there somewhere we can go? To talk?'

'There's the villa where we're staying?'

'Not the villa.'

'Did something happen at our villa?' I ask, thinking about what I read. 'I saw . . . On the news . . . Are they still—'

He exchanges a glance with his colleague.

'Yes, we've found two bodies,' confirms the male officer.

The delivery is matter-of-fact. Doctor and a diagnosis.

My response is the opposite. Thoughts fly up, pieces of paper in a wind machine. *The double murder. Poppy's absence and her silence. Property crime and gangs. Raging figures in balaclavas.*

I picture Poppy at the desk in her room, writing in her short, striped pyjamas with a Diet Coke next to her. Perhaps she had her earphones in, so she didn't hear whoever this was break in.

'She didn't reply,' I say. 'My sister, Poppy. I sent her a message and she didn't . . . She's not answering her phone either. Is that why . . . is that what happened to her? Is it Poppy? Is she . . . ?'

Ruby's face contorts in a way I have never seen in the twenty-eight years of Ruby's life so far. A new expression, reserved for something truly awful.

The officer hesitates, and something in his facial expression makes me pause. I don't have this quite right, but I can't work out why.

'Poppy isn't dead,' he says. 'Not as far as we know.'

A noise, animal, comes out of my mouth at the same time I start to talk to myself, *thank God, thank God, thank God,* incantations. Whatever this is, whatever has happened, Poppy is ok.

Then the female officer delivers the next words.

'We believe, though, that she was involved. We believe it was your sister Poppy who committed the murders.'

COLDER

It's only when I collapse down onto the sand that I realise Ruby has been holding me up. With the words *We believe it was your sister Poppy who committed the murders*, though, my sister's arm has dropped away, the crucial Jenga brick.

And I am grounded.

On the sunbed above me, nine down is half-filled in. Out of the ordinary. PECU—

-liar. Peculiar.

The biro lies in the sand now. Snorkel next to it.

'No, she didn't,' I hear myself say. 'You don't know her, you don't know my sister but you only have to— Poppy couldn't kill anybody.'

I try to stand up but my legs are pea stalks without support.

Down.

'This is a homicide investigation,' says the superintendent, glancing around at the faces that stare at us. 'We need to go somewhere to talk, privately.' He turns to the other officer. 'Dana, can you help her up? We're going to the station.'

I am wrenched from the ground, held again. Not by Ruby this time, but by Sergeant Henry. I am led, lurching and staggering like the local drunk, towards a white police car.

As we move, weird details cross my mind.

The sweat on the male officer's back. My own almost-nudity, towel only grasped loosely at my waist now. What I would be thinking if I were the other people on this beach: *Thank God it's not me. Thank God my day is normal. Who are these people, that they're involved in something so dark? What are they part of?*

Sand on the seat of the police car, transferred from my body. The kind of thing I would normally worry about, apologise for, try to clean up.

The sun, glaring in through the window as the police car starts to move.

And with that, the realisation that at some point in all of this, I have lost my sunglasses. Another thing that would have mattered before.

In the car, Sergeant Henry climbs into the passenger seat as her colleague starts the engine, and then she turns, an awkward angle from the passenger seat, neat ponytail at the nape of her neck, towards Ruby and me.

She can't be much older than me. Late thirties, maybe.

'We need to tell you who the victims are,' she says. 'I wanted to wait until we got to the station, but the situation is moving fast. I'm aware there are news reports.'

I nod. But Ruby just looks out of the window, face set like plaster. I'm pretty sure she's gone into shock.

The officer ploughs ahead, the car moving now. 'One of them is a woman called Robin Sawyer.'

Robin Sawyer is our dad's new girlfriend. We met Robin for the first time on this trip, the one our father had paid for, two weeks' bonding before he and Robin went off on what Ruby called their year-long-round-the-world-spend-our-inheritance cruise together.

I was right then, it *was* our villa on the news.

The next sentence feels inevitable.

I wish, I wish, I wish I had time to warn Ruby about the alert I saw and what that's likely to mean. But really, what good would a warning do?

The words come from the female officer, as we swing around a hairpin bend.

'I'm sorry to tell you that the other victim is your father, Fraser Winter,' she says. 'Our working theory is that Poppy killed him too.'

HOTTER

As the police car overtakes an exhausted-looking cyclist on a narrow road, Ruby has her head in her hands, raucous sobs reverberating around the car. I am trying to lean across, to comfort her.

'We've sent someone back to the villa,' the female officer says gently. 'To collect some things for you both.'

I nod, my face buried into Ruby's side, seatbelt off. 'Ok. Thank you.'

It's all I can manage. *I'm sorry to tell you that the other victim is your father. Our working theory is that Poppy killed him too.*

When I sit up, the car has slowed and we are driving through a small town – a part of the island I haven't been to before. Locals are pouring out of one of the island's plethora of Catholic churches, smartly dressed and laughing.

I stare at them out of the car window.

Normality. How can that exist?

'You have this wrong,' I say. 'This isn't who Poppy is. We'll sue. I don't know what's going on but someone's trying to . . . they're trying to frame our sister or something. This isn't right.'

I hear the desperation in my voice.

Dad.

We hadn't been close in recent years, hadn't always agreed on everything but still. He is Dad. *Dad Dad Dad Dad Dad.* The man who taught me to serve aces; to beat anyone I ever took on in a chess game. He's the reason I eat my steak blue and my custard cold. He is written into my DNA.

A name, just for him.

Dad Dad Dad Dad Dad.

'Can you tell me how . . .' The words don't sound like they are coming from me. 'Can you tell me how my father died?'

But they are the last words I can manage. It starts in my hands but soon ventures further and I am shaking, all over, despite the heat and the large yellow towel with BEACH LIFE! written on it that is wrapped around my body.

'It'll be ok,' Ruby says to me as her own incantation stops and she watches me vibrate. 'It'll be ok.' It's less truth, more recited prayer for a religion you think is bullshit.

She grasps my hand tight. Squeezes until it hurts. 'It'll be ok,' she repeats.

Her eyes are wild and scared.

From the front seat, the female officer speaks again. 'We can talk properly at the station.'

'Is Poppy there?' I ask.

The officers exchange a glance.

'No,' she says eventually. 'We are yet to locate her. Poppy is currently missing. It's crucial we act fast to rectify that, as I'm sure you'll understand. And we think it's likely that you two, as her sisters, can help us.'

In the car, I turn and lock eyes with my sister. I wish we could talk privately, but I know they won't let us, in case we're covering for Poppy. In case we want time to get our story straight.

Poppy's *gone*?

I wish I had a story. Any story. Straight would be great, but curly would do.

◆ ◆ ◆

Twenty minutes later I am sitting in a blue plastic chair at the police station, a huge fan blasting cold air next to me. The sea water has dried but still I shiver like I have the flu.

A giant of a man stands at the door of the room, gun slung across his front as casually as a handbag.

I am wearing cotton shorts and a tie-dye vest after changing in a side room; an officer brought the clothes from our villa, including my underwear.

The room has one tiny window, but it's too high, too small to see out of. The metal table we're sitting at is chipped on the corner, bare apart from a recording device and glass of iced water.

'Can I move the fan so it's not pointing right at me, please?' I ask the officer.

He looks at me for five seconds or more, then ignores my request.

He turns to the female officer. 'Es ou ja palé èk fiancé-la?'

I pick up the word *fiancé*. This is not about the fan.

I don't have a fiancé, I'm single, so the officers must be talking about Ruby's fiancé Emlyn. A thought crosses my mind, fleeting. Walking into the kitchen yesterday. Seeing Emlyn and Poppy – who normally interact very little, don't have much time for each other – deep in conversation. Conversation, or argument? I think back. But even if they'd had an argument, how would that have led to my dad and Robin dying? To Poppy being blamed?

Delice turns on the recording device.

'This is a recorded interview taking place at Daniel Bay police station on 16 January 2018 at 5.12 p.m. I am Superintendent Delice, badge number 18736. Also present is Sergeant Henry, badge number 18233.

'This is a witness interview with June Winter, date of birth 3 August 1988, residing at 4 Earle Court, Edinburgh, UK. The purpose of this interview is to obtain a statement in relation to an investigation into the double murder of Fraser Winter and Robin Sawyer.'

He looks up at me. 'You are not under arrest, and you are not suspected of committing any offence. You are here voluntarily and free to leave at any time. You may also take a break or pause the interview at any moment that you wish.

'Please state your full name, date of birth and current address for the record.'

I hear the shake in my voice now, too. 'June Winter. 3 August 1988. 4 Earle Court, Edinburgh.'

Delice nods, then turns to his colleague. Nods at her too.

'Thank you, June. Now, we want to speak to you about the relationship between your sister Poppy Winter and your father, Fraser Winter, and his partner Robin Sawyer.'

Partner. Ridiculous.

There is a pause, weighted. 'Did your sister Poppy show any antipathy towards your father or Robin?'

A shaken head.

Delice goes next. 'Does Poppy have any history of mental health problems?'

'No.'

'Is your sister violent?'

The questions keep coming, interspersed with their own chats in rapid Creole, me grasping at the odd word I recognise from school French lessons, like they're sweets flying from a piñata. Barely any use.

'Does your sister have money worries?'

Money worries? I laugh at this one. They think Poppy killed Dad for his cash? Poppy, who would live in a hut eating beans forever as long as she could write and climb a mountain. Poppy, who needs such a tiny amount of everything.

Our family isn't old money; we're not *used* to wealth like some of the families who lived near us on sprawling estates growing up. But our school building looked like a castle. Dad developed property through the eighties boom; our late mum was a supermodel.

An ache takes hold of my middle.

Dad.

Poppy.

Mum.

No and no and no and no and no.

Poppy is not violent or angry or in trouble with money or in the thick of a mental health episode. She's a bit weird, sure. We laugh about it. She's the most antisocial twenty-five-year-old, loves animals more than people, but come *on*: we grew up with the massif looking over us like a parent, school classes of eight and close only, really, to each other. A childhood that bred people that way.

I live alone in a studio flat. I can't hold down a relationship.

Ruby is different. She does the things other people do. She's been engaged to Emlyn for a year; is close to his family. She's embraced sprawling family Christmases. She's crossed over, to where the normal people exist.

Poppy, though . . . Poppy is single, happiest with her backpack on and an OS map in her hand. She's spent many a night in a bothy alone in her sleeping bag. Her death row meal would be a dried packet of something, cooked up on her little camping stove on a tiny island somewhere, with only seals for company. That, and a can of Diet Coke, while I'm not there to lecture her about UPFs.

What my little sister is not, though, is a killer.

'What's your evidence?' I ask, eventually, arms wrapped around myself in this stark, basic room – I suspect based on the cabinet in the corner that it used to be an office. 'What makes you think it was my sister?'

I feel it: the shock wearing off, some grit setting in. 'It doesn't matter what it is, anyway,' I say. 'She didn't do it.'

It's true. Even if they have evidence, I have my gut.

But then they show me the CCTV.

COLDER

I lean forward onto a table which is bolted down at each corner, clearly a potential weapon.

The female officer has left the room. It's just me, the male officer and gun-handbag guy. Delice slides an iPad towards me.

'What is it?' I ask.

He leans across and presses play but it's grainy; I have no idea what's going on.

My heart's beating like it hasn't since I walked up Arthur's Seat with Poppy last month. She had arrived at my doorstep the day before without warning. Said she needed to get away.

Now I think about the visit: was *that* anything?

The officer shakes his head. 'Watch,' is all he says. Then, begrudgingly, more. 'It's from just after we estimate the murders occurred. Watch.'

And just then a woman comes into view, the camera only catching her from behind. The body language is nervous. Edgy. She is tall, with a rucksack on her back. She is wearing a long-sleeved sundress but it's hard to see it because she is also, very clearly, splattered in a large amount of blood.

I lean closer.

They think this is Poppy.

I mean . . . she's long enough. Lean enough. The hair – dripping, I realise, this woman is soaked through all over – is right. But that's true of millions of people. Me, for starters. Ruby. Barring the age difference and those ears, we look like triplets.

I fold my arms. 'That could be anyone.'

Except then, as the video keeps playing and the woman moves forward, I spot two things.

First, there is that little hoop in her right nostril.

More importantly than that though, is the tattoo, visible on the back of her neck beneath her ponytail.

The one Poppy had done on her eighteenth birthday.

HOTTER

Poppy's tattoo is a silhouette of a catwalk model. I would never get a tattoo – too limiting for work, I'm an actor – but Poppy's is cute. It looks like it's been hand-drawn and it *means* something. It is an homage to our mother.

The night she got it, Poppy walked into Paolo's, the Italian restaurant where we were celebrating her birthday, and pulled her hair up with her right hand. Turned the back of her neck to us and flashed an I-did-a-naughty-thing grin.

'Ta-dah!' she sang. I suspected she'd had a vodka and Diet Coke before she arrived. 'Happy Birthday to meeee.'

I held my breath.

Dad yanked Poppy down into the seat next to him and scanned around the restaurant. He hissed at her that tattoos were 'for sluts and poor people'. They argued – loudly – and she left.

Dad ordered a double whisky. The rest of us stayed, forked al-dente spaghetti and made small talk. Tried to ignore the eyes on us under the shadow of those huge gold number 18 balloons. Me, Ruby, Emlyn and Dad. No Mum. Our mum had died six years earlier.

Maria Winter – then Gee – was one of the earliest supermodels; doing the job before the term started to be used widely in the nineties. Mum was good friends with Brooke Shields and Christy

Turlington. Her best bedtime stories involved leather jackets slung over her shoulder in dark nightclubs in Mayfair and giant bottles of hairspray backstage at chaotic fashion shows in New York. Flying to Monaco on a private jet for a shoot, before flying straight back again.

The three of us would beg her for more. She'd laugh. Press her MAC red lips together. 'Oh. I've got one,' she would say. 'So Janice was having a birthday party at the Groucho . . .'

'You've seen something?' asks the officer now, pressing pause and watching my face as I take in that tattoo.

I shake my head. 'No.'

I force myself to make eye contact with him.

He presses play.

And there she is again. Poppy – ok, I concede it's her, but only in my head – walking out of the right-hand side gate at our villa. The same one I walked out of to head to the museum yesterday, flip-flop flippant, no idea what was ahead, *how lucky am I*, checking I'd packed my snorkel.

We're not in Scotland now, Toto.

'Anything?'

'No.'

The tattoo. *The tattoo.*

But it doesn't matter. I have to come out fighting for my sister. Even if a voice inside is whispering: *What about your dad? You know, the one who's dead?*

I'm on a battlefield now, though. I can only save those with breath left in their body.

'You can't know it's her,' I say, petulant. I know they'll find out about the tattoo. But I won't be the one to tell them.

He cocks an eyebrow at me. 'Actually, June, we can these days. We are in contact with British police. They've confirmed that the facial recognition is a match.' He pauses. 'I know it's not what you want to hear. But that woman you see on the screen, walking away from two dead bodies covered in blood: that's your sister.'

I am silent.

'She wasn't answering her phone,' I say, after a minute of silence. 'I think she's scared. Scared that you think she did this.' My voice cracks on the words.

He sighs, like he's exhausted. 'I think she's turned off her phone – or more likely got rid of it – because she's committed a double murder, June.

'Her phone last pinged near the villa, at the time of the murder. Nothing since. I think she has gone on the run because she killed two people.

'The reason she isn't answering her phone is probably because it's deep in the sea that backs onto Green Fig, would be my best guess. Easily thrown from up by that pool of yours. And throwing phones away . . . it's something murderers are partial to doing.'

Silence.

The word rings and zips across the room.

Murderers.

I wait him out.

Ruby would capitulate. She's sociable enough to be uncomfortable with silence. Me, though . . . I'm ok with it. Comfortable. On stage, I can deliver a line and let long seconds pass until the next one. I know silence can have power. I know how to use it.

Wait.

Wait.

Eventually, he rewinds the footage back to the start. Presses play.

'I don't need to see it again,' I protest, turning away.

'I think you do,' he argues, watching me watch the screen. 'Because I want to zoom in this time. There's something else interesting. You seem to have doubts, even now. So I think it's worth you watching this.'

My stomach drops. I don't like how confident he sounds.

I need to be ready to defend Poppy. To suggest there is an explanation for whatever he is about to show me. To find a loophole. To raise doubt.

But it's hard to do that, when, on the screen, I see what is in my sister's hand. Half-hidden up the sleeve of her loose linen shirt.

A knife.

HOTTER

A knife that – peering more closely, pinching the screen to zoom in – I recognise. It's unusual, with its neon green handle: I sliced our focaccia for lunch with it two days ago. We ate it with chicken that Ruby marinated and cooked on the outdoor grill by the pool. For what now turns out to have been our family's last supper.

My heart hammers.

Poppy at the scene, her face verified. Knife in her hand, blood down her front.

And two dead bodies.

That could be enough, couldn't it? To charge Poppy, when they find her.

But all I know is the crux of things: it still isn't possible.

Then the door opens and the other officer who came to the beach, the woman, walks in. She says something to her colleague that I can't understand. He replies in English. 'Ok. Thanks, Dana.'

'What is it?' I ask. 'Have they found her?'

He ignores me.

'Nou ni pou nou wètounen nan villa a,' he says to his colleague.

I bristle. Switching back to a language I don't understand feels like a mind game. Though there was one word . . .

I look up. 'Something's happened at the villa? Did you say something about the villa?'

'Wait one moment,' he says, and they both leave the room.

I use the time alone to think. I know Ruby is in the interview room next door, presumably being read identical rights and shown identical footage. I know another thing: Ruby won't doubt Poppy either. Now that our mum's gone, we're the only ones who could watch anything, see anything, and still know in our bones that Poppy couldn't do this.

The door flings open.

The male officer nods at me. 'Let's go. We need to get to Green Fig.'

And then things move fast.

I am up, out of my chair, and we are in the corridor, and there are voices, Creole, English. Heavy accents. There are people. And in the middle of it all, is Ruby.

I reach for her, but we are being told to *go, go, go*. Half-pushed along the corridor.

A door opens and the sunlight is blinding; my eyes flinch.

We are bundled into a police car.

'She didn't do this,' says Ruby in the back seat next to me, eyes wide.

I reach for her hand and squeeze.

'I know,' I reply. 'I know.'

We know.

And then the car pulls away.

There's nothing else to say. We're going back to the villa, but no-one will tell us why.

The potholes fling us up and out of our seat, before we've even had chance to pull on seatbelts. Bends are taken like we're being steered by a nine-year-old in Mario Kart. We pass cyclists at such a close distance that I hold my breath and feel my body strain away from them. All the time, Ruby and I clutch each other's hands.

Half an hour later the police car pulls back into the circular driveway of our holiday villa, Green Fig. I step out next to the huge palm in the centre of it, the witchy fingers of its branches dangling low.

I picture us when we arrived here, only ten days ago. Exhausted from the flight and wide-eyed at the luxury: *look at this place.* A sprawling, modern building with an infinity pool which backs out onto the Caribbean Sea.

We'd shrieked as we pulled suitcases out of the boot and looked at the villa; sweat already pooling in the small of our backs as the temperature hit the mid-thirties.

Now there's yellow tape screaming 'CRIME SCENE – DO NOT CROSS'.

And a feeling too: *a bad thing happened here.*

Delice flips the tape up and motions to us to follow him under it. First me, then Ruby, and Dana bringing up the rear. We walk past the bougainvillea, around the side of the villa and when the passage opens up into the sprawling back garden, my breath sucks in. A tent has been set up next to the pool. Alongside that is a slight, dark-haired man adjusting the height of a tripod.

'Are we ok to be here?' asks Ruby, as she sees it and recoils. 'We shouldn't . . . Is it not . . .'

I hold her hand more tightly.

'We're staying away from the pool area,' answers the officer, steering us to the back door and away from the tent. I glance back to where we came from. To where the CCTV camera is. I see Ruby look at it too.

'It's Poppy's room I'd like you to take us to,' Delice says, following my eyes. 'We need to know as soon as possible if anything is missing from her belongings.'

We go inside. Move through the big, open-plan kitchen with my dad's Lee Child splayed open on the kitchen island alongside a half-drunk black coffee. There is a tiny anklet on the table, thread with shells and stones, that looks handmade and still has a label on. Robin's, I would guess, from one of the jewellery stalls at the market.

We head towards the wide staircase.

The police officer leads.

Other than our footsteps, there is silence.

We walk down the clean, white expanse of the landing, past my room and then Ruby's.

'This one,' I say as Delice takes the next step forward. 'This is hers.'

And he stops, outside the room that our little sister, lifelong resident of the smallest bedroom in the house, had bagsied when we arrived. We'd capitulated easily. It had made sense that she had it anyway; she spent the most time in her room, writing.

My dad and Robin were in the master bedroom, of course, with its teal en suite, rainfall shower and large balcony (reasonable, since Dad was paying for the whole thing).

'Ready?' the officer asks now.

I nod.

We follow him into Poppy's bedroom, all of us crowding around the entrance. My eyes scan around. Oh God. Poppy's lacy blue knickers are on the floor in front of us. I go to pick them up. To put them in the washing basket.

But the officer snaps at me. 'Leave the underwear. Leave everything as it is.'

I hop backwards, like I've been stung.

I see myself in the full-length mirror and I'm alarmed for a second. *Who are you?* A parody of a holidaymaker. Terror in tie-dye.

Next to the bed on the side table is a mug, with a little mark on the rim that looks like the Vaseline Poppy smeared on all the time and the remnants of coffee darkening the bottom. An empty tissue packet. That wood carving – a souvenir – that she'd bought at a market on the first day here. The book she had been reading on a lilo two days ago, her long legs hanging off the end.

How To Kill Your Family.

Unfortunate.

'Can you see anything missing?' asks the female officer, snapping gloves on. She reaches out and pulls the shutters half across, to block out the glare of the early-evening sun. 'We know the sports car out front is gone but is there anything else that jumps out? Anything that should be here but isn't?'

I look around.

'Her laptop?' I say. 'I can't see her laptop and she always has it out. Close by. She's a writer.'

And maybe there's something on there that will show the truth. A time stamp, when she was writing, when she saved something. Anything that proves she couldn't have done this.

'And her phone,' I add. 'Her phone's not here.'

The officer nods. 'We think she had that with her,' she says. 'But like we said earlier, the likelihood is that it's long gone.' She looks out of the window to the sea.

'Her passport was on the side there too,' I say, pointing. 'When I left, at least. I remember because I was badgering her to put it in the safety deposit box with the rest.'

'And it's definitely not in there?' she asks.

Ruby looks up. 'No. I was the only one who had the code. I was looking after all the valuables.'

The middle sister but the adult. That was always going to be a Ruby job.

Delice takes out a notebook. Writes something down.

He sighs and looks up. 'We need something here, girls. Some sort of motive. Is there anything you know? Anything that can help us? Anything that can help us figure out what happened here?'

'Something that explains to us why Poppy did this,' adds Dana. 'You know her better than anyone . . . Any ideas?'

'She must have been forced to do it,' I blurt out, watching Ruby's face contract in pain as I see what she is looking at, Poppy's unmade bed, the pillow still soft with the dent from her forehead. Poppy always slept face down, burrowed in like a mole. 'If you're asking me what . . . if you really think she did it then that's all I have. She could only have done it if she was . . . coerced.'

I continue, warming to my theory. '*If* she did it, and I don't believe that but I'm saying *if*, then that's the only explanation. Perhaps Dad even told her it was ok? A break-in, maybe, and they said it was her or Dad. If it was something like that, Dad would have told her to do it.'

The officer's brown eyes are sceptical; even I can hear it's far-fetched. She fights back a smirk as she says, 'Right.'

'Or she had a breakdown?' I add. 'A psychotic break? I saw this TV show where . . . Well, we'd been through a trauma, losing our mother when we were young. Could you look at that?'

I see the eye roll that threatens. They don't look at each other. Delice speaks. 'Has she *shown* any signs of being under duress? Any mental health struggles that suggest a breakdown?'

I wonder about inventing one or both of those things, but in the end I shake my head. 'No.' I fold my arms across my chest.

'That doesn't mean they weren't happening though,' I mutter.

'Ok. Let's try something different.' He sounds like he is trying very hard to be patient. 'Has anything odd happened to Poppy in the last few months? Any changes in behaviour? Anything out of character?'

As I am shaking my head, Delice looks at his phone. Says something to the female police officer in Creole. Then looks up at me.

'You said Poppy was wearing her pyjamas when you left the villa?'

I nod.

He looks at a notebook. 'Not a sundress with sunflowers all over it in a large print? Blue and yellow?'

Oh. 'No.'

'But she does own that dress?'

My next nod is slower. I'm a rodent, stupidly scuttling towards a trap that will snap me in two.

That dress . . . She's had it for years. And that could have been the pattern I saw earlier, underneath the blood. There was yellow on there.

'Yes, she owns that dress.'

Snap.

His nod is curt. 'Excellent. Because that's the one we just found, behind that mango tree outside. Soaked in blood that we are pretty confident will be confirmed as belonging to your father.'

HOTTER

'How about her behaviour on this holiday?' the male officer presses. 'Was she herself? Happy? Relaxed? Pleased to be spending time with her father? With all of you? Would you say that she was enjoying the family time?'

My breath is coming fast. Shallow.

'I . . . think so,' I force out.

I avoid Ruby's eye contact. We know that this trip has been far from idyllic. Poppy and Dad's relationship was difficult. Poppy and Emlyn were sniping at each other even more than usual. And truthfully . . . something about Poppy on this trip *has* been off.

'And they were close? Poppy and your father?'

'Not especially,' I say. 'Like a lot of families. We all had our own lives.'

'Why were you on holiday together then?'

I'm taken aback. How do you answer that? 'I suppose . . . That's probably why he invited us. Quality family time. A proper catch-up.'

The officer nods.

'When did either of you last see Poppy?' he asks.

'At breakfast yesterday morning,' Ruby says, loud suddenly. 'I was up before everyone else, I always am. I'd made a pot of coffee. She came out in her pyjamas and I poured her one. We stood there for a minute and listened to the birds. You hear turtle doves here a lot.' Her voice cracks. 'It didn't last long – she went back inside to write – but yeah.' She looks at him. 'I last saw her then.'

I didn't know that.

'Sounds magical,' says the officer. 'Was your fiancé there, too?'

They won't notice it, but I do. A tiny flush on Ruby's cheeks. 'No.'

'And you weren't there, June?'

'I'm not known for being an early riser.'

'You don't have children, I take it?'

A flush runs across my cheek; a judgement. 'No.'

'And work doesn't get you up early normally? When you're not on holiday?'

I shake my head. Wry smile. 'Not really. I'm an actor.'

'Wow,' says Delice, nodding, like people do. 'Been in anything I'd know?'

I could tell him about the two episodes of *Coronation Street* and the tour of *Pride and Prejudice* or any of the hundreds of other projects on my CV, but he wouldn't know any of it, and he wouldn't care. I shake my head. 'No.'

'How about your father? Did you see him at breakfast?'

A pause.

They pick up on it instantly. Eyes on us.

'He wasn't there?' the female officer pushes Ruby. 'He didn't have coffee with you?'

'Dad and Robin always had breakfast in their room,' I fill in. 'They have this balcony.' I gesture towards the landing. 'It's got a sofa, looks out onto the sea. You'll see it, if you go through . . . Anyway, Robin particularly liked to eat on there and have her morning coffee just with Dad. Without, you know, small talk.'

An eyebrow flies upwards. '*Small talk*? Is that what it was? Even though you're family?'

'Well, Robin's not family, is she?' I say, snippy. 'We only just met her.'

The female officer makes a note.

I have an image of the two extremes – the idyll of yesterday morning when I ate warm pain au chocolat, chocolate drizzling out of the side, and the hell of now – being physically damaging. Like chilblains when you switch too fast from hot to cold.

As I am thinking this, Delice reaches into his pocket and pulls out his own forensic gloves. His fingernails are long, and I cringe as he pulls the gloves on. Too long for a man, even though that might be a sexist thing to say; Poppy would tell me off for it, that slight age gap – just five years – often showing itself in things like that. *Juno! You can't say that.*

But they *are* too long; grotesque and unpleasant.

'Did she tell you what her plans were while you were out?'

How long ago that feels already – the officers showing up on Parrot Island. Snorkel on the sunbed, pulse in my throat.

Ruby nods. 'She was just getting her words done.'

'Her words?'

Poppy is always trying to hit arbitrary word counts.

'Like we told you, she's a writer,' I say. 'She's waiting for the big break, so she works hard. Even on holiday. She was going to meet us at Parrot Island today, though. We were stopping there on our way back to the villa. We hadn't been there yet and people kept telling us how gorgeous it was.'

'It is pretty,' agrees the officer, with a dot of pride. 'What's Poppy working on, then?'

'What?'

'The writing? What's Poppy working on? Poems? Fiction? What?'

'I'm . . . not sure,' I mumble.

'You're not sure? Your sister's spending big chunks of your holiday holed up writing this thing when you're trying to have family time, and you don't know what it is she's working on? She doesn't talk about it at dinner? You don't ask?'

'She's always writing something.' I sound defensive. 'I haven't asked about this one *specifically*.'

But as I say it, I know I am telling them a lie. I have asked. So has Ruby. We've asked over and over. Poppy has been odd about it; cagey. She's also borderline obsessed with it, whatever it is. I've heard her working on it in the early hours when I've got up to go to the loo. Making phone calls in the evenings. When I ask who she's speaking to, Poppy's cheeks colour and she swerves the subject.

I meet Ruby's eyes and feel the thought fly between us: *something has been going on.*

And it's not just the writing, is it? Poppy's been distant in Saint Aurélie. At the national park when we saw a waterfall that could have made atheists line up for Sunday prayers, I was snapping photos and losing my mind over the colours while Poppy – a nature *nut*, usually – was looking at it but not seeing it. I had to nudge her to notice the hummingbirds circling the flowers.

And the way she'd been speaking to Dad . . . Disagreeing with Emlyn even more than usual . . .

I won't be offering that information up though.

'Poppy's having an amazing holiday,' I say. I need to take control of the narrative. 'It would be impossible not to. The beaches, the food . . . We went to the street party on Friday night and the atmosphere was . . .' I shake my head. 'We were grateful to Dad for sorting this out. For arranging it for everyone.'

'And paying for it,' the officer says, raising an eyebrow.

I feel his eyes on me. Without thinking, I reach out and hold onto the bedstead.

'Can you remember that I asked you not to touch anything, please,' the female officer snaps. Not a question. I snatch my hand away.

'Perhaps your sister had been keeping a secret from you?' says the superintendent. 'Is that it? Is there a chance that your sister, perhaps, is not who you thought she was? It happens.'

I shake my head.

No. Not possible. I know my sister in pink heart pyjamas, frowning in concentration, writing a letter for Santa. I know her together and I know her broken. I know her roots and the depths of their soil.

Then the officer asks us the question he's asked us ten, twelve times now. 'Have you heard from your sister since you left the villa yesterday?'

'No.'

'Can I see your phones?'

I pass mine over first. Think about the in-jokes. The message I sent to a man called Kenny the day before we came out here, ending something before it got started. As usual; my relationships always go the same way.

All of it, the dirt of my life, on show to this officer.

It doesn't matter now.

There's no choice.

Delice opens my messages. Scrolls to my thread with Poppy.

I try to remember what we last messaged about. Not a lot, while we were here. There had been no need; we'd mostly been together. And before that?

Watch this video, hilarious.

Did this walking route, we should try it?

OMG I want this cockapoo.

Can you pack a spare converter plug?

Mundane, inane.

Then I remember. Poppy's deleted message from the day before. The police will see that. I wonder if the phone company can recall it.

And if they can recall it, what will it mean? Could it help her? Or will it get her into even more trouble? Perhaps that's why she deleted it.

The officer hands my phone back. 'Thank you,' he says.

Then he takes Ruby's phone.

'Another phone, perhaps?' he asks, when he's done. 'Did she give you another phone? Ask you to contact her on that, once it was done?'

Once it was done? They think we *knew*?

'What? No!'

Ridiculous. Imagine me, Ruby and Poppy in a world of burner phones and murder plans. Me and Poppy, who'd gone to bed at the same time a few nights ago with Japanese sheet masks on.

We'd laughed: other twenty-somethings came to this island and went on the party boat we'd heard about called The Parrot. They danced in crop tops until dawn. Bought cheap weed in the dodgy bit of the island capital, Jamestown. Sauntered home at sunrise with their shoes off.

But not us. And not just because we were on holiday with our dad, but because it was not who we were.

'Does Poppy use social media?'

I shake my head. 'Not her thing.'

He cocks an eyebrow. 'Really? Aren't they all TikToking like crazy at her age?'

'People are people. Not clichés.'

Delice stares at me. 'Anything else, however insignificant you think it is, that you would like to tell us?'

I take a breath. I picture Poppy on a bike in front of me, Ruby ahead of her, the three of us tracking the edge of Loch Morlich one rare summer day back home.

Sisters' Day, we called it. One day each year, where it was just us. No boyfriends, no parents, no phones. Just us three. White wine by the loch.

It had been four or five years ago, and we'd been spread out by then – I'd got a job on a Pinter play in Edinburgh, Ruby was living in Aviemore with Emlyn. Poppy was the only one still at home, with Dad. Sisters' Day took more organising than it used to but this one had come good.

And then, Poppy flinging her trainers and clothes off and running towards the still-icy water for a dip in her mismatched underwear. Disappearing underneath and then emerging, treading water, staring off into the middle distance towards the end of the lake.

She had run her fingers through the water. Inhaled the air. This is what she did wherever we were. She tasted her surroundings, touched them, heard them. She took it all into her core, as deep as it would go.

The officer asks again. 'Anything?'

And I think. Say something, Junie. Say something to stop this. There has to be *something*.

'Just that she wouldn't do it,' I say, looking up. 'I don't just mean wouldn't, I mean that she *couldn't*. It's not possible. And if you're telling me that there's no doubt, that she did physically do it, then like we said, there's an explanation that means it's not her fault. That she was forced or blackmailed or, I don't know, *something*.'

But before we can talk any more, before he can respond, Henry takes a call and there are loud voices coming from the next room, the crackle of a walkie-talkie, before the female officer begins to steer us towards the villa door.

'On moun ja wè li,' she says to her colleague.

'What does that mean?' I ask, scared. 'What are you talking about?'

The phrase is repeated.

'On moun ja wè li. On moun ja wè li.'

'What are you saying?'

I ask over and over. But I don't get an answer until we are bundled back into the car, speeding down the West Coast highway, putting our seatbelts on as we go.

This time, the sirens are on.

'What's going on?' I yell over the din, though I have a terrible idea already.

'There's been a sighting,' Dana shouts from the passenger seat. 'We're heading straight there.' Then more calmly, almost to herself. 'Looks like we've found our suspect.'

HOTTER

The sirens blaze and blare, the potholes flinging Ruby and me around like we're on a rollercoaster.

'Does Poppy have a temper?' asks Delice from the front, clearly comfortable with the roads. With this speed that's so terrifying for us.

'No,' I say, too quickly.

I feel Ruby's eyes on me.

Lie, lie, lie. Poppy's the most hot-headed of any of us. The most impetuous. I've certainly been on the receiving end of her temper before. Maybe Emlyn was too, when I saw them in the kitchen. Because her temper's been so much worse lately.

But the police are armed, and we are driving towards Poppy. If they think that she will lash out, they are more likely to shoot.

'She doesn't have a temper. Poppy is sweet. Young. Jesus, have you seen the size of her?' A note of begging creeps into my voice. 'If you find her, she'll be scared. Please don't hurt her.'

Delice says nothing.

Five minutes later, we pull up outside a café painted in luminous pinks, sharp greens, vivid orange.

The Arts Cafe, says the sign. Boards stand up next to the rows of palms outside. **Goat in Creole sauce**. And other signs, boasting of rum punch and home-brewed coffee, snapper and fresh roti.

The café's backdrop is the Simons, the island's iconic mountains. Out front, there is a small, shaded terrace with tribal masks painted across every pillar.

All of it pales against one thought. *She's in there.*

In the front seats of the police car, the officers are speaking quietly in Creole. I can't make out a word. Then they turn to me and Ruby and flip to English.

'Right, the plan is this. You go in first,' Delice says, looking between the two of us. 'One of you. *Alone.*'

I squeeze Ruby's hand. 'Me,' I say. 'I'll do it.'

I'm the oldest sister, this is my job. And Ruby doesn't look like she could handle the most basic tasks right now. She's nothing like the woman who steers us round the hairpin bends and looks after our passports.

'But what do I say?' My heart hurtles along a sprint track. 'What do I do when I get in there?'

'You get one chance,' Delice says, pressing his lips together. 'You need to use that chance to persuade Poppy to hand herself in. That she'll get a lighter sentence that way. That's the best thing you can do for your sister now, tell her to come out, hands in the air, and come to the station with us.'

'But how do I do that? What do I say to her?' I ask. I hear panic.

'Your entire aim is to get her to come willingly,' Delice says. 'To come, so that we don't have to go in. Say whatever you need to say for her to do that.'

Dana clips a microphone to my T-shirt.

'We can hear the whole conversation,' she says, mouth set.

She gestures to the officers who are outside the car, holding guns across their fronts.

'So don't do anything stupid.'

Then she nods. Go.

I open the car door. And legs trembling, I walk towards The Arts Cafe.

◆ ◆ ◆

There are not many people inside. Those who are in there chat, laugh, sip hot coffee. They have no idea what's going on outside. Or what may be about to happen inside.

I am dimly aware that there are canvases all over the walls signed by local artists, as well as brightly coloured wooden fish and more, plenty more, of those masks. Something chocolatey is baking. Lots of chocolatey things bake around here, there's a glut of the stuff: we were due to tour the cacao plantation in a few days.

I'm geeky about art and history; Poppy is a chocaholic. The Arts Cafe is a Winter sister dream spot and we should be here, *together*, inhaling cacao and culture. Not like this.

The baking smell suddenly makes me gag.

In the corner there is a pile of books in English and French, and a handwritten sign that says **Book Swap**. Next to the novels is an old man, hair as white as January on Cairn Gorm, a tiny blue espresso cup in front of him. He is staring into the middle distance as though he's trying to solve a crossword. On another table is a couple who give an air of being local, eating identical plates of the biggest shrimp I've ever seen and crisp, rainbow salads.

And then, I see her.

There, with her back to all of them, a young woman in a blue T-shirt dress with unwashed hair. Shoulders hunched. Alone, at a table for two. Hands wrapped around a bright orange glass of juice. Long legs crossed at the ankles. Earrings running down the length of her lobes.

In another life, this woman could be on the last leg of a round-the-world ticket. Hungover from too many mojitos, about to sleep it off under an umbrella on the beach.

In this world though, she is – according to police – Poppy Winter, double murderer.

My sister.

Except, no.

She is not Poppy Winter. Her hair covers her neck but I don't need to see the tattoo's absence to know. That dress is not her dress; that woman is not my sister.

COLDER

When I walk out of the café door, my hand goes to my chest, as though my racing heart can be settled like an excited puppy. *Stay.*

I shake my head at Ruby and the waiting police officer.

Jesus Christ.

They are training their guns on the café, now, in a way that they weren't when I walked away.

Would they have shot Poppy? Poppy, who weighs barely nine stone. Poppy, who's never swiped a lipstick from Boots.

'It's not her!' I say loudly. 'You can put the guns down!'

I push sweat-soaked hair out of my eyes.

'Are you sure?' Delice yells back.

'I know what my sister looks like,' I snap. I eye their guns. 'And you can get them to put them down,' I say. 'I said, *she's not here.*'

I don't care if I am rude; I don't care that they are police.

And what do they think, anyway?

That Poppy killed two people then headed out for juice? I've never been on the run, but I can't imagine that's how I'd play it.

Behind me, customers have started to come out of the café. They have noticed the officers, the guns, and they are leaving, running to cars, panicked faces, talking urgently.

The owner has her hands on her hips and is walking towards us, speaking in fast, furious Creole, then English. All I catch are the words: 'What the hell?'

In front of me, Ruby is sobbing.

I go to her.

Instructions must have been passed on to the gunmen, because they lower their weapons but keep them close. As I pull away from Ruby, Dana shoots me a look; distrusting. Like Poppy is in there and I lied.

And as the officers retrace my steps to check, I realise something.

If I'd seen my little sister in there, that's what I would have done. Lied. So that if anyone finds her, it's not them but us – at least until we have worked out what the hell is going on.

Because I know that Poppy didn't do this. But I also know that, for a reason I don't grasp yet, someone is determined to make it look as though she did.

HOTTER

In the back of the police car, as we drive away from The Arts Cafe, a news alert beeps on my phone and I see the words *Saint Aurélie*.

I click.

> 3.15pm: Suspect's sisters seen entering Green Fig villa
>
> 3.30pm: Suspect's sisters leave villa and climb into police car. They look hurried. Sirens on.
>
> 3.40pm: Suspect's sisters arrive at The Arts Cafe. One of them enters the building before coming out.
>
> 3.42pm: Police officer enters The Arts Cafe, armed.

It's a live blog.

A live blog that is being updated by someone – presumably – in a tabloid newspaper office in London about what is happening right now to my family, here in the Caribbean.

How did they get a journalist or photographer here so fast?

I look out of the window. Hit the door panel with my left palm. 'Fuck.'

Delice looks at me in the mirror.

'Something upsetting on your phone?' he asks.

'You can read my news alerts if you want to.'

When he ignores me, I hold my phone out to my sister. 'Rubes, look,' I say quietly. 'Look what they're doing.'

Ruby scrolls the site – pop-ups every five seconds asking us to pay for this, for that – and grimaces. The phone trembles in her palm.

I lean across the car and read the live blog over her shoulder. We both watch and wait for an update, even though we are living it. Even though we *are* it.

My eyes only move from the live blog to look out of the car, to see if there is someone tailing us, or driving alongside us, to see where those updates are coming from. Because they're close. They have to be.

But there is nothing to see; only colourful houses built into steep hillsides that look like they're on stilts. And the sea, popping in and out of view, that giant wash of a horizon. Images from an alternate universe; a holiday dream world.

I look at the officers. Dana is on her phone too.

Is it possible it's them? Are *they* feeding the information to the press? When I read about the island before we came here, I saw mentions of deep-rooted corruption in police and political office. It's not impossible.

When Ruby's own phone rings, we both start. The wrong thing happening, on the wrong device.

'Emlyn again,' Ruby mutters.

I presume he turned up to collect us as planned at Parrot Island. He will have waited. Waited. And then, started to panic.

Like the last time he called, Ruby just stares at his name.

'Why aren't you answering him?' I say, irritated.

She shakes her head. 'It's . . .' She stops. 'I can't . . .'

We go over a huge pothole. *Up.*

'Just answer it, Rubes,' I say, as we land back down on the seat. I frown. Why doesn't she want to talk to Emlyn?

Finally, she accepts the call.

'Hey,' she says into her phone, then there is a pause. I can't hear what he says, but I can tell his voice is raised, animated. Panicked? 'Yeah. Ok. Ok.' She is answering an instruction. There is a pause. 'In a police car. With Junie.'

Why does Emlyn sound panicked? And what is he telling Ruby to do?

Another pothole. *Up. Down.*

I look at my phone again and see the last live blog entry moving down to make way for a new one.

> 3.47pm: Sisters back in police car. Leave Arts Cafe.
> No sign of the suspect.

Who the hell is watching us?

'Can you come and get us?' Ruby says to Emlyn.

She doesn't explain anything. She doesn't need to. He has obviously seen the news.

I look out of the window, an attempt to give them privacy. We turn, tight down a hillside, and I catch a brief glimpse of the nearly-neon Caribbean Sea. Sailing boats move slowly, louche. Big kids stand up barefoot on jet skis.

Ruby speaks again. 'We'll be at Daniel Bay police station—'

He interrupts her. His voice is audible, even if I can't hear exactly what he's saying. Ruby waits it out. I can hear him speaking again, louder now. She sighs. 'We're on our way back there now.'

Delice looks at Ruby in his mirror. 'You do know you can't go back to Green Fig, right? We can find you accommodation. But you can't go back there. You need to tell your fiancé that too, straight away.' He turns to his colleague. 'Can you get someone back at the station to sort the accommodation out?'

Green Fig Villa had been booked for another three days, even though Dad and Robin would have been on their year-long round-the-world cruise by then.

Now, though, the villa is a crime scene.

'Emlyn,' Ruby says into the phone. 'Don't go back to the villa.' Pause. 'Stay away.'

'How do we get the rest of our stuff?' I ask, while Ruby hangs up and slips her phone into her pocket.

'Someone will bring it,' Delice says. 'Once they've finished up at the scene.'

At the station, someone on the reception desk gives us a piece of paper with the name of a hotel written in biro. She tells us we're to stay there until we leave the island in three days; they've booked us in. That way the police will know where to reach us if – when – they need to ask more questions.

And then they let us go, into the unrelenting heat that would melt butter to a puddle. We wait outside the station for Emlyn. Ruby doesn't listen to a podcast; I don't do a crossword. We just stand. Too scared to speak openly this close to the station, to the officers.

'Rubes!' shouts Emlyn, as he runs in walking sandals from the car, a seven-seater Suzuki we've hired for the trip. Robin and Dad had hired a sports car too, for when they went out on their own, but this one was big enough for us all. In reality, we only went out in a group once, for dinner.

'Are you ok?' Emlyn hugs Ruby tight. When he pulls away, his face is taut with concern.

'Let's get in the car,' says Ruby, mouth pursed.

Emlyn looks at the station building. He goes to speak but before he can, a shadow appears behind us. Delice.

'Actually,' Delice says, 'as I've just told Mr Jones on the phone, we need to speak to him too. If you want to take the car, we'll sort a taxi out for Mr Jones when we've finished.'

Emlyn nods. Ruby looks scared.

'But why do you need to speak to—' she begins to ask.

Delice cuts her off. 'Standard procedure. Mr Jones was also staying at the villa.'

'It's fine, Rubes,' says Emlyn, but his face is white.

Ruby kisses him hard on the lips and burrows into him tight – it's unusual, they're not a PDA couple – before he peels away. I frown. *What's going on?* Emlyn follows the officer towards the station, while Ruby and I climb into the Suzuki.

As I get into the passenger seat, I turn to put my seatbelt on and over my shoulder see Emlyn speaking fast and focused to the officer as they walk towards the station. I watch. What's he saying? Surely *they* should be speaking to *him*? Bringing him up to speed. Leading this. But it looks like the opposite is happening, and a thought crosses my mind: is he getting his narrative out there quickly, because he has something to hide?

But no. Jesus. Not Emlyn. What is this day doing to me that I suspect the man Poppy and I call Mr Vanilla of committing murder?

When Ruby's phone beeps in the back seat, I jump.

'I'll just check that,' she says. 'Before we leave. In case it's . . .'

We know what she isn't saying. *In case it's Poppy.*

When she shows me the message, I look up at her.

'It is,' I tell Ruby, wide-eyed, heart racing. I point to the phone. 'That's her. It's Poppy.'

HOTTER

In front of me is a list of digits, 502150, all in a line, no breaks, from a number that Ruby doesn't have saved.

'What do you mean?' asks Ruby impatiently. 'It's just numbers. It's nonsense. Spam. It's not— What makes you think it's from her?'

It's a sauna in here now, without the air con, and I feel the sweat dripping down into the back of my knee.

'Is it a phone number?' she pushes. 'Is that what—'

'No,' I interrupt. 'Look at it, Rubes. It's not long enough for a phone number.'

She stares at it again. 'A code?'

'A code for what?'

'I don't know, Junie!' she snaps. 'A code for a safe?' Ruby huffs, irritable. 'Why don't you tell me what you think it is since you seem so sure it's from Poppy?'

And I feel relieved that Ruby is speaking to me normally again. This is better than the staring, broken Ruby of earlier. That Ruby terrified me.

I lean over and turn on the ignition. Twist the air con to full blast.

'It's backwards but . . . look. Fifth of the twelfth '05.' I wait for recognition but there is nothing. I say it quietly. 'It's the date Mum died, Rubes.'

On 5 December 2005, our mum Maria Jean Winter was one of four people to be killed in the worst avalanche ever to hit the Cairngorms. The avalanche happened at 2.33 p.m. in the northern corries, just a smidge north-west of Cairn Gorm mountain. It was a big story in the local news but quickly dropped out of the national press when a terrorist got early release and there was a fire in a tower block in Stevenage.

No-one else would store that date away. No-one else would remember it. No-one but me and my sisters.

There's no doubt in my mind that Poppy sent this message.

Now I need to work out why.

COLDER

Outside the window, a grey and white donkey wanders by, ears at attention and docile. Roadside stalls are loaded with fresh bananas and huge mangoes, stallholders sheltering under the relief of blue umbrellas.

Then, the roads get busier. We head through one of the island's liveliest towns, gift shops showcased outside their shopfronts with island tote bags and Saint Aurélie caps. Churches, grocery stores. Bustling bars and shacks. Every high stool taken, every hand holding a bright cocktail, a coffee, a steaming burger.

I watch it all, with my phone attached to my ear.

Redial.

Again.

Again.

I have been calling this number repeatedly since we were in the police station car park. In the end, I told Ruby to drive. I would keep calling, but we couldn't sit there all day.

Every time I call, though, the number rings out. No voicemail but not disconnected either. Someone is there.

After we have checked in at the hotel, Ruby sits, her body sagging, on the crisp white sheets of my hotel bed. I look out at the car park.

And I call again.

Again.

Again.

And again.

'She isn't going to answer, Junie,' says Ruby, tired.

But I ignore her. Hunch over my phone and send texts instead.

Call me.

Is that you?

I know what that date is.

But there are twelve messages on there now, and fifteen calls. And they've all gone unanswered.

I throw my phone down next to Ruby on my bed.

Our dad is dead. We aren't in touch with any of Mum's family or old friends, barring the odd straight-out-of-a-pack-of-fifty Christmas card.

I know that message is from Poppy. A message that looks like meaningless numbers to anyone else – even to the police who are likely tracking our phones. But it's a message that her sisters understand.

I message again.

CALL ME.

This time though, I get a message failure notification. The number is not recognised. A noise comes out of my throat, guttural.

She's gone. The breadcrumb's been vacuumed up.

◆ ◆ ◆

The next morning, I walk down the long hotel corridor towards the lift, pulling my plain black sun cap down low and listening to chatter from excited British kids in flip-flops who are going to the water park at Coconut Bay today. One of them dangles a pair of green goggles from his wrist. Hops up and down like he's downed three espressos.

I step into the lift. Head low, no eye contact.

For me, now, Saint Aurélie is not the holiday idyll it is for most people. It isn't water parks and white sand beaches and cacao tours. It's hell.

I am locked in only one thought. *My dad is dead. They think my sister killed him.* I am desperate to get off this island. At the same time, the thought of leaving is unbearable. Because when I leave Saint Aurélie, I leave Poppy. And then what? We give up on her?

Our flight is in two days.

With a lurch, the lift moves and heads down towards the ground floor. In my pocket, my phone beeps.

I take it out.

Not again.

This message is from a cousin of Robin's, who's flying out to the island today. She wants to meet me and Ruby; wants to know why Poppy did this.

The message is aggressive. Nasty.

I block them, like I have all the others. (Robin seems to have a fuckload of cousins.)

I am getting messages from other people too. People I haven't seen in ten years, but who are suddenly my best friends.

I can't turn my phone off though, in case there is news.

The lift door opens and my phone is still in my hand. Now I've picked it up, I've fallen down a rabbit hole and I am scrolling the news app.

We're a big enough story that we're still making the British news. A story about something Robin posted on Instagram the day before she was killed. Selfies with her Cartier watch and Chanel handbags in prime position. The name of the villa in the background. Enough detail, speculates the newspaper, that a local – actually, anyone with access to the internet – could have figured out where it was. Could have gone to Green Fig with the intent to burgle it and the knowledge that there were valuables there.

Yes. Someone else. Another suspect.

There are quotes, too, from someone who saw my dad buying baguettes at the food market on the morning of the murders. Someone who says he looked distracted. That he nearly left without paying because he took a phone call that looked heated.

It's a story that's obviously getting clicks. Which means it's being fuelled and fuelled and fuelled and fuelled. High-profile comment writers opine on what they think happened. There are detailed, picked-apart timelines.

> Did alleged St Aurélie killer have connections to the island's drug scene?

Drug scene? What the fuck?

> Evil Stepmothers: Why daughter/stepmum relationships can be so tricky.

I wince.

While there are the other angles and occasional suggestions of other suspects, the overriding view – I presume coming from the police press department – is that they are only looking for one.

Poppy.

Her character is being ripped apart. *She liked being alone. She went on solo hikes in the mountains. She wasn't into sport at school.*

I feel the fury surge in me as the lift moves. Big fucking woo. Some team captains kill people. Some loners don't.

But as I step out of the lift on the ground floor, and click on another tabloid site, I see a different kind of update. My brow furrows.

This one isn't opinion or speculation. This is a video – grainy CCTV.

The police haven't shown us this one, so I doubt it's come from them.

I stop, in the middle of the lobby. A woman walks around me, pulling a large suitcase and muttering something at me in Spanish.

I carry on staring at my phone.

The piece claims that this CCTV is the last recorded sighting of Poppy before the murders, taken the night before Dad and Robin died.

I click play and my belly lurches. It *is* her. She's walking down a wooden dock next to the sea. Then she pauses, slips off her tan sandals – *my* tan sandals actually, she borrowed them a few days ago – and climbs into a dinghy.

The video is narrated. The voiceover claims that the video footage shows Poppy walking away from Bleu, the most well-known and lauded restaurant on the island. It has two Michelin stars. Jesus Christ, me and Poppy had *joked* about that restaurant. A writer and an actor; as if us two could afford to go there. Better stick to whacking burgers on the grill.

What had my sister been doing at Bleu?

I keep watching. After Poppy boards the dinghy, the narrator says she is heading towards a giant yacht which is anchored in the next bay.

Another thwack to my middle.

A *yacht*? Whose yacht?

I think of people we knew at school – rich people, sure, but not yacht rich. It wasn't Eton.

Except . . . Perhaps it belongs to him.

Because Poppy is not alone in the video. Poppy is with a man.

On an evening when she told us that she had been at the villa, writing. Alone.

HOTTER

The man is tall – Poppy is tall, we all are, and he looks tall next to her so must be a good 6'3" – with posh-boy hair. Long-ish. Well acquainted with expensive conditioner.

There is no colour on the CCTV but this man is in a short-sleeved shirt, chino shorts and deck shoes.

And that's all I get.

I watch it again.

That, and the fact that he is clutching Poppy's hand tightly.

Too tightly?

I walk to the table that is set up by the sliding doors of our hotel, pour myself a glass of the complimentary Prosecco that's next to the bowl of bananas and apples and down it in one. Then I sit down on the cream leather sofa. I am the only one here. It's 7.30 a.m., still early, especially at a place where most people are on holiday. Those who are early risers are at breakfast or doing lengths of the pool while it's quiet. No-one else is sitting in the lobby alone, drinking and reading the news.

I press play.

Watch it again.

And I try to spot something. A clue in her body language, or a facial expression. *Something. Anything.*

Most of it is shot from behind, though, and nothing stands out.

Did Poppy talk about a man? Any man? A guy she'd spoken to in Adeline's, the coffee shop where she went to write? A mate who happened to be island hopping over here at the same time?

But I don't remember her mentioning anyone.

Which means there must have been a reason to keep this guy a secret.

Black-and-white chequerboard tiles gleam beneath me as the air con in the lobby blasts. My arms spring goosebumps. A woman in her sixties walks past and stares at my empty Prosecco glass. I haven't even got the energy to feel embarrassed.

I message Ruby.

Where are you?

It's 7.35 a.m. now, we were supposed to meet here five minutes ago.

Need to show you something ASAP.

Maybe Poppy spoke to Rubes about this guy. Maybe she knows something.

But the message sits unread.

I rest my head back against the sofa and feel a rise of irritation. It's all right for Ruby, having a lovely time in her hotel room with her fiancé. Too distracted to answer messages. Not staring at her phone the whole time like I am. Not alone.

I call Poppy's number again. *Fuck, Poppy.* I need her to get back here; I need her to explain all of this to me. How can I help her when I don't understand what she's doing? When I can't even begin to get my head around what happened that day. And why she's run.

I am watching the CCTV from the villa again when my phone rings in my hand.

Ruby, finally.

'Can you come up?' my sister says, before I can speak.

We don't live a life of pleasantries now, just information and need. But even by those standards, Ruby's tone scares me.

'Aren't you coming down?' I say. 'I thought we were meeting for breakfast.'

'Junie, just come up,' she snaps. 'Dana called.'

'What did she say?' She doesn't answer. 'Rubes, what did she say? You're panicking me.'

A pause.

'They've found her, Junie,' she says eventually. I hear a sob on her words, and realise why she didn't speak at first. Because she couldn't. She barely can now.

They've found her.

But there's an important omission.

Ruby doesn't say if they've found Poppy alive, or if they have found another body.

HOTTER

Two minutes later, we are in Ruby and Emlyn's hotel room, where we have been told to wait. Emlyn and I sit in silence; him on the edge of the unmade bed, me on the uncomfortable cream chair by the dresser. There is an atmosphere in here that isn't just about Poppy. I suspect they have been arguing.

The bathroom door opens. Ruby comes out and dabs gently at the corner of her mouth. Her face, despite the length of time we've now been in the Caribbean, is pale.

I watch her eyes. 'Hey.'

'Hey.'

'Did they say . . . ?'

She shakes her head.

'Not even if she's—'

Ruby shakes her head. 'No, Junie,' she snaps. 'Nothing more than that they've found her, and they're coming to speak to us.' Her eyes dart to Emlyn's and I think about his raised voice in the car. That conversation with the police officer. The atmosphere between him and Ruby.

And I look at him again, Mr Vanilla, still sitting on the end of the bed, his finger and thumb rubbing at a couple of days' rare stubble in a deep V.

In the end, I slide the balcony door open and go outside. At least there I can breathe. Think.

Ruby and Emlyn's balcony looks over the car park, like mine. I guess we were a late booking; the garden view rooms taken by people who didn't turn up at the last minute because their dads got murdered.

Then I hear Emlyn inside. 'Yeah, come in.' His voice is shaking.

When I go back into the room, my hand grips the first thing I find to hold onto, the handle of Ruby's red suitcase.

'Is she—' I begin, as the female officer from yesterday looks towards me.

But I still can't say it. Can anyone ask if their little sister is dead? It's like trying to make myself jump out of a plane: my body is saying no, no, no. The words won't form.

Thankfully, the officer fills in the gap.

'She is alive, June. As far as we know.'

My body resumes its usual functions. Breathing. Moving. Poppy is alive. Anything else is manageable; Poppy is alive.

Henry has her moments but she's definitely the kinder of the two officers. She's younger than Delice by a couple of decades. Perhaps she can relate to us more. Perhaps she has a sister.

'Now, I need you to be honest with me when you answer the next question,' she says.

I nod. Tighten my grip on the suitcase handle.

'Did you know that your sister got a flight back to the UK yesterday?'

What?

'Your dad's rental car is parked at the airport. We lose track of her after CCTV caught her landing at Gatwick and a passport check, which happened just before the bodies were discovered by the housekeeper,' says Henry, eyes flitting between Ruby and me.

'The housekeeper whose schedule you all *knew*, of course, as it was taped to the back of the kitchen door. So that's interesting timing.'

Poppy has gone back to the UK?

Poppy was booked on the same flight as I am, the same one as Ruby and Emlyn too. The one that leaves, as we always planned to do before this, in two days' time.

When Ruby would look after our boarding passes and Poppy would mainline Diet Coke and I would slap her grubby bare feet off an airport chair.

When we would waste time before they called the gate, buying crappy Saint Aurélie souvenirs and giant bars of Toblerone and taking the piss out of the grossly cute way Dad speaks to Robin, now that we were away from them.

That was the plan. To be on *that* flight together.

Dana asks again. 'Did you know that?'

Of course I didn't know that.

But something different comes out of my mouth.

'Actually, yeah.' My chin is jutted forward, defiant. *Challenge me, I dare you.* 'Poppy did say that she had some things that she needed to do back home. That she may need to get an earlier flight.' I make direct eye contact. 'I remember that now.'

I'm not sure if Sergeant Henry believes me. My heart is hammering. But I have to do *something* that makes it look less like Poppy killed our dad then fled the country. Something that reclaims the narrative that Poppy Winter is a dangerous double murderer. Something that lets her exist as what she really is: our antisocial, Diet Coke-loving, wild little sister.

It's an outright lie to the police.

But we're in a race now, to find her first. And races only have one winner. So I know with certainty: this lie won't be the last.

COLDER

Sergeant Henry stares at me. Eyes that bore through me, and make my cheeks flush pink. She has curled her lashes this morning. She is wearing subtle brown mascara, the kind of classic make-up look that Ruby normally goes for.

Out of the corner of my eye, I see Ruby frown at me, the tiniest hint of a creased forehead, and I know what she is thinking. *Poppy was never flying back early. Why did you lie?*

Why did I?

I try to work it out.

I just wanted it to sound as though Poppy hadn't made a rash decision. Or, even worse, planned in advance to take the earlier flight for another reason. Because that would sound suspiciously like it had been part of a much bigger plan.

To come to Saint Aurélie, to do her writing and bide her time. And then, when she was ready, to wake up in the sunshine one morning and end two people's lives.

◆ ◆ ◆

Two days later, with the police accepting that we don't know anything about where Poppy has gone, we are allowed to get our flight home as planned.

The live blogs have stopped now; the top spot has been vacated to make way for NHS waiting lists. Still, you don't have to scan far down the news agenda to find the terrible tale of the Winter sisters.

Now, we are in a taxi to the airport. I am in the front and Ruby and Emlyn are in the back, silent. There is an odd atmosphere between them again: one minute the PDAs are excessive; the next they are snippy with each other, fraught.

I usually guzzle every bit of Saint Aurélian scenery I can when I'm in a car on this island. Glimpses of the chilled-out Caribbean or the moodier Atlantic on the other side of the island. Of goats bleating as they wander the streets. One of the island's endemic iguanas that Poppy loves so much, crossing the road as brazenly as a London fox. Those spiky mountain views.

Today though, my head is down. Let's just get on with this.

Airport security is the kind of thing that Ruby normally finds stressful, marching us through hours too early, with everything in her bags labelled, sectioned and ordered. Today her eyes are glazed as we pass through the scanners.

I've realised something since this all happened: we can only have one dominant emotion at a time. Ruby and I are terrified. That means that we don't have room for anything else. I think it's why I haven't started grieving for my dad yet.

But it also breaks me, that thought.

What if we never find Poppy? Does that mean all I will ever feel is scared? I want a breadth of emotions. This shitty, *shitty* emotion can't be the only one.

We board the plane in silence, and I am convinced everyone's eyes are on us. Convinced everyone knows who we are and what our sister is accused of. I see a woman whisper to her husband and think: *She's talking about me.* This'll be a claim to fame when they get back: *Guess who we got a flight home with, Rita?*

When we land at Gatwick, we pull jumpers out of our bags. The temperature is three degrees. It's a shock to the system after the Caribbean but a sauna compared to what will come next: in six hours' time, we'll be back in Scotland.

'How long's your wait at Waverley?' I ask Emlyn, for something to say as we walk through Victoria station.

The train up to Edinburgh – after we get to King's Cross – will take four and a half hours. Then, for me, it's a fifteen-minute Uber to my flat in Leith. Ruby and Emlyn's journey is more gruelling. They'll get a connection to Aviemore, another three hours north.

Ruby's head whips round. 'You're not coming home with us?'

I feel a flicker of irritation. She *always* does this.

Leith is where I live. Where I have lived now, on and off, for nine years, since I left drama school in London and arrived back in Scotland, mild Scottish accent eradicated, clipped RP in place (wouldn't happen now, of course, people actually rate regional accents).

It's home. But because I don't have a *fiancé*, because I am single and show no signs of wanting to procreate and because I rent, Ruby treats me as though I'm a student, living a half, temporary life. She is the matriarch; the Cairngorms is home.

'No. I need to get home.'

'Why?'

We have stopped outside the eighty-seventh branch of Pret A Manger I've seen since we landed.

'Because . . .' Because what else is there to do but get on with normal life?

'Well, there's work, and—'

I have an audition coming up for a part in a play. They've picked up on the line on my CV that says I can play the flute. Now I need to remember how to play the flute.

'Please don't leave me,' she says, reaching for my hand. Emlyn stares at his phone. 'Not yet.'

And when one sister is missing but the other is in front of you saying *please, don't* – that middle sister who never asks for help because she is so keen to show you that she is nailing life – you can only make one decision.

As the train pulls away, I write an email to my agent, Carolina, and then to the casting director, Bobby. Try my best to explain something that is unexplainable.

Bobby replies quickly.

> Oh God, Junie. Don't worry. We can push it back a week? I saw the news. Of course you need to be with your family. Anything I can do, just let me know.

We know each other well. He's cast me in tens of shows over the years, at the same theatre. They're known to be super-cliquey but . . . well, I'm in the clique. And unless you get a gig on *EastEnders*, regular work isn't common in our business.

Emlyn stares out of the window. Ruby puts her AirPods in and closes her eyes. Opposite them, I lean my head back. I am exhausted. But again, I know sleep won't come.

◆ ◆ ◆

The next morning I sit on Ruby's leather sofa, too-hot black coffee in my hands, in my sister's flannel pyjamas and thick socks. I have nothing with me, barring swimwear and T-shirts. Flip-flops and shorts.

It's minus four degrees outside.

Ruby is crouched down in her slippers with a box of matches, lighting a stacked wigwam in the wood burner with shaking hands.

'Morning,' says Emlyn, appearing at the bottom of the stairs in a dressing gown and slipper boots, still unshaven. He heads to the kitchen. No small talk. No eye contact. I remember Morning Emlyn in the Caribbean – up early, getting a run in before the sun got too high. Here, Morning Emlyn is a ghost.

'There's coffee in the pot,' Ruby shouts after him, shoving a credit card bill into the fire and slamming the door shut as it roars. 'I've put toast in too. I'll come with you.' There are dark circles under her eyes that are not normally there.

Ruby follows her fiancé out of the living room and I can hear them whispering in the kitchen. I sigh. *What a stupid thing to do, to come up here.* I pull a blanket over my lap. Their Victorian semi is colder than my flat too.

When Ruby comes back in, she's holding a dinner plate loaded with buttered toast. She is crying.

I take the plate and put it on the coffee table and wrap my arms around her. But I feel a jolt of panic. Ruby never loses it. Never. Now though, she is heaving with sobs.

After a minute, she pulls away from me. Sits down.

Then I notice her do something. The spread of her fingers around her belly button. A minute movement.

Oh.

'I'm eight weeks,' she says, following my eyes to her belly. We both stare at it. 'I found out on holiday.'

I grasp for social cues. 'Congratulations,' I murmur. 'You found out before . . . Oh God, I'm so sorry this has been . . . with Dad. Poppy . . . Oh, Rubes, the timing, this is so unfair. But I am so happy for you. So happy.'

And don't we need something joyous to focus on? Maybe this will save us.

'Emlyn says you want to look for her,' she says.

I nod, slowly. Since we got back, I have been focused on Dad's funeral. Whether we hark back to his lapsed Catholicism or go for no-frills humanist. Wondering whether I can deliver the eulogy, without somehow mentioning the murder charge that hangs over my sister. Wondering, with a turn of my stomach, if Robin's awful and angry gaggle of cousins will turn up at the wake. Although, to be honest, I don't think the coroner's going to release the body any time soon, anyway.

I also still hold onto the hope that Poppy will call us and explain, somehow, how the whole thing is a misunderstanding.

If she doesn't, though, I know something. I will look for her. For however long it takes. Even if I have no clue where to start.

Except then my phone rings, and I have one.

I have a clue.

HOTTER

'Do you know a Lewis Williams?' I ask Ruby, as I end the call. In front of us the fire licks and flicks. Ruby is shovelling in slice after slice after slice of toast, washing them down with coffee.

It would be funny, her ravenous pregnancy hunger. If anything was funny.

She speaks through a mouthful. 'Who?'

I start at the beginning. 'That was Dana,' I say, nodding to my phone. 'The police officer from Saint Aurélie. She wanted to know if we know a man named Lewis Williams.'

'In what context?' Ruby frowns. She takes another huge bite, then speaks through her food. 'I don't think I know a Lewis . . .'

I interrupt her. 'They say he's Poppy's boyfriend.'

Ruby puts her toast down.

'Poppy hasn't got a boyfriend.'

I sigh. 'Well. She doesn't have a boyfriend *that we know of.* But they say there is one.'

'Is he the guy from the CCTV?'

I nod. Check my email and then hold my phone out. 'I think so. They sent me this. To see if I recognise him. It looks like the same guy to me.'

Ruby's breath sounds strangled.

'Oh,' she chokes out.

Because the picture on my phone is not just of this man, Lewis; it is also of our sister, looking completely like herself, white snow jacket and yellow bobble hat, somewhere up a mountain in the snow in Scotland, and cuddled in close to this guy. Eyes wide and bright with happiness.

It halts my breath. I haven't looked at pictures of Poppy since the murders.

'She didn't meet this guy in the Caribbean then,' says Ruby, frowning. 'She was already seeing him.'

I bite my lip as I reply to the email, giving permission for this man to contact us directly.

Fuck.

When it came to dating, me and Poppy told each other the grim and the hilarious. We told each other *everything*. How could this have been going on without me knowing?

A while later, my phone pings. I read the message.

I can't leave the island.

Police need me here for more questioning. But if you are still here, or you come back for anything to do with your dad and Poppy, I would love to meet up and chat.

Then a sign-off.

Lewis.

And so, less than forty-eight hours after we arrived home from the Caribbean – already exhausted, already jet-lagged and already spent and already *done* – Ruby and I pack our bags.

And we get ready to head back there.

HOTTER

It's thirty-seven degrees outside Rémy International Airport and I am wearing thick socks and a hand-knitted jumper made from merino wool that I picked up in a charity shop in Aviemore.

'An odd choice,' my sister mutters, gesturing at my weird clothes then blinking into the blinding sun. I dig for my sunglasses in my carry-on.

She's not wrong, I look ridiculous. But it seemed better this way round than walking to the car on Scottish ice at 4 a.m. in flip-flops. I stop and take off my jumper.

The Caribbean. How are we back here?

The clothes are manifesting my garbled mind.

I look around, for a sign towards the Car Rental, and nudge Ruby – *this way* – before we head towards it, pulling small cases on wheels behind us.

'Are you ok with that?' I ask her.

'I'm pregnant, not ninety.'

But Ruby is distracted. Wheeling her suitcase with one hand and typing to Emlyn with the other.

She stops on the pavement and stabs more words into her phone. I see Emlyn's reply over her shoulder.

You need to leave this

he writes.

I frown. Why would he want her to leave it? Because she's pregnant and he is worried about her? Or – I think about their hissed whispers, the awkwardness between them – is there another reason?

'Coconut Beach, right?' Ruby asks, as she climbs into the driver's seat and I open Maps on my phone. She is fiddling with the seat, moving mirrors.

'Actually, no,' I say, hand on a lever under my own chair to give myself more legroom.

'Change of plan.' I check my phone. 'We're meeting him at . . . The Reef Café. Which is on the way to the hotel, so we might as well go straight there.'

Ruby nods but she's distracted again. She picks up her phone and starts typing.

While she deals with Emlyn, I stare out of the window at the families wrestling luggage onto trollies, handing snacks to overtired children. I feel the familiar lurch of my stomach. As tangible as a piece of food I've swallowed, the anxiety sits there, a constant buddy now.

Eventually, Ruby throws her phone hard onto the back seat, hits the steering wheel with her palm and turns on the engine. We head out of the car park at a screech and I am forced back in my seat.

'Left-hand drive, Rubes!' I yell, as she moves off to the right. 'Same as at home, remember. And slow down!'

'Balls, balls, balls,' she mutters, and swings over sharply, muttering angry swear words at the beeping Honda coming towards us.

I direct her, reading out instructions on my phone, until we get to the West Coast highway. After a while, Ruby pulls off and our speed slows. A town, now. Street sellers handing out coconut water, feral chickens running across roads like escaped toddlers.

Ruby changes gear as we leave the town and start to climb. This island is one of the hilliest in the Caribbean; I had planned to cycle around it on our holiday but one afternoon with a rental bike had given me a reality check, especially in the heat. I'd swiftly switched to the air con of the Suzuki.

I look across at Ruby. Her hands are gripping the steering wheel. The road winds.

'You ok?' I ask quietly.

She nods, stoic. 'It's just hard. Being back here.'

Then she looks at the bright orange puffer coat that's on my lap. 'I can't believe you brought *that* as well as the woolly jumper, you mad woman.'

She is trying to be light, trying to be my sister. But something in Ruby is changed.

I prod various buttons, attempting to turn down the air con. 'If I don't work out how to do this in a minute, I might put the jumper on, to be honest.'

Loathing the cold is something I get from my mum.

Poor Mum, dragged kicking and screaming from London by Dad in the late eighties to the freezing wilderness of the Cairngorms, hacking the ice off her car every morning when all she wanted was pedicured toenails in wedge heels and a fancy cocktail on the beach. When her soul was still in a miniskirt on a roof terrace in Kensington.

A repeated promise from Dad: *It's not forever, Maria.* But then they had us and we started school, met friends, joined clubs, formed lives and suddenly it was. It *was* forever.

It was her forever.

Mum told me this not as a child of course, but as an – almost – adult. When she came to Edinburgh to see a play I'd been cast in at the Fringe. A version of *Gangs of New York* at

Pleasance Courtyard. I was seventeen and I'd just done my application for LAMDA.

We went out for dinner afterwards, tapas in a rammed Spanish place at 11 p.m. Mum ordered champagne and I wore heels and a short skirt that swished, and the whole place was lifted off the ground with the festival buzz and I felt, for the first time in my life, like a grown-up.

'You were magnificent,' Mum said, beaming as she speared an olive. '*Magnificent.* Star of the show!'

I'd had two lines.

She topped up my champagne. I felt it go to my head, and loved it.

'Magnificent!' she repeated, a bare arm reaching for my face, cupping my cheek with her glass aloft in the other hand. 'My baby, so talented. I could *burst.*'

She was so close to me I could smell her Chanel, floating across the table with a fog of Elnett and garlic. Red lips, as always, and dressed up to the nines.

She died four months later.

Mum would have loved it here.

Who came instead? *Robin.*

And Dad, whose most anticipated stop on his upcoming round-the-world cruise was Greenland. Who started to sweat at fifteen degrees.

I look out of the window. Graffiti sprawls across a stone wall – something to do with the right-leaning political party that's got a stronghold in this part of the island, I think. I'd read up on it before we came: the social democratic bastions that sat right next to conservative-forever towns, a small island population reliant on IMF loans and over-dependent on tourism.

'I can hear her voice,' I tell Ruby. 'The last time we did this journey, in the taxi. I can *hear* it.'

Ruby hadn't been with us on that drive. She had followed on with Emlyn, on a different flight because he had an important meeting at work.

'What did you talk about?' she asks.

I shrug. What do you ever talk about when you don't know it's one of the last times? When you think you have a million conversations left.

'That graffiti,' I say, nodding towards it. 'And how we were going to survive nearly two weeks with Dad. We thought the rum cocktails would be key.'

Poppy had barely spoken to Dad since she had moved out of home four years before. She was more nervous than any of us about the trip.

I slip my sunglasses down off my head and back on to my eyes, the glare bright even through the car windows.

'She thought Dad had an agenda, inviting us here,' I say quietly.

Ruby turns fleetingly. 'An agenda?'

'I don't know.' I shake my head. 'She was on one. But then maybe she was right . . . none of it made much sense, did it? Dad paying for this luxury holiday when everyone knew what a massive tightwad he is.' I catch myself. '*Was.* The fact it was thirty-five degrees and Dad liked being in places where he was only one lost shoe away from frostbite.'

Ruby answers. 'I guess it was close to the port where they were sailing from. It's hard to find ice near Florida.'

Something pulls at my insides then.

Dad. He's been lost in the melee, grief on pause. I know Poppy didn't kill him but there is no doubt about the other part: he is definitely dead.

'God, her face when Dad sent us that text in the taxi,' I say, wincing at the memory.

Heads up, chicks. I brought Robin xxxx.

Poppy's eyes had darkened when she read it. We were here. We had no time to change our minds now, and he knew it. Poppy had said the words we were both thinking: 'Who. The. Hell. Is. Robin?'

The driver our dad had booked to pick us up, Andre, had looked in his mirror, hearing the darkness in her voice. Wondering what – who, surely, it was the kind of emotive response that can only be caused by another human – had triggered it.

We never found out the answer to who the hell Robin was. Sure, we saw her bum up close as she sunbathed in her thong bikinis around the pool. We ate seafood salads with her at lunch and made small talk about reality TV shows – she had an almost-encyclopaedic knowledge of *Below Deck* and was *very* excited about the cruise. Even if it baffled me how someone who hated water and couldn't swim would want to spend that long on a boat.

But we didn't *know* her, know her.

Maybe we would have done eventually. But there was no time because then . . . well, then she was dead.

My phone beeps.

'Him again?' asks Ruby.

I nod.

Dad kept secrets, yes. But he wasn't the only one.

Now, we are about to unpick one of Poppy's. And work out where this boyfriend fits into things.

I reply to Lewis, just a few minutes away, and feel it again: that sense of foreboding.

There is so much more to this story – there has to be. And I'm desperate to unpick it all.

But I am also terrified. I'm terrified what I will find out if I go digging. I'm terrified what I will find out about my little sister Poppy, and the lies that she's been telling us.

COLDER

'This is it,' I tell Ruby.

I've finally worked out how to lower the air con in our hired Toyota Yaris and thrown my orange puffer into the back, but we have gone to the other extreme and there's a puddle of sweat in my lower back.

Ruby pulls a face. 'Is that it?'

We've driven half an hour to a sketchy-looking café, grubby plastic white tables on arid land out the front, unkempt dogs lolling in the heat under tables with dried-out bowls of water in front of them. Scrawled menu on a board.

INTERNET

SHAKES

BURGERS

'It's no Bleu,' I mutter.

Ruby says nothing.

We head inside. It's quiet. There's a pool table in the corner, two cues lying askew on top.

The man at the counter, young with wavy blonde hair to his shoulders, looks up as he snaps a puffed-up croissant with tongs then slides it onto a plate.

He nods towards a pile of menus instead of making eye contact. 'Grab one of those, girls,' he says in an American accent. 'The special's the mahi mahi.'

Then his eyes come up. He watches us, scanning around the place. 'If you're looking for someone, you know we have tables behind too, right? It's packed out back. Most likely they're there.'

We do as we are told, and head out of the back door. And here's where the café springs to life. More scrubland, but it backs onto the beach where there's a windsurfing school; a crop of people in wetsuits crashing off their boards into the waves out at sea. The heavy *dud-dud-dud* of a bass; a DJ playing on decks under a palm tree.

There must be twenty-five people outside the café, sitting in wicker chairs under the shade of fruit trees, squirting bottles of ketchup on chips or sipping long cocktails, tapping their bare feet with sandals slipped off to the music.

A waiter walks to a table, announcing an octopus stew and a pizza and looking harassed. They're understaffed; the whole place needs a tidy-up. One table has six empty beer bottles on, flies buzzing around it.

I look at every face, one by one. And then again.

But I don't think any of them are Lewis.

I think how many miles Ruby and I have travelled. How much we've spent on this flight to come back out here, so soon. My stomach dives.

'He'd better turn up,' I mutter to Ruby.

But then, I'm distracted. On a stool under an umbrella, there is a woman staring at me, lips attached to the blue straw in her drink. She wears more make-up than she does clothes but beneath it, I can see, she's still a kid. She raises her eyebrows at me, combative. *Yeah?*

Something about her makes me think of Robin.

I shake my head.

Ghosts.

Robin was nearly naked when we met her, too; standing with her hand on the waist of Dad's Hoff-esque red swim shorts wearing only thong bikini bottoms and a bandeau top. There had been two empty stubby beer bottles on the table.

'Girls! You're here! Meet the lovely Robin.' But my dad, as Poppy and I had registered how *young* this woman was – barely older than me – would not meet my eye contact.

I'd been too furious to look at him anyway. Too furious to hug him. He'd tricked us into coming on this holiday. He hadn't mentioned that he *had* a girlfriend, let alone that she would be here.

And I knew it wasn't her fault, but still, I hated her and her stupid bouncing bum cheeks on sight.

It had been twelve years since Mum died. That may sound like a patient timescale to meet someone else, but in reality (and is anything more of a reality than grief?), years take on new forms after a big loss. They're decades and seconds. No time and all time. Even after all these years, we needed *warning* before we saw our dad with someone else.

I'd steered Poppy – even more livid than me – to her room, muttering something about unpacking. I knew why Dad hadn't told us about Robin. Because even for a free holiday in the Caribbean, he knew we'd have said no.

I had clutched Poppy's arm tight: *Calm.*

In the café, now, Ruby nudges me out of my memory. 'Let's sit down. It's only just half past. He'll come.' But she bites her lip.

We grab the only free table – with the empty beer bottles and those bloody flies – and I scan around while Ruby goes inside to order our drinks.

After Lewis messaged me, we flew out on the first – painfully expensive – flights that we could get. I'd heard enough to know that Emlyn didn't want us to come here; didn't want us to meet Lewis.

'It's just because of the baby,' Ruby said, but I wasn't sure. Emlyn was different after Saint Aurélie. I kept coming back to the atmosphere in the hotel room. Did he know something? And whatever it was, had he told Ruby?

Then the other question I asked myself: someone had to have done this – so however vanilla I found Emlyn, could it have been him?

'Still no sign?'

When Ruby speaks, my cheeks flush. *Jesus. Imagine if she knew what I was thinking.*

Fifteen minutes later, the table has been cleared and Ruby is back but there's still no sign of Lewis. I call him.

No answer.

'Now what?' Ruby asks, setting her half-empty coffee cup on the table. She's got that look again, like she's about to throw up. Her hand rests on her tummy.

I pick up my phone. 'We keep trying,' I mutter.

I leave Lewis a second curt voicemail. Because if he doesn't show, so much has been wasted on this. My credit card is maxed out. I've lost the job; even as a mate, Bobby couldn't wait this long for me.

And then there's Ruby. I look at her little belly.

'Have you drunk enough water?' I ask her. 'Shall I get you something to eat?'

She says she's fine but I order us sandwiches anyway.

I look at every face on my way back to the table, one by one, in case I've missed Lewis. In case he's been here the whole time. But with every blank face I make eye contact with, this has more of the feeling of a wild goose chase.

'Anything?' Ruby asks as I get to the table.

'Nothing.'

Then she looks past me, towards the door. 'Hang on.' She nods her head and I turn and see a man so gorgeous, he could lead a movie. In the CCTV, Lewis is blurry. In his WhatsApp picture, he has sunglasses on and is in profile. Unlike most people's chosen shots, it does him a disservice. In real life he has curls that sashay; eyes that glint like a mirror.

He stands by the door, phone clutched in his palm. Then he spots us.

'Junie? Ruby?' He takes a large, rattling inhale as he arrives at the table. 'God, you both look like her, don't you? Sorry I'm late, I'm so bad at . . .'

He shakes his head.

'Anyway, I'm Lewis.' His accent is English and fancy. Silver spoons and private school, which makes sense with the yacht. Not to mention dinner at Bleu.

I look at him closely. *Interesting.* He's not at all who I would have thought Poppy would have gone for. Then again, what do I know? I thought she was single.

'Can I get you a drink?' he asks. 'I'm just going in to grab a coffee.'

'Americano, thanks,' I say, as our sandwiches arrive and Ruby bites straight into her cheese and ham hungrily. 'I'm Junie, by the way. We've come straight from the flight so . . .'

'Double shot?' Then his face flips to serious. 'I really appreciate you coming back. I would have come to you but the police don't want me leaving the island just yet.'

I try to keep my face neutral. They don't want him to leave. *Interesting.*

'Decaf for me, please,' says Ruby, as she finishes chewing.

'Got it.'

As he walks inside to the counter typing on his phone, I watch him.

Slim, toned calves.

A tan.

His non-typing hand is in the pocket of his board shorts. The watch on his wrist, not that brands are my expertise, looks expensive.

He doesn't look as smart as he was on the CCTV, but then he's not out for a fancy dinner.

Lewis is strong. Muscular. He could overpower a man past his prime, and certainly tiny Robin, who weighed about eight stone.

Does he look like he's devastated? Like his girlfriend's just been accused of murder and then disappeared? Like catastrophe has struck his life? *No.*

He's friendly. Inside at the counter, I imagine he's chatty with the barista as he orders our coffees. But it would be crazy to take him at face value. A man who was captured on CCTV with Poppy; the last sighting and a night she lied about even to us before she turned up wild-eyed with a knife at Green Fig.

A secret boyfriend. Jesus.

I feel guilty about the thoughts that crossed my mind earlier. *Emlyn.* This guy is a lot more likely to be involved than bloody Emlyn.

As I take a bite of my own ham and cheese sandwich, I turn to Ruby. I keep my voice low. 'Why wouldn't Poppy have told us about him? He's not some down-and-out. It doesn't make sense.'

'What part of this makes sense, Junie?' she replies, playing with the salt shaker. 'What part of this makes even the tiniest bit of sense?'

The door is pushed open. Lewis thwacks back out in designer flip-flops towards the table. Lands back on his seat hard. 'They'll bring them over,' he says. He looks us both right in the eye. 'Wow, you really do look like her. Both of you.'

I watch him as I take another bite of my sandwich.

Like this is news to us, a lifetime later. I see Ruby with those fingers splayed again around her belly button. Maybe whoever is hanging out in there will look like us when they're born too. But will Poppy be back by then? And if she is – unless the police find another suspect – what the hell will be happening to her?

As I finish eating, I lean forward. Take the lead.

Lewis has to be the answer. Has to be.

'How did the police find you then?' I ask, wiping a crumb from my mouth. 'If *we* didn't even know . . . How did they know you're Poppy's boyfriend?'

I don't take my eyes off him.

He nods. 'I guess it was that CCTV,' he says, fingers playing with his light stubble. 'I was in Grenada and off-grid. Didn't hear the news. But I travelled straight here when they called me.'

Do his cheeks colour slightly then?

I wait him out.

'I suppose . . . Well, I was going out with her and I was one of the last people to be seen with her, so I get that I'd be a person of interest.' Earnest. 'And I was *glad* they called me, in case they found her. So I could speak to her. Support her.' He shakes his head. 'Then I found out she'd flown to the UK.'

I watch him.

He must believe she's innocent. Otherwise, he'd run a mile, surely. Distance himself immediately from being the boyfriend of a double murderer.

Believe she's innocent or *know* she's innocent, though? Does he know she's innocent because he was there? Because he *isn't* innocent? I study him.

'So you've been together about a year?'

He nods. 'Thereabouts, yeah.'

'And how did you meet?'

He bows his head, then, and when he looks up his expression is darker.

'Oh, it was . . . I guess it was Spencer, really.'

'Spencer?'

'Sorry, Spencer was my best mate.' He smiles, then it falls away. 'Since we were three. Spen died trying to break up a fight between two guys in Notting Hill one night. We'd had some beers but it wasn't his . . .' He looks up. 'I wouldn't want you to have the wrong idea. Spen was trying to do the right thing.'

'And Poppy was there?' I scan my mind for a trip Poppy took to London a year ago. It does ring a bell . . .

Lewis is shaking his head. 'No, she wasn't there . . .' He pauses. 'I didn't know her then. We met later.'

He puts his drink down.

He nods. 'The truth is I didn't handle it well, when Spen died. I fell in with a dodgy group, being with our old mates without Spencer was . . .' He shakes his head. 'It was too much. Easier to lose myself in a new crowd.'

I wait him out.

'I decided to get away,' he says. 'Put a backpack on. Go travelling, indefinitely. I realised that I wanted out of London life. I was in banking, if you can believe it.'

I think about the boat shoes he was wearing on the CCTV. I try to flash a 'no shit' glance at Ruby, but she's staring into space again.

'I wanted away from that scene,' he says. 'I wanted something different.'

'And you met Poppy while you were in Scotland?'

He smiles. 'That's right, yeah. Cairngorms was my first stop.'

'How did you meet her?'

'Café she was working in. It was quiet, not many customers. We got chatting about hiking routes.' He smiles, looks up at us.

'She knew her stuff, didn't she? When she was on her break, she sat down to help me map a walk.'

Her writing never paid enough. Poppy – same as me, as an actor – did shifts in a plethora of bars and coffee shops over the years. The odd Amazon delivery driver gig.

'I might have replaced booze with caffeine,' he says, wry smile. 'Or maybe it was because of Poppy. But either way, I was in there all the time.'

'Is it serious?' I ask him. 'I mean, I guess . . . if it's been a year.'

He cocks his head to the side. 'Well . . . most of that I've been away. Like I said, I'd decided to live this nomad kind of life. I really like your sister – she's amazing – but I don't stay anywhere long. She flies to meet me, when she can, when she's saved up a bit.'

I remember a few trips. Times she said she was going to meet a mate who was travelling. When she disappeared for a while, not much notice. But I never questioned it: that was Poppy.

'I guess we're serious, but in our own way.'

I frown. What does *that* mean?

'Why didn't we know you existed?'

Lewis takes his time to answer. Then he looks up. 'I respected her wishes, I guess.'

I feel like I've been punched. Her wishes to keep the fact she was in a relationship from us?

'Poppy is a secret keeper,' he says, sighing. 'You must know that, right?' He picks up his cup. Whirls the final dregs of his coffee around the bottom. Drains it and chuckles to himself. '*Man.* Poppy Winter. That girl is a live wire. Unpredictable. More secrets than anyone I know.'

The words cause a jolt to run up my spine and back down again. I turn to Ruby, who looks equally shocked.

Does she?

HOTTER

Half an hour later, Ruby's eyelids are drooping. I reach out and touch her wrist and she jolts.

'I'm fine,' she says, blinking at me. 'I'm fine.'

The decaf she's switched to in pregnancy isn't coming close to fighting the exhaustion and the jet lag and the human battling for fuel and energy. She needs to sleep.

I look at her, and my stomach lurches.

Oh, Rubes.

This is not how pregnancy should be for her, after all this time. She should be at home having her feet rubbed and the bath run. She should be with Emlyn.

And then I feel guilty again, for thinking he could be involved.

'You ok?' Lewis asks, looking edgy. He glances at Ruby. 'Is she . . .'

Ruby stands up abruptly and walks fast towards the door to the café.

'She's fine.' I sigh. 'She's probably going to the loo, to throw up.' He looks alarmed. 'She's pregnant.'

'Oh.' There's a pause. 'Did Poppy know, before she . . .'

I shake my head.

He smiles, sad. 'She'd have been so excited.'

But I'm too distracted to get emotional about that.

I'm fired up on double shots and adrenalin and I want answers, and I don't want to pause this, whatever state Ruby is in.

I let my pregnant sister chuck up in a cubicle again and come back to the table, and I don't march her to the car. Because *I* want to stay. I need to find Poppy. Just like I needed to come out here again.

More secrets than anyone I know.

How can I leave now?

I lean forward onto the plastic table and feel the leg wobble on uneven ground. Lewis takes a receipt out of his pocket, wedges it and shoves it under the table leg. Every second, I watch him.

'Go on then,' I say, as his handsome face reappears from under the table. 'Why did she keep you secret? Are you married?'

Lewis laughs. 'No, not married.'

'But?'

He ponders. 'But I guess Poppy knew that there was no *point* introducing me to family anyway, because it wasn't that kind of vibe. And we were both ok with that, you know?'

Ruby comes back to the table, sits back and rests her eyes.

I lean forward. Up close, I realise that Lewis isn't as young as I'd thought. There are lines around his eyes. Thirty-five or thirty-six, perhaps?

I stop myself from rolling my eyes. I wish Poppy had told me about this guy. I'd have passed on older sister wisdom: this, right here, is your bog-standard commitment-phobe dressed up as some sort of bullshit romantic nomad who is definitely too old to pull this off. I bet he writes poetry. And I bet it's bloody awful.

'I was always honest with her about it,' he says, defensively, and I wonder if he can read my expression. 'I was never going to be the guy who puts the bins out.'

'So that's why you didn't come on the family holiday, then? Not a meet-the-in-laws situation?'

Because he'd have been welcome. I remember Dad's words: *Feel free to bring plus ones. Green Fig is huge.* I remember it because Emlyn *had* come. I remember it because I was irritated knowing how smug Ruby would be about being the only sister with a plus one. Like it was some sort of adulting victory, getting a mortgage broker from Llandudno to agree to hang out with you for the entirety of your existence.

Lewis nods again. 'Exactly, yeah. Not my thing.'

My stomach twists. I picture Poppy. Putting herself out there. Inviting Lewis along on a family holiday. Then trying to be Cool Girl, *no pressure, it was only a thought*, when he said no.

I want to punch him.

'But you came to the Caribbean anyway?'

He smiles. Looks out towards one of the many rocks of islands that pepper the coastline. A whoop goes up behind us to a club classic I recognise but can't name and a group of girls in their twenties start dancing between the tables. 'Just briefly. On the way to Grenada for the environmental project. I suggested we caught up for the night.'

I nod.

'It's disconcerting, though,' I say, eyes on him even though his are still out to sea. 'That Poppy has never mentioned you at *all*, even if you are casual. I'm sure she told you that we're close.'

I watch his breath catch. His eyes are back on the table. He opens and closes a ketchup bottle again.

'And I have another question,' I say, not waiting for him to answer. 'Why did it take you so long to contact the police? I know you've been a bit off-grid being a nomad or whatever but it's been international headline news. And casual or not, she's your girlfriend. Someone *must* have mentioned it to you, surely?'

I pause before I say, 'That, to me Lewis, is a bit suspect.'

And at the word *suspect*, Ruby seems to wake up. Her eyes flicker open. She sits up straighter.

Of course she does.

Because another suspect is exactly what we're looking for. And here is one, sitting in front of us holding an empty coffee cup. Panic flitting and dashing across his movie-star face.

If we give the police a suspect, they can let go of their only current one: our sister. And then she can come home.

I watch Lewis.

Finally, I think, we have an offering.

COLDER

His eyes are cold now. Lewis is less attractive when he's angry.

'This is bullshit,' he says, standing up. 'You sound like you're . . .' He shakes his head, curls shaking like a damp mop. 'Like you're *accusing* me.'

Before I can answer, he speaks again.

'I was trying to help. Look, I didn't *need* to contact you. Either of you. I've answered every question, I've been an open book. I just wanted to meet you both and try to . . . And you've turned it into . . .'

He bites his lip.

'Poppy would hate this,' he says. 'She'd hate that you're doing this to me. She'd want us to get on, she'd . . .'

I laugh. '*Would* she? Then why didn't she introduce us?'

He pushes his plastic chair backwards with his body. 'I'm leaving.'

I watch him.

I get the vibe that no-one ever criticises Lewis. That he bolts before he's challenged. Before life gets hard.

Great choice, Poppy. As if the boat shoes weren't a clear enough red flag.

I push my own chair backwards too.

The DJ plays '*Lola's Theme*'. People close their eyes. Raise cocktails in the air. Dance barefoot and whoop.

A woman on the next table turns, mouth still on her cocktail straw and an eyebrow raised, curious about us. *What sort of idiots argue in a place like this?*

'No,' I say, blocking Lewis's path. 'No, you're not leaving.'

And that feeling that's swept over me occasionally in the last few days, creeping up past the layers of devastation and frustration and fear, comes again now. Rage. Unfiltered and ballistic.

'And please don't tell me what my sister would hate,' I snap.

What happened that day? I told the police that nothing unusual was going on when my dad was murdered. That everything was the same as usual.

But that wasn't true. There was Poppy's secrecy over her writing. Her attitude – not just about Robin – towards Dad. The hissing in the kitchen with Emlyn. Flashes of temper. But it's more than that. Something must have been *more* unusual, mustn't it? Because things like this don't happen out of the blue. The story always unravels; there's always more than at first appears. Layers to peel back.

The yacht trip and the fancy dinner have to be a layer. *Lewis* has to be a layer.

Now, I have to unpeel them all. Because otherwise it's a life of never knowing. Life lived on an open question.

Lewis hasn't sat back down but he hasn't left either.

We stare at each other.

'We came all the way out here to meet you,' I say. 'Ruby's fiancé is barely speaking to her. I missed out on a job that I could really do with to pay my rent.'

Ruby has her head in her hands now.

'We've both maxed out our credit cards,' I continue. 'We came back to the Caribbean, when we'd barely got back to Scotland. I wore a jumper because I can barely keep up with what sodding distance I am from the equator. Have you got any idea how exhausting and expensive all of this is, even at the best of times and let alone when someone is pregnant and grieving and should be at home relaxing and . . .' Ruby is sobbing now, audibly. I look at her belly, then back at Lewis. 'You. Are. Not. Leaving.'

And then, shaking with fury, I place a hand on his left shoulder and push. There is authority in being tall sometimes and I watch him – just over six feet – and feel a power I wouldn't have if I was five foot two, if I was petite like Robin.

'Sit.'

Then I position my body in the way of Lewis's exit.

'Ok,' he says, eventually, sitting down now. 'Ok. Fine. You're right, you've come a long way. Honestly, I don't want us to be enemies. Just . . . tell me what I can do. What gaps can I fill in? What do you want to know?'

I stay standing. 'I want to know everything. The truth. Something that will give us answers about what happened to Dad. Something to help clear her name, so that she can come back. Something to help Poppy.'

Something to help me, I think. Please, someone help *me*.

'But mainly?'

'Mainly, we want to know where she is.' I look at Ruby, who is still crying. 'Ruby and me, as her sisters. Whatever the truth is, we can deal with it. But we need to know where she is.'

I know Ruby is looking at me, questioning, but I don't look at her because I'm following it: this instinct I've had since we got here, since I first saw Lewis's face.

Since I watched him dodge my eye contact.

Since I thought about the messages that he and I exchanged, when he asked us to come back out here and meet him.

Since that question ran through my mind: who gets someone to fly all this way unless they have something to tell them that is unmentionable in messages? No-one does that just to chat over coffee.

I know the police are tracking our phones, in case Poppy gets in touch. Lewis would know that too. Anything important would have to be delivered in person.

'I think you know something,' I say slowly.

'What?' says Ruby, eyes snapping upwards. Something darts across her face but I can't think about that now. I am watching Lewis.

He puts his head down.

But when he looks up at me, he nods.

HOTTER

I stare at what Lewis is showing me on a phone that looks out-of-the-box new.

'Oh my God,' I whisper.

I turn to Ruby, who is upright now, back in the room. 'You see what this is?'

Not a confession from Lewis. Not an admission of his guilt. Not what I wanted.

But still *something.*

Ruby shakes her head. 'No. What is it?'

I look at Lewis. '*You* see it, though, I'm presuming? This is why you got us out here?'

He cocks his head to the side. 'I don't get exactly what . . . well, that's why I wanted you two to look at it,' he says. 'But yeah, I get that it's *something.*' He looks directly at me. 'Something from Poppy.'

Ruby's eyebrows shoot upwards.

I snatch his phone from him and look at the message again. In front of me is a jumble of numbers and letters. I think about the last time I saw something like this: the date of my mum's death. But this is different.

'I still don't get it,' says Ruby.

‘The first part is OS co-ordinates,’ I tell her, pushing her coffee cup out of the way and putting Lewis’s phone on the table. I poke at the screen. ‘It’s just put in a weird format, see, so it doesn’t look like them. But if you move the space to there. . .’

57.14 75 N, -3.7550 W

My mind whirs to catch up. OS maps and co-ordinates. We’re all familiar with them; we grew up with maps in our leggings pockets.

All of us. Including Poppy.

‘The most important part though,’ I tell Ruby, ‘is this.’

She looks up at me and I point to the second sea of digits.

‘It’s a *date* and *time*, Rubes.’

‘Meeting instructions?’

‘Exactly.’ I pick up the phone and copy and paste the first part of the message into Maps. ‘But this is the important bit, Ruby, the mad part. Because look at where the meeting instructions send us.’

I zoom in and hold it out to her.

‘I knew you’d get it,’ Lewis says, victorious and a little smug. ‘This is why . . . I know it’s a long way for you to come, I know it’s too much and the money and everything but *this* – this was why.’ Then he looks at me. ‘Where is it, then?’

‘If you knew we’d get it, why not show us the *moment* we walked in?’ I snap, looking up from the phone. I still don’t trust him, even with this. But I don’t have many options. I need to see where this goes. Keep Lewis close. ‘Why didn’t you tell us straight away?’

Lewis sighs. ‘I didn’t know if I was being ridiculous, if it was nothing. Or if it was sent by a crank, even . . . And then you seemed to . . . well, as the conversation went on, you seemed to *suspect* me and I got scared. I didn’t know if you’d get me in trouble with the police and—’

Jesus, he's such a kid.

But then he speaks again. 'And I wanted to chat to you first, to be honest. Check that I trusted you.'

'*Trusted* us?' I spit, but Ruby puts her hand on my arm and I consider it. Lewis might view us in the same way we view him: as potential suspects. Perhaps more so. Unlike him, we had reason to hate Robin. Unlike him, we had reason to be angry with Dad. For Lewis, those feelings don't exist; as far as I know, he never met either of them.

Still, I am sure he's hiding something.

I look at him, then out at where some men about Lewis's age are trying to windsurf and failing. 'And do you?' I ask. 'Trust us?'

There is a pause before he answers. 'I think so, yeah. Even if you got pissed off with me . . .' He smiles, sad. 'But you remind me of Pops.'

I stare down at the table.

'Emlyn is going to kill me,' Ruby mutters. She puts a fingertip on her belly. For a while, all three of us just watch the terrible windsurfers. 'If we go to this place as well . . . It's exactly the kind of thing he didn't want me to do.'

'Well, he might get his way,' I say, thinking. 'I'm not sure it's even possible to get there in time, from here. It's only three days away. Can we do another flight that quickly? Then get all the way up to the mountains?'

Because if we're right, then the co-ordinates take us to Scotland.

Poppy has gone home.

◆ ◆ ◆

'If we're even considering this, then I need more coffee,' I say, pushing my chair back to stand up, a vicious *screeeeakkk* as the legs brush the floor. 'My round. Same again?'

There are absent-minded nods.

'Decaf, remember,' mumbles Ruby, downcast. Then she mumbles lower. 'Bloody decaf.'

I put a sympathetic hand on her arm.

I head to the counter, leaving Lewis and Ruby staring at their phones. Lewis is back on the message, on those co-ordinates. Ruby is looking at flights.

'I take it you called the number?' I ask Lewis when I sit back down. 'The one that sent this message?'

He nods. 'Dead. Which means it's even more likely it's her, right? On a burner? She sends the message, then ditches the phone straight afterwards. She wouldn't risk keeping it.'

Still, I call the number again from my own phone.

'This number has not been recognised.'

Ruby sips her coffee. Winces as it burns her mouth.

'How far is this place from where you live then?' Lewis asks Ruby.

I look at Google Maps again and answer for her. 'Less than half an hour.'

Ruby explains the geography. 'But you know it a bit anyway, right?'

Lewis nods. 'Yeah.' He peers at my phone over my shoulder. Points. 'I think we've been round some of those parts. We stayed in a bothy one night which must have been . . . I love it there. But I guess I'm not familiar with up that way . . . Poppy does all that stuff, when we hike. Maps and routes and kit. I just turn up with a packet of biscuits.'

Shocker.

'I hadn't realised,' he says, wincing. 'I'm so sorry. I didn't know you'd have to fly straight back.' He trails off. 'I just thought it was a weird message, and that it must be something to do with Poppy.

That it was too random to be a coincidence. Especially when the number disconnected.'

He is convincing. But still everything in me is screaming: *You're lying about something.*

As I try to work out what, Ruby stands abruptly.

'Cake,' she says. 'I need to throw sugar at this situation.'

The hand's on her belly again, and she looks at me, as I type Saint Aurélie to Gatwick into Skyscanner. 'Find out if there's some bloody loyalty scheme with this airline as well. We must be *racking* up points.'

But then her face straightens. I put my hand on her arm. 'Three days, Rubes. Tell the baby. Three days and we could have Auntie Poppy back.'

But Ruby looks like she is going to be sick again.

We know we need to find her first. We know we need to find her before the police do. What we don't talk about is what we will do then.

If we meet her. *If* she's there. Because we both know that this nightmare won't end with Poppy coming back. In a lot of ways, as she faces a double murder charge in a country that still has the death penalty, it will only just start.

Unless, of course, the police have another suspect.

Lewis looks up at me. Smiles.

And I look back at him.

You.

COLDER

In Scotland thirty-five hours later, I break. In the last seventy-two hours, I can't have had more than ten hours' sleep. And most of it has been upright in an aeroplane seat with someone interrupting it to ask me if I want to take advantage of the special two-for-one offer on an indulgent and luxurious Charlotte Tilbury anti-ageing cream.

I think I'm tired at the end of an opening night. When it's 1 a.m. and I'm still not off-book and the callback is tomorrow.

I think I'm tired when we have a lock-in at the pub next to the theatre and the young cast members who drink kombucha have gone home but the rest of us are half-cut on house red.

None of it compares to this.

I am exhausted, to my bones.

The day's structure has done what it does when trauma happens; it has disintegrated. The meals I usually think about so much, defrosting and balance and protein, eating the rainbow and plenty of fibre, now consist of beige carbs and vending machines and functionality.

'I'm worried about you,' Ruby says, as we wait for Emlyn outside Aviemore station.

I groan. 'Oh God, Rubes, don't say that. I can't let you worry about me. You have enough to worry about.' I'm not pregnant. I didn't just throw up at 30,000 feet in a BA toilet. 'Please don't be worried. I'm fine.'

But I can feel it and she can feel it too, sharp as ice on bare toes.

I need my habits and my order and my space. Always have.

Without them, I've toppled off my tightrope.

'There's Emlyn,' she mutters, as a grey Volvo pulls into the car park, and she glances at Lewis. She looks wary.

As we approach the car, pulling our cases behind us, Emlyn gets out of the driver's side. Takes our bags and puts them in the empty and pristine boot. Then he notices.

'Oh,' he says, looking at Lewis. 'Oh. Hi.'

I try to read the look that passes between him and Ruby, before he flicks on his standard Emlyn politeness. 'You must be Lewis,' he says. He slams the boot closed – the car is so clean it's gleaming too – then puts a hand out. 'I'm Ruby's fiancé, Emlyn.'

'Good to meet you, mate.'

Emlyn walks back round to the driver's side in silence. We all shut the car doors behind us and pull on our seatbelts. In the car – Lewis in the front with Emlyn as per some outdated male/female car rules, and me and my sister twisting our long legs into the back – there is silence.

There's a light frost outside the window. It isn't as bad as the one inside.

Is he ok? I mouth at Ruby, after poking an elbow into her middle to get her attention.

She shrugs.

Really, his reaction's not surprising. Emlyn likes to make Christmas plans in June. He favours holidays booked two years in advance so he can set aside cash and pay them off monthly.

And now, here we are, throwing Lewis onto him not only without warning but without any opportunity to object, because we're all in an enclosed space. He's also probably worked out that Lewis is sleeping in his spare room tonight. And no-one has asked what he thinks about that.

Now, as we turn out of the car park, I can only see the back of Emlyn's head. But I still know what his facial expression is.

He turns on Radio 4.

'Where is it from here, then?' asks Lewis, turning to me and Ruby as we come off the main road and descend into the darkness of the more rural lanes. Emlyn flicks the full beam on. Lewis looks around. 'Will we come back this way?'

I feel Ruby twitch beside me. *Oh God.*

Lewis presumes Emlyn knows what happened in Saint Aurélie. He presumes that Ruby filled him in.

But Ruby clearly hasn't told him any of it.

'Come back this way for what?' Emlyn asks.

'We think Poppy's messaged to arrange a meeting,' Lewis says, somehow not picking up on the tension or the mood, typing on his phone. Distracted by something, everything, always.

For a hippy nomad, he's one of those people whose phone is an extension of their hand. Who doesn't think it's rude to speak to you while looking at it and checking, checking, checking everything.

Emlyn looks at Ruby in the mirror. I see it again: that look that passes between them. Unreadable. 'What?'

'Will you be you coming with us, mate?' Lewis asks, oblivious, head still down.

Emlyn just grips the steering wheel, tighter and tighter and tighter as he eyeballs Ruby in the mirror. 'No, Lewis, I won't be coming with you,' he says. 'I'll be at home being the grown-up. As per.'

My eyes stay focused on the mirror.

One thing is clear. Emlyn doesn't want us to look for Poppy.

But what I can't work out is if he is just worried about Ruby's health and their unborn baby. Or whether he has another reason to want us to leave it alone.

HOTTER

A terrible night's sleep, then a day of unpacking and various attempts at naps, and Ruby, Lewis and I are on our way to meet Poppy.

'Here?' asks Ruby, who's driving, through a yawn. 'You sure?'

The co-ordinates 57.14 75 N, -3.7550 W take us up to broad high ground way up in the mountains. We leave Ruby's Fiat Panda tucked half into a hedge on the curve of a country road, wing mirror an almost certain casualty.

I look around.

Oh. I know this place.

We came up here when we were kids; it's sledge paradise. You even get the odd learner skier, or mums and dads teaching their kids to snowboard. Once we persuaded Mum to let us bring an old rug that was in the garage and flew down on it together – Mum included. A few hours later, we'd picked up a gaggle of other kids and a sausage dog in a jumper named Mavis to join us on the 'magic carpet ride'. Mum was still the only parent.

'Do you remember?' I ask Ruby now, smiling. 'We were up here for hours.'

'I remember,' comes the voice as she turns the engine off. The internal light comes on and I see her face, pale. She isn't smiling.

'I don't know if this is . . .' But she trails off. The silence echoes. There is nothing here. No-one.

But hopefully, one person will appear soon.

About two miles down the road behind us, there is the coolest après-ski café where I've drunk a thousand marshmallow-laden hot chocolates and a fair few beers; shovelled down bowls of spicy chilli. It will be long closed for the day now. A mile or so up the mountains are the ski fields. Extremely weather dependent – especially in recent years, as the world heats up – but when they have a good day, world-beating.

Here though, in the middle of those two, there is reams of nothing. Now the car lights are off, the place feels like an undiscovered planet. The blackest of black.

I pull my gloves on. Hit my watch to light up for the time. It is 9.50 p.m. but it feels like the early hours. We're still crawling through the world's longest January.

Ten minutes until our meeting time.

'Did you bring a torch?' asks Lewis from the back seat.

'We're going to go without for now,' I tell him. 'Draw as little attention to ourselves as possible.'

He looks out of the window.

'But—'

'Your eyes will adjust.' I sound impatient. I watch him. Touch the Swiss army knife in my pocket. 'Ready?'

Ruby, lit up by my watch light, touches my arm.

'Is this definitely a good idea?' she asks, frowning.

'Don't worry,' I reassure her. I nod downwards, giving her the tiniest glimpse of my knife, and alarm dances across her face. We open the car doors.

The three of us trudge across fields that have seen a thick dumping of snow in the last twenty-four hours, towards the co-ordinates; as close as we can pinpoint it. The whole time, I keep my eyes on Lewis.

I can barely see in front of me. I've lived in cities for a long time and my eyes have adjusted as though I've started wearing glasses; I forget how dark this place can be.

Time to rope in the other senses. I listen hard.

'Be careful where you step,' I say, turning to Ruby. Her pregnancy is so early. So precarious.

'I'm going to have to turn the torch on,' she says, ignoring me and trudging forward in her sturdy snow boots. She's lent me a spare pair, but they are a size too big and my feet slide around in them. 'I'll keep it low.'

The light might spook Poppy, but we don't have a choice. The dark is too absolute.

When the torch is turned on and Lewis and I fall into line behind Ruby, I look around. Get my bearings. The mountains ahead, just visible, and the frozen loch down there through the thicket. In between that though, there is just an expanse. As meeting places go, it's as barren and isolated as there is.

It's perfect.

I congratulate Poppy in my head. She plans our routes when we hike together, the most adept at mountain craft and reading OS maps and putting a tent up in bad weather out of the three of us. Of course she would get this right.

It makes me feel better too; *she'll be ok. She can survive.*

I check my watch: 9.56 p.m.

But as I look at it, I slip again in the badly fitting boots. Ruby reaches out and grabs me.

I keep walking.

I can hear the ghost of kids' shrieks with every step. A toddler Poppy in a thick snowsuit being pulled by Mum down the hill. The three of us building ramps to make obstacle courses then hopping in our sledges to take them on, getting stuck halfway down.

Hopping out in bright yellow wellies to shove each other over the ramps and keep going. Zero fear.

I check my watch again: 9.57.

'Shall we shout her?' Ruby whispers.

I shake my head, then realise that's useless. 'No. Best to stay as quiet as we can, I think.'

9.58.

'Stay still?' I whisper. 'Or keep walking?'

She looks around. 'A little further from the road maybe? It's more hidden.'

We walk towards the trees, the barrier between the field and the drop that we had walked around so many times as kids.

9.59 p.m.

'Here?' I ask Ruby.

Lewis is silent, out of his comfort zone and following our lead in a pair of not-in-any-way-snow-proof trainers. My eyes scan back to him regularly.

We're in a dense blanket of trees now.

'Let's stay still,' Ruby says. 'We'll hear better that way.'

What will we hear? Footsteps? A car? But Poppy's own second-hand black Mini is still in the driveway at her shared house a few villages away.

I shake my head. It doesn't matter what the logistics are. Poppy said she would be here, so she will. She has a plan. We can get the details later.

I check my watch.

And now we're there.

10 p.m.

I clutch Ruby's arm. Keep her close. We stand, still and silent, like it's the eleventh day of the eleventh month.

And we wait.

10.01.

10.02.

10.03.

And at that point a thought creeps in. What if that message was faked?

I glance to my left. Lewis is still on his phone.

My heart speeds up.

What if Lewis has set us up? We're out here in brutal temperatures, in the middle of nowhere and we followed him blindly – despite my suspicions – never checking that the breadcrumbs that he scattered for us were real.

But there are two of us. We are tall. Fit. He has snow seeping into his socks. He can't do anything to us, can he? Even in the middle of nowhere. I touch the Swiss army knife again.

Can he?

Emlyn knows we're here but I suspect Ruby didn't give him the specifics of the location, considering the atmosphere between them. And anyway, Lewis might be dominating my thoughts, but *do* I fully trust Emlyn? I think of him, speaking in a flurry to those police officers outside the station in Saint Aurélie. Of the way I feel like Ruby is holding something back.

Every time I think *But it can't be him, not Emlyn*, I think: *Well, it can't be Poppy either.* And there were two bodies; it has to be someone.

Emlyn went straight to bed when we got back from the train station last night. Ruby, embarrassed, showed Lewis to the spare room.

I heard him, once the door was closed, making a call. An update to a parent or friend, I presumed, or someone back in Grenada. *I'm in Scotland. Flight ok.*

But *was* it that?

I can't see Lewis in the darkness but my eyes have adjusted enough to make out his outline. He's a big guy. Muscular.

I slip my phone out of my pocket and hold it in my hand. Though it's fully charged, it only has one bar of reception and no sharp edges so I'm not sure how it's going to help me. They're just comfort blankets really, aren't they? We think they'll save us; most of the time they do the opposite.

I try to hold the shivers inside my body. I don't have enough layers on. I berate myself for being unprepared – this is my domain, I know how to dress for Scottish winters – until I remember I'm grieving and jet-lagged and traumatised and I don't have my own kit. *Give yourself a fucking break, Junie.*

10.05.

And then I jump. Scream.

Because there is a hand, pushing down on my arm.

'Get off me!'

'Sorry!' Lewis says quickly, stepping backwards in alarm as I brandish the knife at him. 'Sorry, Junie. I was – I was just going to offer you my coat. You're shaking so much. Jesus.' His eyes glance downwards. 'Knife's a bit much, mate.'

He stares at me.

'Can you blame me?' I snap, slipping the knife back into my pocket.

At 10.09, as I press my lips together to stop my teeth from audibly chattering, as I keep my eyes trained on Lewis, watching in case he reaches into his pocket, takes out a weapon, or even just grabs a large stick from the ground, Ruby interrupts my surveillance with a whisper.

'How long do we wait?'

But I put a hand on her arm. Because there is something. 'Sssh,' I tell her. 'Listen.'

I hear it again. The crunch of footsteps.

Unmistakable, in an empty field, this late in the evening in the middle of the mountains.

10.11.

'Poppy?' I let myself say, quietly. I feel the cold of my breath; the relief of calling to her and saying her name. It makes me brave enough to say it louder. 'Poppy!'

But Ruby stills my voice with a hand on my arm. 'Stop. Hold on.' Then, more urgently. 'Listen.'

Because coming through the trees, through the cool night air, there is the clear sound of a reply.

COLDER

A voice.

Except not quite.

No, not a voice. More like . . . A yap?

A yap.

Just a yap.

It had *sounded* like a person. But when the noise comes again, it's clearly a dog. And the crunch of footsteps: its owner, of course. Walking their dog at night because they are in the office during the day, perhaps, or they just prefer the solitude of the late evening, cutting through trees in their boots in the stillness.

Not our sister.

The yaps get quieter. The footsteps pass and disappear.

10.15.

10.16.

We still say nothing.

Could the dog and its owner have scared Poppy off? Maybe she *was* here, as planned, but then she heard that man – a man, surely, to have the option of walking a dog in this darkness, this isolation – and she was scared? She may have heard the yap too. Could even have thought it was a police dog.

If she sent the message, that is. *If* any of this is real.

I look at Lewis again. Still on his phone.

10.17.

At 10.20, Ruby turns to me.

'I think we need—' she says.

'A bit longer.' I sound like I'm begging.

But I look at Ruby. It's so brutally cold out here; so harsh. It's not even a still kind of cold – the kind that leaves you alone, gives you a chance to wrap up – but that invasive howling kind, that gets into your nose, ears, down your throat. That infiltrates, via any route it can.

We can't leave though. We can't.

'Five more minutes,' I plead, teeth still knocking against each other, body vibrating. I bury my gloved hands deeper into my pockets.

'But then—'

'Yes, Rubes, I know. You don't have to spell it out.'

Sisters, in the end, still speaking to each other in snapped words and over-familiarity, whatever is going on.

I stand silently and wait.

10.22.

10.23.

10.24.

At 10.27 my body gives in.

I don't need to say the words: *She isn't coming.*

They speak themselves though, as we walk in silence back to the car. As no-one shouts for us to stay, to wait. As the only sound is the wind. I pass Lewis the torch and let him go ahead because I want to keep my eyes on him, because I don't trust him to be behind us.

My mind goes back to where this chase started. To the café in Saint Aurélie.

What if this was a set-up that didn't pan out? What if Poppy never sent that message at all, but Lewis sent us here, on a search that was only ever fake?

I follow behind Ruby, who is behind Lewis, toes numb despite the boots.

Perhaps the dog walker interrupted Lewis's plans. Perhaps we were supposed to be alone.

Perhaps he wasn't giving me a coat, but he saw the Swiss army knife and backed off. Perhaps Lewis harms people.

Robin.

My dad.

Poppy, even.

Perhaps there is a motive, I just don't see it yet.

And I cling to that idea. Because if that's true, if Lewis has a motive, if Lewis did this, then it means I was right all along.

My sister is innocent, and she can come home.

HOTTER

A week later, I'm back in Edinburgh.

Partly because I have an audition in a few days and partly because I can't bear the atmosphere that exists between Ruby and Emlyn. God, I'm glad I'm single. The need to escape their house bit at me like a horsefly.

It is 11.30 p.m. and I am lying on my sofa, phone out – even though I usually have a *no phones after 10 p.m.* rule that I am stringent about. But the usual cares of life have left the building, since our life became about the big things. Dead dads. Murder. Survival.

I know I need to go to bed but I can't stop reading everything that has been written about our family. I've been contacted by a journalist called Francesca Plowman, who has asked me to tell my story. I know Ruby would be appalled but I am thinking about it. I need to do something, and what if it could help us figure out who did this? Someone has to know something.

Next, I search for Lewis. It's a common name but once I find Lewis Williams the heavyweight amateur boxer and Lewis Williams the philosophy researcher at Oxford, there's nothing. Online, Poppy's Lewis Williams is invisible.

Huh.

Is that weird? For a thirty-something in 2018, it feels weird.

Eventually, I put my phone in sleep mode and take it into the living room. Then, hours after I should have done it, I go into the kitchen to shut the blinds.

'Oh!'

I jump backwards from my kitchen window.

I swear I . . .

No.

No.

But I did. I saw someone move in the near darkness outside my ground-floor flat into the alley behind.

Before I know what I am doing, I open the back door. Go out there in my slippers. Feel the rain seep into the fur on the front of them; the damp in my hair as I yell.

'Hello! Who's there?'

What the hell am I doing? If there's someone dodgy there, I should stay inside and call the police, not come out here shouting like this. But I don't go back in.

Lewis claims he has left Scotland now. Headed off to London where he is going to catch up with old friends, before he flies back to Grenada to finish his environmental project. But of course, he could be lying.

Anyone could be lying.

Someone *has* to be lying.

I'm about to lock the door and come back inside when I hear it. The *clap, clap, clap* of footsteps.

Not heavy, but there.

'Poppy!'

I don't even know it's what I'm thinking until it's out of my mouth. Lewis had been a conscious thought; my sister hadn't. But there it is. That's why I ran out. That's why I didn't huddle inside, safe. In case the person who was lurking outside my flat was Poppy.

'POPPY!'

This time I shout it on a loud, desperate sob.

Then the back door opens on the flat next to mine in our Victorian terrace.

'Did you hear a noise too, June?' says Saz – my neighbour who does Pilates in the garden, and whose invites to drink rosé, to barbecues, to her annual yard festival *Saztonbury*, I ignore – sticking her head over the fence. She is frowning at me. I wipe my face and duck my head.

'I thought I did but it was probably—'

'No,' she says, shaking the dark curls that ring her face all the way down to a fringe; a lion's mane. 'My outside light just came on when I was in a bridge. Saw it through my legs. There was 100 per cent someone there.'

Now, she looks at me, frowning. 'I thought I heard someone last night too, you know . . . I'm going to call 999.'

And in she goes, before I can object. Before I can think of a reason why a person *would* object to the police coming out when they live alone and there's an intruder in their yard.

An officer is at my door half an hour later.

'Can you give me a description of the person you saw?' he says. 'We've just been round to your neighbours.' He looks at his notes. 'Sarah and Dan? They said their outside light came on but that they didn't see anyone. They said you did though?'

I shake my head. 'Oh. Not really. It was just a . . . shape of someone.' I hesitate. 'It was dark. And all very quick.'

If Poppy was in my yard, the last thing I want to do is give her away.

But what if it *was* Lewis? Wouldn't I want the police to follow it up then?

I wonder if the officer knows what happened to me in Saint Aurélie. I wonder if he knows about Poppy. Saz might have told him, thinking it could be relevant. But if he does, he doesn't mention it.

Instead he glances behind me through the open front door into my flat. 'Do you live alone?'

I follow his eyes. What gave it away? Was it the single pair of shoes lined up by the back door? Or the empty cardboard box from a pad thai for one, waiting to be put into the recycling?

I want to defend myself; explain that I normally batch cook healthy one-pot meals, thanks very much. That it's just been a rough couple of weeks, officer, a bit of an anomaly what with my sister being accused of murdering my dad and an almost daily commute to the fucking Caribbean.

That all the buckles and locks have come off, and I'm now attached to my normal life only by a loose thread. That the noodles for one are the least of my fucking worries, actually.

I don't say any of this.

'Most likely an opportunist,' he says. 'Looking for an open door. They tend to grab any electronics that are out on the side and run. You could think about getting cameras installed?'

He doesn't wait for a response.

'And you seem to have good neighbours, at least. Keep doing that, keep looking out for each other.'

I feel guilty then, for my antisocial ways. For never taking an hour of my life to eat a burger with Saz. For scuttling home without saying hi when I see her and Dan buying Pinot in Tesco on a Friday night. I socialise with work people, after shows. I do *Cabaret* on Bobby's karaoke machine. But I don't make much effort with anyone outside my acting bubble.

'Well, call us if anything else happens,' the officer says, looking ready to leave. 'Day or night. Always happy to pop out and check on things.'

When he leaves, I walk into the kitchen and pull the thick grey curtains across. I glance out of the back window. By now, though, whoever was outside my flat will be long gone. Scared away, surely, by neighbours and outdoor lights and police and yelling.

I think about how I felt when I was out there. How convinced I was, for that few seconds, that it was her.

Was it you, Poppy?

But I shake my head.

Of course it wasn't her. Most likely it wasn't Lewis either, but an opportunist, like the officer said. Looking for an open door or window. Looking for some cash to grab, or an iPad. Someone who had eyes on Saz and Dan's place, as much as mine.

Except, I don't believe that.

I double-check all the locks. I pull the blind down in the lounge and I walk from room to room, checking windows, putting bolts on, looking behind doors.

And then, I call the direct contact we've been given in the Saint Aurélie police. 'Could you look again at Lewis Williams? I think he's lying about something. I think he's sending fake messages, pretending to be Poppy. And I think he's just been outside my flat.'

THE SUSPECT

THE CARIBBEAN

The suspect looks up, dazed. Yawns. She taps her phone. It's 12 p.m.

She scrolls down the pages of writing in the document that is open on her laptop. There are hundreds of them.

'Holy shit,' she mutters, looking at that time again, and at the work. 'Holy shit.'

When she opens the shutters, the daylight makes her blink. She plunges her knuckles into her tear ducts. They burn, red like she is in a horror movie.

When she closes the shutters again, she pushes her long, dirty blonde hair out of her eyes and sighs. There is a self-help book splayed on top of her chest of drawers. The cover says something about being *tired and wired.* Next to it is a box of herbal tea and an eye mask.

On her desk though, surrounding her laptop and where she has just been sitting, the story is different. On the desk, there is a mess of empty Diet Coke cans, as well as empties from a local energy drink called *Turbo* and the dregs of a cup of coffee.

When she walks barefoot into the kitchen, her body jitters and flicks. She sits down on a wooden stool, long legs dangling. She glances at the almost empty instant-coffee jar on the island, then puts her head in her hands.

She stays there for a few seconds, until there is a noise. Then, her face snaps upwards.

Her eyes go to the open bifolds and she grimaces. 'Oh God, no,' she murmurs to herself.

They are there on the terrace. Nearly naked and wrapped around each other. The bum cheeks are out. A champagne bucket sits on the table, the bottle sticking out of it like the Leaning Tower of Pisa.

None of that's unusual.

But there is one thing that is.

Her dad, normally a good six, seven or eight inches taller than his girlfriend, is not at the height he should be. He is lower. He's at knee-height. He is proposing.

She stands up, trying her best to be quiet but as she moves, her dad looks up and sees her. Makes eye contact.

She turns and runs up the stairs back to her mess of a bedroom, stumbling not once, but twice.

She slams the door behind her, like a child.

PART TWO: RUBY

HOTTER

SEVEN YEARS AFTER THE MURDERS

'Mum? Can we grab you for a second, Mum?'

I turn, slowly. Feel the wave of rage.

I am not your mum.

I try to smile but my mouth refuses. The best I can do is force it upwards into something that looks like constipation.

God, when did I get so negative? Maybe I need to up my anxiety meds. I make a mental note to speak to the GP.

Or maybe it's more about what's happening this weekend.

I shake my head. Try to block that out, like I've been trying to block it out for so long.

I try again with the smile, gritted teeth burrowing into the top of my scarf, as I stand in front of my daughter Seren's teacher, Mrs Halliday.

I am alone, which is standard. Conversation dries up when I arrive at the school gate. The other mums are peppy and enthusiastic. I can't be bothered to look interested when they tell me about the chicken they bought from Costco. I don't ask how the new extension is looking.

The old me would have. Not now.

None of these people – mostly women, let's be honest – know me. They don't know that I'm a woman whose sister was accused of murdering her dad. We moved to this village when I was six months pregnant. Still in Scotland, still near the mountains, but far enough to start again. Emlyn and I got married when I was pregnant and I took his surname, so did Seren. The story faded away.

There is no reason to link me to the Winter sisters.

Or there wasn't, until now.

Last autumn, I had a call from a TV producer in the States called James Fisher. He told me that he was the producer on a show called *Hotter/Colder* and he wanted my input.

I stood in the chiller aisle in Tesco, basket in my hand, frowning in confusion.

'I think you must have the wrong—'

But he didn't have the wrong— James Fisher was working on a TV series that had been sold to Netflix, due to air in 2025, and which was loosely based on a real story.

Our real story.

The real story of me and my family, and what happened to us seven years ago in the Caribbean.

This weekend, that show will be on TV.

◆ ◆ ◆

When James Fisher finished telling me about the show – how the names and key details would be changed – I put the phone down. Blocked his number.

No. I couldn't do this.

Over the next few months, Junie messaged me updates about it. She was calmer than me. When James Fisher called her, she heard him out and then she got to work. She told me about the emails she had written trying to get the show pulled; the wording she had drafted by expensive lawyers.

Then eventually she told me about the lawyer who took pity on her and told her to stop: that the TV company would make what they wanted. Who told her that she would be in a much better position if this was the BBC but that US streamers' libel laws were nowhere near as stringent as the UK's. Who told her she would never win.

Junie sent me other messages:

> They said they would run a statement at the end saying that we as a family protest Poppy's innocence, if we want, but if we do that we are announcing that it's based on our story. So I've said no.

Then a final message.

> They're making the show, Rubes. There's nothing else I can do. It's going to be on Netflix in Feb.

◆ ◆ ◆

Last week, when Seren was in bed, I turned on the TV and saw it: a still from the show, a *coming soon* banner across it.

Of course. *February.*

Now, at the school gate, I look around. Here, rumours spread faster than chickenpox.

Gill Bright, head of the PTA, who gets to the school gate twenty minutes early every day to max her social interactions and whisper about the dad of the Year Four kid who had the fling with the woman from the tanning place.

The alarmingly chatty dad who wears running shorts every day, even in the snow, and is cousins with the caretaker.

Fee Murray-Smith, whose tops are worth more than my house.

They are everywhere, teeming around me with their similarly recognisable kids; Seren's classmates.

By next week, they could know. They could all know.

'Mum?'

'Sorry, yes,' I say, eyes back on Seren's teacher.

'It's the wildlife park trip money? We still haven't had Seren's. The deadline was three days ago.'

'Oh. Yes. I'll do it as soon as I get home. On the app?'

'Aye. Same as always.'

A tight smile. They're used to it; I drop more balls than a drunk juggler.

Mrs Halliday walks away, and I turn to my daughter, who is playing in her Mary-Janes and thick black tights with her friends.

'Warmer, warmer . . .' I hear Seren say.

'Colder!' Seren shrieks. 'Freeeeeeeezing!'

'Snowy! Like our mountains!'

This is Seren and her friends' favourite game, picking a spot and telling each other when they get near to it (warmer) and further away (colder).

Seren whispers her spot in my ear, warm breath on a cold lobe as her little pink glasses graze my face. Co-conspirator now, I join in, giving Seren's friend Frederick instructions. 'Warmer! Colder! Icier than an ice-cream! Frederick, you have essentially moved to the Arctic.'

The four of them slowly migrate towards the gate, a swarm of pleats and grey and Ninja Turtles backpacks and bobble hats.

As I usher Seren off school grounds, my phone vibrates in my pocket. *Who calls these days*?

Then I see her name and jab at the phone to answer.

'Junie?'

'Hey. Yeah. Hi.'

'Everything ok?'

I shout over the sound of the kids.

'Bye, Seren!'

'It's my birthday tomorrow!'

'You're freezing!'

I stick a hand up to wave. Seren's friends are drifting away but they are still shouting to one another, dragging out the goodbyes.

I put a gloved hand on my daughter's red duffel coat; steer her one-handed towards the field that we cut across for home, like I am manoeuvring a car.

And I go there fast.

This is it. After all these years, Junie is phoning to tell me that they have found her.

'Ow!' says Seren.

I am gripping her shoulder too hard.

'Sorry, my love. Sorry.' I kiss her head.

But she is over it. Runs ahead on the route she knows so well, chasing birds, picking up sticks, coat flailing open as she refuses to zip it up despite the end-of-January chill.

I turn my attention back to the phone call. 'Junie?'

'Can you talk?' My sister pauses. 'I mean, *talk* talk.'

I put a hand over the ear that's not listening to her, over my bobble hat. 'What?'

'I said can you talk? Properly?'

The line isn't great. Her voice is faint. And we're on the farmers' field now, the one that is so open, so wide, wind whipping across it and drowning out most sound.

'Rubes?' Junie raises her voice. 'Ruby, are you still there?'

'Yeah, I am but . . .'

But then I glance behind me and realise there are other kids heading in the same direction as us – the family we call The Tinies who live opposite us on the cul-de-sac – and any conversation I have now will be in front of them.

'Actually, give me twenty minutes, Junie. We'll be home then and I can speak properly. I can't—'

'Ok,' she interrupts. 'No problem.' But she sounds deflated.

'Hold on,' I make myself say. 'Before you go. Just tell me if they've found—'

'No. Sorry, Rubes. If I made you think that, I'm so . . . No, not that. Sorry.'

Seren runs slightly too far ahead in the field with her friend. Tiny Mum passes me, a Super Mario backpack over her tiny right shoulder.

This is when parenting is hardest. When you have your hands tied. When there are things that need doing but you can't do them because it doesn't matter if the world is ending; keeping your child safe is the priority.

And then there is my sister, all those miles away in Liverpool where she moved four years ago for a fresh start. Where I picture her now, sitting on her Ikea sofa with her legs tucked under her next to a bowl of granola and a half-filled-in puzzle book. Or the newspaper clippings that she keeps; everything that's written about our story, including the interviews that she gives protesting Poppy's innocence. The ones that we fell out about. I never believed anything good could come from Junie talking to the press; she claimed that someone had to speak up for Poppy. Or that maybe someone would see them, and it would make them remember something. Give us another suspect. That it would root out Lewis, who has disappeared without a trace. Or that Poppy would see one of the interviews, and knowing her sister believed in her would give her the strength to come home. Tell us what really happened. Let us help her.

And all the time I thought: *And what happens then?*

'But it is about . . .'

There is a mist of thin drizzle coming down now and I try to put my hood up, still holding the phone in one hand and Seren's bag in the other.

A pause then, loaded as a nacho.

Her voice drops low. 'It's about Poppy.'

Junie has sent me messages about the lawyers and the TV show, yes.

But I answered the phone so quickly because it has been so long since we had any other communication.

So long since I heard her voice.

This is the first conversation I have had with Junie in four years.

COLDER

Fifteen minutes later, Seren is under a thick blanket in our living room with her blue fluffy slippers on. She laces her hands behind her head, cookie crumbs scattered down her front, and sighs.

I laugh.

'What?' she says, not looking at me but at the TV.

I shake my head. 'Nothing, chick.'

But I am laughing because I can picture my mum in the same position. Just add red lipstick. Swap that semi-skimmed out for a large Shiraz.

My mum was always cold, always in need of a wool blanket or her ragged old sausage dog hot water bottle. Seren is the same, especially now in winter when the cold in this part of Scotland is still brutal and the walk home has whipped wind and drizzle into every crevice of our faces.

'Can you light the wood burner, Mum?' Seren asks, eyes still on the TV as she burrows down into her nest.

It's what we often do when we get in from school. I sit next to her on my laptop – finish my work or scroll mindless celebrity gossip while she gets cosy. But today I don't have time. I need to speak to Junie.

'I'll light it in a bit,' I tell Seren, with a kiss on her head, pulling my phone out of my pocket. 'I've just got to speak to Auntie Junie.'

Blank face.

Auntie Junie. God, that's a stretch, for an adult she would barely recognise. *Four years.*

'You know. Mummy's sister.'

She makes a vague noise, completely lost now to Lego *Ninjago,* series 3085. I've been careful that she's in the child's Netflix profile so that she won't see the ads for *Hotter/Colder*. Those stark images, heads bowed low, tears streaming down faces that are meant to represent ours. Not that she'd even know what it was, of course, but the idea of Seren being aware of that show at all is anathema to me.

I pull the blanket up around Seren's chest and walk out of the room in my slippers, stepping over toys and Seren's school backpack. I reckon I have about twenty minutes before she needs something. Twenty minutes to talk to my sister.

I remember seven years ago, when Junie was still in Edinburgh. When she called me, her voice charged. *Rubes, there was someone outside my house.*

But it was probably nothing, she said afterwards. The police said most likely an opportunist.

They never came back. We moved on. A couple of years after that, Junie got cast as Olga in *Three Sisters*, which was doing a tour and then a long run in Liverpool. She got some other job at a theatre there. Then another. It seemed as close as actors get to a reliable gig, so she moved there.

A fresh start, Rubes. What have I got to stay in Scotland for anyway? I can do what I need to do anywhere.

Because, God, she was still determined. Still did the interviews on the anniversaries. Still searched for Lewis. Still asked the police to look into him, over and over, even though he had an alibi and there was no evidence, no motive. The police never took her seriously. Lewis isn't a person of interest to them: only to Junie.

Once, Junie got an anonymous tip-off that he was living in Madrid and she went over there to ask around, but it was like looking for a needle in a haystack, especially for a man who had no social media. Online, it was like Lewis didn't exist – which only ever made Junie more suspicious.

I don't get involved.

Now, I click on Junie's number.

She answers with the words: 'I've seen the show.'

'How?' It's not out until this weekend.

'Badgered them for a preview and they sent me one, like the ones they send to reviewers at newspapers or whatever. Only episode 1.'

I've ignored the interview my news feed's served up with Hugh Grant, discussing the complexity of playing a role based on my dad. I've ignored the billboards I've seen on buses, at train stations.

Now, though, I get a reality check. I can't keep ignoring it. This show is coming.

'But they . . . they can't do this.'

Junie sounds irritated. 'I told you this, Ruby, *yes they can*. This has been going on for . . .' She huffs. 'I've begged them not to air it. Threatened lawyers. But it's impossible, they're mighty, they can do this and they can weather any pushback. And they've changed enough detail that they can legally get away with it.' She pauses. 'Ruby, it's going to be on TV and I don't want you to watch it on your own.'

I don't say anything.

'I want to be with you. When you watch it.'

I sigh. 'How's that going to happen?'

It's my fault we haven't seen each other in so long, I know that. I could leave Emlyn at home with Seren and visit Junie, any weekend. I could jump on a train and eat the kind of authentic Japanese food we can't get in the sticks and let Junie drag me around museums or art galleries to cock my head and stare at pictures I don't understand.

There is no excuse.

Other than the truth, the grim truth, which is that the odd time that I am not with Seren – if Emlyn takes her down to his mum's in north Wales – all I do is take a Xanax and go to bed. That I get it together just in time for Seren returning.

'About to get on the train,' says Junie.

And it's only then that I notice it – the background noise, the announcements, blaring over my own internal din.

When she speaks next, she is slightly out of breath, like she's walking. 'We should be together when—' I hear someone announce a delay to the 16.17 to Birmingham. 'I'll message with my ETA.'

And I go to object, but she has already hung up.

In the living room, Seren greets me like I've been gone for six months, warm soft arms popping out of the blanket.

I light the wood burner and climb under the blanket with her. She nestles into my armpit and I try to be present, and I try to be happy, and I try to make this enough.

But really, I just wish that Seren was with Emlyn in north Wales – he's helping his mum out after her hip replacement for a few nights – and Junie would leave me alone. So that I could take the Xanax. So that, again, I could make it all stop.

COLDER

'Ogres are like onions. Onions have layers. Ogres have layers. You get it? We both have layers.'

Seren, in her pyjamas now, shrieks with laughter at *Shrek*, then looks at me with shiny eyes. I kiss her head.

It is later the same evening and we are back under the blanket; Emlyn would be furious if he knew she'd had this much screen time.

I feel my eyes droop. Then I remember: it's nearly time to leave.

I tried to put Junie off. I sent messages as soon as we got off the phone telling her that I'm not watching the show anyway, so I don't need a babysitter. That I'm busy; it's not convenient.

But she wouldn't budge and as if that's not bad enough, with Emlyn away at his mum's, I have to go out on a winter night to collect her from the bloody train station.

I move my arm from out behind Seren, irritation prickling as physically as sunburn.

'Where are you going?' she asks, stifling a yawn.

'To check what we have for tea.'

'I *had* tea.'

'Not your tea. Auntie Junie's tea.'

There's a pizza in the freezer. Healthy-eating, overnight-oats-face Junie will hate it but it'll have to do. Serves her right for springing this visit on me.

The old me would have had a lasagne prepped and in the oven ten minutes after I got off the phone to my sister, flinging the vacuum round as it baked, fancy candle lit, wood burner roaring so that by the time Junie got here, there was a clear message.

I am the sister who has got my shit together. The adult. I am on this.

The new me can't be bothered.

The new me pops a sertraline and looks around the living room thinking that I should stand up. I should do something. Then I pick at a bit of cuticle that's hanging from my thumb and stare at the wall.

The old me wore subtle blusher and SPF. The new me has looked at the same cobweb on my living room window every day this week and done nothing about it.

Sometimes, the new me has to run out of rooms because there is music playing and something on TV at the same time and I can't take it, I can't take the noise, the noise, all that noise, and God, my heart has sped up and I feel like I may break, smash into pieces. Stop it, stop it, stop it, stop it, stop it.

The new me lies awake with dread churning in my belly if I have to drive anywhere further than the school gates. Sometimes I check out entirely, so that I arrive somewhere after a half-hour car journey and have no idea how I got there.

I hide as much of it as I can from Emlyn, but what he sees, he has no patience with. We have to move on, he says. He persuaded me out of seeing a therapist. I think he was scared I would say too much.

There is a daily knot in my stomach. My own body broadcasts fear every second of every day. Sometimes I have no clue what I am scared of; other times it feels acute and clear.

That is what trauma does to you, I've learnt. It resets your entire body. Your entire self.

There is the me before Saint Aurélie, and there is the me after. I can never reset that clock.

The pills helped. *Help.* But I am not the person I used to be, and I am running out of energy to pretend I am.

'When are we going to get Auntie Junie?' Seren asks, on a full yawn now, as I come back in from the kitchen. It's past her bedtime.

'We'll head off in one minute, chick,' I tell her.

I glance at my phone. Click on a news story without even realising I'm doing it. And there is another one: an advert for *coming soon Hotter/Colder*. Fake me, fake Poppy, fake Dad, fake Junie, fake Robin, fake show.

This can't be right, can it? It can't be right that they can do this.

And suddenly I feel so stupid for ignoring it for all that time.

The familiar sensations start. A tightness, across my chest. The tremble of my limbs.

A few years ago, I was signed off work for three months with generalised anxiety disorder and PTSD. I never told Junie. The worse it feels, the less I speak to people. To anyone, but especially people I love. It's easier. Because talking would be pointless, when I can't say what I want to anyway.

Junie copes better, unsurprisingly.

After Saint Aurélie, she did the things you hope you'll do if life turns to shit. She walked and walked and walked through the mountains. She gave up caffeine. Signed up to sponsored this and charity that. Made batches of lentil soup and daily green juice.

When she moved to Liverpool, she sent selfies up in the skies on day trips in Snowdonia. The Berwyns. Weekends in the Lake District. On blustery local beaches. Toned thighs and big smiles. The view across the Mersey. Her tattered crossword puzzle books next to her, *still* not switching to an app, as she took a break from rehearsals in the park. Her apartment was tiny but gorgeous and bright and hers. Owned. That wouldn't have been possible on an actor's salary but, like me, she inherited money from Dad.

And through it all, she carried on standing up for Poppy. Pleading her innocence. She has a couple of good journalist contacts now so that whenever a story comes up that has even a tenuous link to ours, or an anniversary comes around, Junie is their first port of call for an interview. She refuses to let Poppy's guilt be accepted as fact.

She chases the police. Asks for updates. She tries, despite zero leads in so long now, to track down Lewis Williams.

Many people – usually the ones who contact Junie on socials with their conspiracy theories and their insights – have told her there is a lot of corruption on Saint Aurélie. That there is a huge question mark over how the police system is run, and who really controls it.

Junie delved into that too, of course, like she's delved into everything. In between suspecting Lewis's involvement, she became convinced that someone framed our sister then paid off the police to make her the prime suspect. To my horror, she talked about that theory loudly in a newspaper interview. I know she touted Lewis's name too, but the newspaper wouldn't print that. *Defamation*, or something.

'Come on then, chick,' I say to Seren with a gentle nudge. 'Time to go.'

I grab my car keys. Strap my girl into her car seat in her pyjamas and dressing gown and tuck a blanket over her. Her eyes droop in the mirror. I can't believe Junie's turning up this late, when I have a small child. She'd messaged earlier.

It's fine, I'll get a cab.

I'd rolled my eyes. Idiot. She's forgotten what it's like here. Cabs are as likely to turn up as a heatwave.

Now, on the way to the station, I glance in the mirror again. Seren has fallen asleep and one of her slippers has slipped off her foot. Her tiny sock breaks my heart.

At 9.34 p.m., Junie walks out of the station wheeling her case behind her, just as I am coming into the car park. I pull up next to her and rap on the front windscreen.

'Oh!' says Junie, as she opens the back seat to put her bag in and spots Seren.

'Hello, little mate.' She goes round to the other side, opens the door and plants a light kiss on her niece's forehead. 'God, she's getting big, Rubes,' she whispers as she shuts the door and climbs in next to me. 'Sorry you had to bring her out so late. Where's Emlyn?'

At least she's acknowledged it. My irritation dissipates, as I explain about his mum and the hip replacement.

'Hey,' I say, turning to her as I indicate right and pull out of the car park. 'Nice hair.'

She has dyed it bright orange. In truth I hate it – it's a colour I would never choose, why would you? – but it does weirdly suit her. And what else do you say? It's too out there to ignore.

'Thanks.' Junie glances back at my daughter. A fabric of sadness falls across her face. 'It's for a part. But I think I might keep it?'

She is still looking at Seren.

'How is she? Does she know anything about—' Then she changes tack. 'Do you think she'll remember me?'

I know what Junie was about to ask. Have I told Seren anything about my family? Does she know about Auntie Junie? Auntie Poppy? About Grandpa? Grandma? That woman we barely knew who would have been her step-grandma?

'I'm sure she'll remember you,' I lie.

I ignore the other part.

The thought of people telling Seren that Auntie Poppy was accused of murdering her grandpa keeps me awake at night. I've always known I'll have to tell her the story before the internet does, but now, with the TV show, I worry I'll have to face it sooner.

We live in a small village. If one person watches *Hotter/Colder*, then delves into the real story behind the show and finds the link to us, it will be minutes before everyone knows. And once that has happened, Seren could hear anything, any time. From classmates who've heard their parents' chat and repeated something without understanding it. From Gill Bright and her mum crew at the school gate. '*She's* a Winter sister?'

At home, I swerve into the drive and open the front door before I run back and scoop up Seren, her legs snaked around me, arms circling my neck, barely stirring.

On the doorstep, Junie touches my arm lightly. 'Hey,' she says, pointing at the sky, and a line of three stars. 'Look at that. Orion's Belt. Three sisters.'

I stand there for a second, eyes on the sky.

Three.

Not two.

My eyes burn.

'I need to get her to bed,' I say, mumbling into Seren's hair and stepping inside.

As I come back down a minute later, Junie is waiting in the hall. 'You could have gone through,' I say, surprised. 'You know where the kitchen is.'

We moved in here when I was pregnant. When we were still in touch. Junie – even if it has been a long time – knows her way around.

'I didn't want to just—'

I walk past her and head for the kitchen. Junie comes in behind me, pulling off her beanie and gloves, then her big parka. It hangs in the air: the lack of hug, the lack of familiarity. Her standing awkwardly in the hall like a stranger collecting a bike I've just sold them on eBay.

But I get it. I don't know what will happen to me if I get close to her either.

In the kitchen, I take the pizza out of the freezer, wait for the oven to preheat and whack it in. I look through the oven door and feel queasy. Greasy cheese, slowly thawing.

Behind me there is the screech of a chair. Junie sits down at the kitchen table.

She sighs. 'Can we talk about—'

'I don't think you get what it's been like.' I am still facing the oven. *Stop talking, Ruby.* I give myself a warning.

I picture me and Junie walking back to the car seven years ago with Lewis; those yaps of the dog in the distance behind us, the charge that ran through my body.

After that, I waited.

I thought she would appear again.

But after all those clues, that activity, there was nothing.

Junie went on tour and was consumed by work. The show landed in Liverpool, and she relocated. She travels a lot, though. If someone sends her a message to say there has been a sighting of Poppy in Dublin or Birmingham or Winchester and she can manage it with work schedules, off she goes. Scouring the streets. Asking and asking and asking.

'I don't get what it was like?' When I turn round, Junie is staring at me. 'Are you serious?'

In my brighter moments, when the pills are working, I picture my nomadic little sister living a life that suits her, with a boyfriend she loves. On a beach in Bali. Roaming, free. A gaggle of mates who may not know her real name but who know her spirit, her heart. A dog, a couple of cats. I picture her happy.

But my brighter moments take up around 0.005 per cent of my life. In the rest, I think Poppy's living an unhappy, scared existence on the fringes of society. Without us and lonely. Desperate.

Scared.

And then, I can't breathe.

My own life is smaller now. I don't run any more but Emlyn does. In the mornings, he slips out to do a 5K before work. I make porridge for me and Seren. On Sunday evenings, I iron my daughter's small blue uniform and batch cook the week's meals. I turn down the invites that drop in occasionally from old mates suggesting a catch-up. When Seren goes to bed at 7.30 p.m., I climb under the duvet too, while Emlyn finishes work downstairs.

I don't listen to true crime podcasts any more.

And now, here is Junie. Watching me. Trying to make me leave my small life behind. Making me open closed doors.

We sit in silence.

'I'm not watching it,' I tell her, eventually. 'I know you want to talk about it, I know you want to think about it, but people are different and I just want to move on.'

The oven beeps.

'This is not like a sighting, though,' she says with a sigh. 'You might be able to ignore those. But this is in our homes. Have you seen the ads? This show is going to be everywhere. I don't think you have a choice with this one, Ruby.'

And I look at her and think: I always have a choice.

That's why seven years ago, when someone asked me to keep a secret, I said yes.

I made a choice.

What I don't know, despite all this time passing, is whether that choice was the right one.

HOTTER

I am sitting opposite Junie now, three slices of limp steaming pizza on each of our two plates – God, I haven't even thrown on a few salad leaves, I'm a disgrace – and she puts her phone on the table between us.

'There's something I want to show you.'

'How much clearer can I be?' I snap, ignoring the phone. '*I don't want to see it!* I don't want anything to do with this bloody TV show. I just want to get on with my life.'

She laughs.

'What's funny?'

She looks around and gestures to my kitchen with her hands. 'What life?'

'I'm a mother.'

She laughs again. 'Oh, ok then, my mistake,' she says, voice dripping with sarcasm. Then she moves the phone towards me again. 'Look at it,' she orders, and my eyes can't help it, they scan down.

I glance at the comments written below a five-star preview of the show.

'So?'

Junie huffs like I'm a moron and I bristle and for a minute it's just normal sister stuff.

'Look at *that* one,' she says.

You know the story this show is based on? Saint Aurélie, seven years ago. They were Scottish, I think. Three sisters. Dark stuff.

And there it is. The link, made already.

'How have they even seen it?' I ask, looking up at her in panic. 'The show's not out yet.'

'The reviewer's seen the first episode, like me, but I guess the person in the comments has just seen the trailer.'

I stare at her. 'They figured it out from the *trailer*?'

If someone can get to us from the trailer, then when all six episodes drop at the weekend, our family's pain will be everywhere. Known to everyone.

'There are others,' Junie says quietly. 'If you scroll down. We need to get ahead of this, Rubes. Are there people you need to tell? Do you need to . . . do you need to talk to Seren, in case someone mentions it in school?'

My fingers rub at my forehead. 'Stop.'

As I rub at my temples with my thumb and forefinger, Junie waits for me. She takes a bite of her pizza and stares at me as she chews, a tiny bit of sauce in the corner of her mouth. More lines around her eyes than I'd noticed. A few that wiggle across her forehead.

Finally, she puts down the pizza and sighs. Pushes her plate away from her. 'I know it's awful,' she says. 'But I think it's better not to be chasing this. We could even release a statement? *We still protest our sister's innocence. We deny the narrative that this show presents, etc etc.* I think that might be a good idea.'

'But then we're acknowledging that it is based on us!' I say. 'Isn't that worse? Aren't we best to stay as distant as we can? I thought you said that, when you decided not to let them run the statement at the end?'

Junie nods. 'Yeah. I did think that. Then.'

She prods at the comment and looks at me with something that I can't unsee: pity.

Quietly, and with her long fingers on my forearm, she says: 'Now, though . . . now, I think it's too late for that, Rubes.'

HOTTER

I eat the rest of my paper-pizza in silence. Junie doesn't touch another bite.

Eventually, she changes the subject.

'How's Emlyn?'

I shrug. 'Fine.' I take a sip of water. 'Good. Fine.'

After Saint Aurélie, Emlyn and I began to disagree on every fundamental. Every conversation hummed with suppressed rage.

But now . . . well, none of that is new. I don't point that out though because that will only draw attention to the gaping chasm of time that Junie and I haven't spoken for.

'We're going to Lanzarote in a few weeks.' I force a smile. 'All-inclusive with Emlyn's family.'

I loved it when I found Emlyn's big and chaotic family, with the crew of aunties and uncles and cousins. Maybe it overrode any doubts I had about him. The fact that I knew Junie – and especially Poppy – barely tolerated him. That I had heard them call him that nickname, *Mr Vanilla*.

My family is too small. Too quiet. Too smashed to a million pieces. Even if she doesn't know the details – *yet* – I hate that Seren is starting to realise that.

'Seren's never met Poppy.'

Junie ducks her head. 'No. I'm sorry.'

'Or Mum. Or Dad. That's getting hard, as she gets older. The other grandmas are at pick-up, helping on the tombola at the school fair. She asks why she doesn't have grandparents like her friends do.'

When my voice cracks, Junie leans over to hug me. But I shake my head, lips stuck together to stop it all coming out. It's not a hug I need. It's numbers. Recruitment, like an army.

'Emlyn's mum is still in Wales?'

I nod. 'And old, now. Bad health, it's the hip this time but there's always something. And Bryn passed away five years ago.' I pause. 'Mum would have been the glam granny, wouldn't she?'

Junie laughs. 'Yeah. But she would never have let *anyone* call her granny.'

'I'm sorry it's such a shit dinner,' I say, a minute later. I look at the remnants of pizza. 'Especially when you've schlepped on a train this far. I'm sorry that I'm not more . . .'

Junie watches me closely. 'It's fine, Rubes, I didn't come for the catering.'

If she thinks it's surprising that the sister who would always whip her up a paella or roast a chicken and put fresh roses on the table and light a Jo Malone or two just gave her junk food from the freezer, she doesn't say it.

And in that moment, I wonder if Junie knows more than she lets on about how I've been feeling. If she knows why I bury my head so deeply in the sand. If she could feel my desperation when she hugged me.

What life?

'Tea?' I ask, when I've cleared the plates. 'Sorry, I don't have any vino.'

She looks surprised.

'I've quit drinking. Just . . . for a bit.'

Junie keeps her face neutral. 'Ok.'

I like that she doesn't ask. I like it so much that I tell. Head dipped low, like I'm at confession. 'It wasn't helping with how anxious I was feeling.' That's part of the story. The other part is that I was scared. Scared of what I would say, if I had one glass too many.

'Makes sense,' says Junie, steadily. 'A lot of the younger guys at work don't touch a drop for the same reason.' She chuckles. 'It's how I know I'm old, when they go home for green tea and we're on the fourth bottle of red.' She chuckles. 'I'm firmly in the old theatre lushes camp now.'

Junie's only two vices: rare steak and red wine.

She smiles, and I wait.

I wonder if she is about to tell me that she's suffered too, alone in her apartment without a Seren to drag her out of bed and school drop-off to do and lunchboxes to fill.

I wonder if she's about to tell me that there are pills in her bag.

That she sometimes takes too many as well.

THE SUSPECT

THE CARIBBEAN

'Open the door, love,' her dad says, rapping on it for the third time.

But the suspect is lying on her huge double bed, face down.

'Come on, this is *silly*,' he says from outside the locked door. 'It's a happy thing, love! An engagement's a happy thing.'

When she looks up, she sees the empty energy drink cans. Six. Seven?

She reaches for her bag. Finds what she's looking for. She stops for a second and waits. The banging on the door has stopped and there are footsteps now, padding away from her room down the hall.

The suspect lowers her face down, nose first, to the side table next to her bed, and inhales.

◆ ◆ ◆

The next time there is a rap on the door, she yells before he can: 'Leave me alone!'

But when the door – left unlocked when she came back from the toilet, she realises, kicking herself – is pushed open, it's not her dad. No. It's *her*. Her dad's new fiancée. In her green thong bikini and Miami Dolphins baseball cap, her hair poking through the back in a dark brown ponytail so that she looks about nineteen.

'Did I invite you in?' the suspect snaps.

'No,' the other woman snaps back. 'But I did pay for this villa so I guess I am entitled to go into any room I want to.' She sits on the end of the bed. 'Your dad's gone to the shops.' She sighs. 'Let's talk, girl to girl?'

The suspect starts to laugh.

'*You* paid for this villa?' she says. 'No, you didn't! My dad did.' She reaches for a tissue to wipe her nose. 'He pays for everything.'

A calm smile. 'What's mine is his.'

'Not quite.'

'No. You're right. But from two days' time.'

When the suspect looks up, the other woman nods.

'Yeah, he's booked the wedding. Wanted us to do it while we're here in such a beautiful place. All planned. That's why he invited you all out here. Surprise!' She pauses. 'But if you can't face it, that's your prerogative, and I will cope.'

Then her eyes dart over to the side table. A rolled-up dollar. A trace of white. She raises an eyebrow. 'Interesting twist from the baby of the family.'

The suspect stands up and walks out, but she is followed. 'Wait. I'm talking to you.'

She runs down the stairs.

When she gets to the bottom, she whirls around. 'I think you're a money grabber,' she says, out of breath. "You think with the amount of steak he eats and whisky he drinks, you'll get your hands on his cash quickly.'

The other woman laughs. 'Are you *moronic*?' she says. 'If I wanted to find an old guy who was about to cark it, I wouldn't pick one who still runs marathons.'

But the suspect is already heading out of the back door towards the pool.

'I don't think you know your dad well, do you?' the other woman says, grabbing her arm. 'You're not around a lot.'

She is shaken loose but it doesn't stop her.

She comes close to the suspect and hisses in her ear: 'You're pretty morally superior. For a loser addict without a proper job.'

COLDER

Junie has been staying with me for two days when I take the call.

The severity of the allegations against Poppy meant that the British police were involved with our case, even though it happened in the Caribbean. We were assigned a family liaison officer – a FLO – called Heather Mars.

'Heather?'

Junie, imaginatively, calls her *The Mars Bar*. Heather is a mouse of a woman with a pixie cut and a voice so soft you have to strain to hear her. It's been years since we last talked.

'Hi, Ruby. Is it a good time?'

'Oh. Yes. Sure.'

Junie pauses a cooking show; the screen freezes on a jus reduction. She frowns at me in question.

'Are you on your own?' asks Heather.

I press the phone closer to my ear to hear her.

'I'm with my sister.' Then I realise I had better clarify. 'Junie,' I add. A pause. 'Shall I put you on speaker?'

'Yes, great, I've been trying to get hold of Junie, too. So that would be helpful, to talk to you both at once.'

When I put my phone on the coffee table next to my cup of tea and Heather's voice comes through it, realisation flies across Junie's face.

'Is it about the TV show?' she asks. 'Sorry. It's Junie. Hi, Heather.'

Junie and I both lean in close to the phone, my sister's mug clutched between her hands. I see it tremble slightly.

'Hi, Junie. No. It's not about the TV show. Well, not directly.'

In the early days, there was the odd crank who claimed to have met Poppy, to know something. The occasional vague update from the Caribbean. But nothing now, for so long.

As Heather speaks again though, that changes.

We get the first update on our missing sister that we have had in many long, silent years.

HOTTER

'There's been a sighting,' says Heather. 'A credible one.'

Junie inhales sharply.

'You know we get a lot of this stuff, people claiming to have seen her,' she says. 'High-profile cases like yours, they bring out the cranks.

'So we don't tell you about all of them, or even *most* of them because we know how hard that would be, to be constantly getting your hopes up.' She pauses. 'But this one . . . Well, we've corroborated it and had it verified as credible.'

I stare at the wall.

Breathe.

The feelings mix and confuse.

I look at Junie, who looks overjoyed.

Then I picture Emlyn's face, when I tell him this news. It's what he's dreaded, since we heard about the TV show. He has been through it and through it, fearing all the ways that this show airing could upset our careful family equilibrium.

'Where was she seen?' asks Junie, snapping into action as the lead on this, as she always has been. 'Has this come through Interpol, Heather?'

'No. No Interpol.' A beat. 'Actually, the sighting was in Scotland.'

'Scotland?' asks Junie, grabbing the phone. 'Where?'

Heather pauses, like she is looking at notes. 'Near you, Ruby. Near where you live. Near where you all grew up. The part you told us Poppy loved.'

Because Heather *knew* our sister. She had never met her but she knew her. We turned Poppy inside out with this woman.

'But in a town?' I push, my mind racing. 'A village?'

'No,' says Heather slowly. 'Actually, she was spotted in the mountains.'

I almost laugh.

'You haven't heard from her?' Heather says.

'Of course we haven't,' I snap.

'And you'll tell us if she—'

Junie and I meet each other's eyes.

'Absolutely,' I say.

Lie lie lie.

Because if Poppy is found, it can't be the police who find her, it has to be us.

No. More specifically than that, it has to be me. So that I know how many lies I need to tell this time.

HOTTER

Two days later, I have dropped Seren off at school and I'm picking up hot drinks for me and Junie in our local coffee shop, Mountains.

The crowd is mostly pre-school kids with colouring books, bounceable tablets playing *Peppa Pig*, and their heavy-eyed mums clutching coffees as tightly as they do their own children.

Mismatched chairs jut out at angles from the tables. A baby wails, raging, from the carroty chaos of a high chair. A plastic beaker flies through the air.

On the counter, there are plump cakes preening under domes, crammed full of chocolate chips and dried fruit. *Look at me. I'll make you feel like you didn't get up three times between 2 and 5 a.m.*

I look at these women and feel a wave of nostalgia. I remember those years.

I've not been into Mountains for a while. The smells are familiar though: fresh coffee, those cakes. Pains aux raisins that are still warm, stacked up high on the counter.

All of it is comforting.

Except then . . . I am spinning out. Spiralling. Flying round this room in circles.

Because in front of that counter with her back to me is a woman in a black Dryrobe, damp blonde hair running down her back and a plain black tote slung over her right shoulder. A wild swimmer, most likely. Warming up after a winter dip in the loch.

'And one macchiato.' The barista hands her a takeaway cup.

My heart beats a trace faster. A *macchiato*?

Before I know it, I move fast and desperate across the café.

'Excuse me, excuse me,' I mutter as I squeeze past. Even past the baby, who has a banana squeezed firmly in her fist. I brush past the high chair, tilt it slightly.

'Can you watch where you're going?' snaps the mum.

But no. I can't.

Me. It has to be me.

The woman with the baby mutters under her breath.

But then there is no more thought, no more awareness of what is happening because I am gone, I am there. I grab at the woman's Dryrobe. Her wet blonde hair moves and she turns to face me.

'What the fuck?' she says, stepping backwards. I see her take me in. Unwashed hair. Bags under my eyes.

My hand falls loose.

Shit.

Heather shouldn't have told me about this sighting of Poppy, somewhere close to me, so recently.

This woman has an English accent. Clipped and private school. This woman is not Poppy.

'Sorry,' says Junie, suddenly swooping in to place a hand on my shoulder. 'My sister mistook you for someone else.'

She steers me away. Carries on apologising for me even as we move towards the door.

The woman with the baby is still glowering at me but also now watching with interest: *Well, today just got livelier.*

'God, Ruby,' Junie mutters, as we leave the coffee shop.

'She did look like her though,' I mutter, heart still racing. I can't place the emotion. Sadness? Terror? Relief? I think of Seren.

And then I picture Emlyn's face if I told him what just happened. *Ruby. You have to leave her behind.*

Now, we are walking fast back down the high street. Junie has a paper bag in her right hand from the charity shop she nipped into while I got our coffees. She's steering me along with her left.

'She was drinking a macchiato *and* she'd been swimming,' I say.

My sister huffs. 'Lots of people drink coffee. Lots of people swim. I'm all for looking for her – Jesus, if anyone understands that urge, it's me – but you can't just go around grabbing—' Then she speaks quietly. 'She didn't look anything like her, Ruby.'

This used to happen a lot. Seven years ago I used to see Poppy everywhere. Then Seren was born and Emlyn begged me to close the door, and I did. Outwardly at least.

I had to close it, to protect my marriage and my family. But with the TV show and the sighting, the door has been barged open. And with everything I know, wasn't that – in the end – inevitable?

HOTTER

When we get back to my house, Junie slips her boots off and wanders into the kitchen, more comfortable here now. I follow her in and put the kettle on, sliding my feet into old battered slippers.

'Since we didn't get our coffee,' I murmur, sheepish now.

She doesn't reply. Instead, she just stands there, looking at a picture in a frame of Seren as a baby, beaming in her nappy in a paddling pool.

'Do you ever wonder if Poppy has kids?' she asks quietly. 'If Seren has a cousin?'

I wince. Shake my head.

I dream up lives for Poppy all the time, often when I can't sleep. *Eat, Pray, Love* stories in Bali. Starting again in Melbourne or Vancouver or Oslo. Living on farms, surrounded by animals. I dream of her being relieved that she can live a nomadic life. That she can be free.

But never children. None of the lives I imagine feature children.

Because I know Poppy wouldn't have brought someone else into this mess. She would know how vulnerable that would make her. She needs to be able to run. To flee. To hide.

What I do get is a swathe of guilt, regularly. I get *this* – this experience, motherhood – and she doesn't. And as I pop pills and climb into bed, look at me – I don't even appreciate it.

Everything Poppy has given up; everything I have. And I can't even enjoy it.

The kettle boils and I spoon instant coffee – decaf for Junie – into a BFG mug for her and one with Seren's baby footprint on the side for me.

'No. I don't think she has kids.'

Junie doesn't reply. Just stands, still staring at that photo of Seren.

'Right, I'm going to get the maps out,' she says eventually, and she heads for the bookshelves in the kitchen. 'OS maps on there?'

As she looks at me for confirmation, I nod. Junie has made a plan. She is going to spend this weekend in the mountains, covering as much ground as she can. Looking for our sister, in the place where the sighting was made.

'*Not* in a bloody coffee shop,' Junie mutters, head tilted to the side as she finds the map she is looking for and slips it out.

As I pour the boiling water onto the granules and take the milk out of the fridge, I feel my face flush with embarrassment.

Because she's right. We're not going to find Poppy on the high street, ordering a macchiato in her Dryrobe and wondering which cake she fancies. But the mountains? Yeah, we might find her there.

Poppy is being hunted like a wild animal, so she will do what wild animals do. She will stay in the mountains. For solitude. For isolation. Figuring out how to live off-grid, but still, to feel in some way like she is home.

I feel it again, that seven-year-old conflict.

I watch Junie spread the map out on the kitchen table. Make noises as she suggests routes.

And I don't say a word.

I am going to go with her; I can't let her go alone.

But in my head, I wonder if the best thing to do would be to leave Poppy in her hiding place in the mountains. In solitude and in isolation.

Maybe that's the safest thing for her.

The safest thing for everyone.

COLDER

'You know this isn't a good idea,' Emlyn hisses at me down the phone. 'What the fuck are you playing at, Ruby?'

There is panic in his voice.

When he speaks again, he is almost begging. '*Please*, Rubes. I know Junie has turned up there and she's thrown you and you're . . . But if you go down this path . . .

'We've talked about it so many times. Think of what it could do to Seren. Think of what it could do to me.' His voice cracks.

'The sighting is real though, it's being treated as legitimate,' I tell him.

'So what!' I hear him rub at the uneven beard he has these days.

Junie looks over, and I wonder if Emlyn's voice is audible to her from down the phone.

I leave the room. Lower my own voice when I think it's safe to talk to him. 'Isn't it better if I find her? At least then it would be me, not the police?'

'Why does it have to be anyone? Even if the sighting *is* real – which I doubt – the mountains are a vast space. It's been seven years. No-one is going to find her now, Ruby. She's gone.'

I bite my lip. 'I can't not go,' I say. 'Junie won't understand it. I can't let her go on her own.'

'And then what?'

'I don't know. I'll figure it out.'

He waits a few seconds and I hear his breath, heavy. 'Ok. Then I'll speak to Mum, and I'll come back earlier to look after Seren.' He pauses. 'But you are playing a risky game, Ruby.'

◆ ◆ ◆

On Thursday, I pick Seren up from school and take her for cupcakes and chocolate milkshakes. In the café, she eyes me suspiciously. 'Why am I getting this? It's not even the weekend.'

'You're onto me,' I say, winking at her. 'It's nothing big. Just that I won't see you much for a few days, chick. It'll mostly be you and Daddy this weekend.'

She looks up from her long slurp, chocolate around her face, and frowns. 'Where are you going?' She eyeballs me closely. 'Oh biscuits, you're not breaking up, are you? Dylan K's mum and dad are being divorced. Are you being divorced?'

'No. We're not *being divorced*.'

And I am about to give her some bullshit about catching up with an old friend but I stop. Watch her face. It's lengthening, losing its baby roundness. Her two front teeth are missing, those lifelong adult ones about to pop through and dominate her face for a while. I feel my chest contract.

Deep breath.

'You know how Auntie Junie's been staying with us?'

She nods and grins, showing off her gap. 'Yeah. I like it.' The missing teeth give her the hint of a lisp.

Seren and Junie bounce on the trampoline together and play Uno while they eat their pasta. They sneak extra Hobnobs and watch *Harry Potter* under Seren's *Minions* blanket. Junie's the closest thing Seren's ever had to a sister.

'Well, me and Auntie Junie are going to see if we can work out what happened to our other sister,' I tell her. 'Auntie Poppy. Remember we haven't seen her for a while? We want to catch up with her, you see.'

'Oh. Ok.' She eats a mouthful of her pink cupcake, smearing it all over her face. 'Can I stay up late with Dad?'

◆ ◆ ◆

As we walk up our road, me with Seren's *Harry Potter* backpack over my shoulder, she stays close, her hand in mine.

We walk past the park, past the swings and the slide that comes out of the lion's mouth and she doesn't ask if we can go in.

'Did Auntie Poppy do a bad thing?' she asks, out of nowhere.

My stomach plummets. We have never had this conversation and somehow, even after this long, I'm not prepared. I stop and crouch down next to her. 'Who said that, chick?'

The school parents don't know I am a Winter sister. They would barely remember the story after all this time, and to them I am just sullen, disorganised mum Ruby Jones. They don't – as far as I am aware – know anything about what happened to my family. But then I think about the trailers I've seen for *Hotter/Colder* over the last few weeks. The billboard I saw at the train station. The advert that flashed up when I was reading some trashy celebrity news online. The interview I know was in *The Times* this weekend with the Australian actor who plays Robin's equivalent, *Wren*.

I think about those comments under the preview that Junie showed me.

We could easily have been exposed, already. And if one school mum knows, they all will: I live in a small community; people's misery is shared like a side dish. The story isn't old now; it's out-of-the-packet new again.

'Was it someone at school?' I ask.

And this perfect little human tilts her head to one side, very adult, and that tiny motion does the thing so many tiny motions of Seren's do: it slices straight into my insides. 'No,' she says. 'It was Daddy.'

Emlyn? Why would he—

Though of course, I know the answer to that.

'Well, Daddy is wrong,' I say, forcing a smile. 'Auntie Poppy didn't do a bad thing. I know that.' For God's sake, *he* knows that.

'How do you know?'

'Because she's good! She doesn't do bad things. And she's my sister, so I would know, right?' I think. 'Who knows Amelie better than Livvy?' I'm talking about the twins in her class.

'No-one!' she says, aghast. 'Amelie and Livvy are *sisters*.'

A swathe of guilt. Seren doesn't have a real non-Junie sister, but it's what she wants most in the world. It's never happened.

'Exactly.'

She walks on a little skip. 'What else is Auntie Poppy like?'

I try to work out how to sum up Poppy, how to boil down her essence in a handful of words delivered as I walk past a camper van and a ginger cat who is looking at me right in the eyes like I've hurt his youngest kitten.

'She's tough.' I start to laugh. 'Far tougher than Mummy. Unique. A big adventurer. Loves chocolate even more than you do. *Obsessed* with animals.'

Seren grins.

'She has this mind that just . . .' I shake my head. 'I don't always get it. But I think it whirrs, constantly. And I think that causes her problems sometimes, like it's a bit much, she's impulsive, I guess, but she . . .'

Seren is frowning at me now, and I pare it back. 'She has all kinds of incredible ideas. She's smart. But I think it means that sometimes, she needs to be alone. To withdraw a bit.'

She grins. Skips again. 'She would like my cosy spot.'

I picture the den that I make for Seren on Fridays when she finishes school. Biscuits and pillows and the TV paused at the start of the movie, remote control right where her hand will be. How she burrows down deep into it, how I watch her body loosen.

'She would *love* your cosy spot.' Something forces its way up my throat. 'She'd love *you*.' I cuddle her, hard, with one arm, as we walk.

'If she had a baby, would it be my cousin?'

I swallow. 'Yes.'

'Oh biscuits, *does* she have a baby?'

'No.'

Seren smiles and nods and doesn't dwell – kids don't, thank God – and she hops and skips the rest of the way, gappy grin, talking about the plot of *Dog Man: Unleashed* instead. We don't stray near the topic of Poppy again.

At home, Seren runs straight up to her room, to grab her pens and colouring books and forget all about the conversation that will replay in my mind for months. Which I already know I will beat myself up about, wondering if I should have said something differently or if I should have done this months, years ago, getting ahead of the narrative. Before anything else had chance to stick.

When I walk in, Emlyn is in the kitchen, pouring a bag of pasta into a pan of boiling water.

'Hey,' he says without looking up.

'Did you tell Seren about Poppy?'

Without looking at me, he shrugs.

My teeth clamp together.

'Well, I told her a kids' version.' He sighs.

'Yes, but not—'

'What's the alternative, Ruby?' he snaps, finally looking at me. 'She needs to know something, if you're going AWOL. And especially with this bloody TV show coming up. People will gossip.' He pauses. 'It might reach her and I want to make sure—'

I interrupt him. 'I'm not AWOL, it's one weekend.'

We stand in silence. 'Look, you always say it yourself,' he says, sighing. 'It's best to tell kids the truth, or they fill in the gaps.'

'But it's not the truth!' I say, voice raised. 'To say she did a bad thing. That's not the truth. You know that.'

'You tell me what I should have said then,' he hisses.

I feel every bit of energy leave my body.

'If she needs them over the weekend,' I say, changing the subject. '*Dog Man: Grime and Punishment* is in her rucksack. *Dog Man: Lord of the Fleas* is in her room. And *Dog Man: Tale of Two Kitties* hasn't got a bookmark in, but she's on page 37.'

He nods, as though this is a normal way for two adults to speak to one another. '*Dog Man: Fetch-22* still missing?'

'Yeah.'

He *tsks*. 'It's a library book too.'

Then he looks at me. 'You're really doing this?' he asks. 'I thought you agreed it was for the best to move on.'

I stare at him, my insides churning with the conflict. 'Junie—'

'*Junie* can't make you do anything.'

But how do I tell her no, without her wondering what the hell I am playing at?

'The forecast is extreme this weekend too,' he says, hand in that V on his beard again. 'I know you're used to it, I know you think that you—'

'I've checked. It's only forecast to get down to minus one. We're not camping. Coming home to sleep.'

He looks at me like I'm insane. 'Yeah, that does make sense since it's *the Cairngorms in February*. It means you're slightly less likely to die from hypothermia.'

'Emlyn!' I look over his shoulder for Seren.

'It's fine. She's upstairs.' A snorted exhale, as he turns the hob down to a simmer. 'And let's be clear about something. I'm not the one damaging her here, Ruby. *I'm* the one trying to move forward.'

◆ ◆ ◆

In the hall, I find Junie on all fours, with the cupboard under the stairs open, pulling out rucksacks and walking poles.

'Are we doing the right thing?' I ask, speaking to her bum. 'Should we be leaving her be?'

Junie sits back on her heels. She puts a walking pole on the floor, then holds a hand out for me to pull her up. 'She's our sister,' she says, as though that is an answer.

'Coffee?' In the kitchen, I take a packet out of the cupboard.

'Ooh, posh stuff.'

'It's not decaf though.' I turn to my husband. 'Emlyn, d'you want one?'

He shakes his head. Leaves the kitchen, and heads upstairs. Junie's eyes follow him, in a way that makes me nervous. *Why is she watching him like that?*

'Secret incoming,' she says, snapping her gaze back towards me. 'I do drink the odd real coffee again now. Caffeine me up.'

As the coffee brews, I let myself imagine it for a moment. Poppy – a little older, a few lines around her eyes now she's in her thirties – walking towards us across the massif. Sitting next to me in a bothy, walking boots crossed in front of her, telling me her stories; of sneaking around the Cairngorms, of meditating in Indonesia. Of a new name, maybe. A new identity. Maybe she's met someone, fallen in love, and told them everything. Maybe there is someone there for her; someone who is on her team. Maybe she's ok.

I bask in it for a minute.

Then I remember the reality. What will begin to unravel if Poppy comes back. How we view that as the finish line, but it would only be the start.

The coffee pot whistles. I pour the coffee and see my phone light up on the kitchen table. Emlyn.

I open the message.

What the hell?

From upstairs, he has forwarded me a link, with the title: *Declaration of Presumed Death.*

'What's up?' asks Junie, but I can't speak. I feel like I've been winded.

'I don't want to say this in front of Junie but this might be a better use of your time than running around the mountains,' he types. 'After seven years you can do this, you know? Declare a missing person dead. Move on. And then you and Junie can split Poppy's share of the inheritance too, and that might seem callous but that's money for Seren. Let Poppy be, Rubes. She's gone, and she doesn't want to be found. And that's for the best.'

I stare at it. Shake with rage. And even though moving on had been my stance before Junie arrived, I had never, not once, considered declaring my sister *dead.*

How dare he suggest that?

Emlyn, of all the people on the planet.

HOTTER

The next morning, I slide my backpack in next to Junie's in the boot of my black Fiat Panda. Slam the door shut.

On the windscreen, de-icer dribbles down the windscreen. Junie has an ice axe in her backpack; there are spikes on our boots.

I climb in. Junie is in the passenger seat, lighting an OS map up with the torch on her phone as the heaters blast noisily at their maximum.

Outside the car, dawn is breaking. Dim light trickles in through the window but the car lights are still on; a helping hand required for the emerging sunshine.

I turn the engine on.

'Ready?'

Junie nods.

I drive up the steep road out of the village, climbing towards the spot where we will start our first search.

I fiddle with knobs to turn the heating away from the windscreen and onto our shivering bodies. Warm air starts to blast from the vents.

'Walking poles, head torch, stove,' Junie mutters, reading through her list. 'Water, snacks, more snacks, extra snacks, all the snacks I could fit in.'

But I am somewhere else. Thinking about Emlyn's message. We had a hissed argument in bed last night; he'd have slept in the spare room if Junie hadn't been in there. I was too wired to drop off until nearly 3 a.m.

The money I inherited from my dad means that we are safe and secure, despite my erratic earnings. To inherit half of the same amount again – Poppy's share, divided between me and Junie – would mean a solid university fund for Seren.

It would mean letting go of the constant worry of losing my job to the internet or the ether.

And yet, despite that, there is no way I would even consider doing what Emlyn says. Because this isn't about money, it's about my sister.

'Rubes – the herd,' Junie says dreamily, looking off to her right. We have been driving for ten minutes by now and the sun's a little higher. We can see them now: the Cairngorm reindeer, grazing under the sunrise. That image, so familiar, but still able to snatch the breath from my throat. It could surely chill out dictators.

'I'm afraid to tell you that this is not a school trip,' I tell her, but I'm smiling. 'Gorgeous though they are, we can't fit the reindeer in today.'

I remember when we could fit them in, often. We went to visit that herd so much as kids – there weren't a lot of day trips available up here in the sticks in the nineties unless you wanted to climb yet another Munro.

'God, Poppy loved them.'

'That's not saying a lot, though,' Junie says, smiling. 'She could get mushy over a goldfish.'

It's true. The closest family member to our childhood cat Ollie, Poppy's was always the lap he went to, the only one that diva seemed vaguely interested in. And it was because she adored him. Him, and every animal she saw. She nearly cried when she saw a lone goose, out of formation and away from their flock as they migrated south. Once, at the Highland Wildlife Park, she said the pigeons were her favourite animal because no-one else liked them and she felt bad.

'I can picture her,' says Junie, eyes still out of the window, even though we have left the herd behind. 'Hand-feeding the littlest reindeer in her yellow wellies.'

Little gloves slipped off. Me and Junie firmly in the cynical eye-rolly years but Poppy still all in.

Sometimes I think it would be easier to leave – to go further than the twenty minutes away we relocated to. To not see Poppy's ghost everywhere. I think it would be easier to do what Junie's done: find a new place and start again.

It would have been safer too, to be further away from anyone who did remember the story of the Winter sisters.

But I remember hearing a theory about grief. What our brain needs is not to rebuild but to repeat. Repeat the old habits. Go to work. Do the old hobby. They're the familiar things that will get us through. And there's no doubt about this feeling: for the last seven years, it's felt like grieving. Not just for Dad.

There's no way I could have left the Cairngorms.

Tears spring up but I won't let them fall; instead I hold them there like children at the top of a slide. *Wait. Wait.*

'Right. Here we are,' I say to Junie, turning off the road and slowing down.

We aren't the first car.

'They probably went up for sunrise.' Junie sighs, nodding at the black Dacia across the car park. 'Nothing like it.'

The car park is at the ski centre, where we'll start today's climb. We both sit in the boot to put our walking boots on, spikes for the ice added to the bottom of them. We turn on our head torches.

'Ready?'

Junie ducks her face down into her snood. Slips on her gloves. 'Ready.'

I lock the car and bury my keys in my backpack. Shake it onto my shoulders.

And off we go.

We walk past the café, ski fields to our right and away from the funicular railway, and then into a wide expanse of heather. Onto hard ground, covered in thin ice. We tread carefully. The wind hoots like an owl and I bury my face into my coat, pull my worn old bobble hat down onto my forehead. There are a lot of hours ahead: this is going to be brutal.

And then the real climb kicks in. Up the windy ridge path, avoiding the ski slopes. The map dangles from Junie's gloved hand and I follow. More slowly now, as the incline gets bigger.

The views, though. They pay off quickly, as the sun comes fully up. Below us is mythical Loch Morlich, where Poppy used to swim in all weathers. It's a partial ice rink today, slabs floating like glass. Even Poppy would have drawn a line.

'This place,' murmurs Junie, and I realise how long it's been for her.

'I know,' I reply quietly. 'I know.'

One foot. In front of the other.

One foot. In front of the other.

But I am out of breath already.

There is no choice though and slowly, slowly, one foot in front of the other begins to feel like a meditation.

Overhead, a ptarmigan circles and swoops. Then there is a flash of white, darting behind the granite boulders.

'What was that?' I ask, stopping.

'Mountain hare,' Junie tells me. She takes out her binoculars. 'Juvenile, I'd guess. Hiding in the boulders, bless it. They turn white for snow camo too, the ptarmigan do the same. Wait until we get a bit higher and you won't notice them. The camo does an amazing job.'

She slips her binoculars back into her rucksack and starts moving again, the crunch of the ice beneath her feet. 'Come on,' she says. 'Not a time for wildlife spotting. We need to get this ground covered.'

The more ground we cover, the more chance there is that we will find our sister.

I remember Emlyn's words. *You are playing a risky game, Ruby.*

Still I go. One foot. In front of the other.

When we pass a bothy, we stick our heads in and look for signs of life. Of someone making a more long-term base there. But there is nothing; even the hardiest hikers go home at the end of the day in February. And – rightfully – they observe Leave No Trace anyway.

'Shit,' says Junie, looking up. 'This wasn't forecast.'

There is a flurry of sleet coming down. Visibility gets trickier, and Junie takes out a torch. And then there is a noise above us. Out of place and unnatural.

'Rescue helicopter,' says Junie quietly, face to the sky. 'Hopefully no-one's in too much trouble.'

But we fall silent. Because we know that this is a place where people can get into too much trouble. Six months ago a solo walker was found dead by mountain rescue dogs. And then, of course, long before that, there had been our mum.

◆ ◆ ◆

'Do you know what Emlyn told me to do before?' I say to Junie, a couple of hours later.

We are sitting on a boulder eating snacks, hoods pulled around us as the sleet continues to fall. In the distance we can see bundled-up snowboarders and skiers, goggles in place, battling on despite the weather.

Junie pauses eating her pot of nuts, and *hmmms*. 'Well, you two don't seem friendly at the moment so I'm going to say . . . Go fuck yourself?'

'Swearing?' I raise an eyebrow. 'You know Saint Emlyn would never say something so rude.'

Junie laughs from her belly. It sounds like she's been waiting to let that laugh escape. I remember that nickname they think I don't know: *Mr Vanilla.*

'True. What, then?' She shoves a banana into her mouth while she speaks, devouring it in two bites.

I look up. 'He told me to declare Poppy dead.'

'What?' says Junie, through her food. All remnants of her laugh have left the mountain. She stares at me from inside her hood. 'He said that?'

I nod. 'Yep. You can do it, apparently. After seven years. Even without a body.'

'Apart from anything, I'm sure I remember Francesca telling me that you can't defame the dead, so imagine what a field day the tabloids would have then,' Junie says, wincing.

A noise comes from her throat. 'What the fuck would you be manifesting, too? If you declared her *dead*. Dickhead.' She stands up, sharply, and tucks her banana skin in the side pocket of her bag. 'Sorry. I know he's your husband.'

I nod. 'It's fine.' I am regretting saying anything. Those divided loyalties, all the time. 'Anyway, let's go.'

One foot.

In front of the other.

We climb higher and higher and higher. There is another white-blue mountain hare over to the side and a golden eagle, gliding like a paper aeroplane above us. Nature, blowing our minds at every step and resetting us, after Junie's rage over Emlyn's idea. Nature slowing our breathing; soothing our souls. In that way Poppy always loved.

The sleet comes down harder, though. It's blizzard-like now, visibility down to a few centimetres in front of our face. We walk in silence for a long time, traversing over towards the next mountain, until I can barely see in front of me.

Shit. It's got so much worse, so quickly.

'I don't know which way . . .' I begin, starting to panic. I think of that rescue helicopter. Of Mum. It can happen so quickly. 'Junie, how do we know we're not . . . ?'

We're close to white-out.

But Junie takes my hand. 'Stick with me,' she says, soothing. 'We're fine. It's the plateau, all good, easy from here, Rubes, I know this place.'

'But you haven't been here for—'

'Doesn't matter. I'm like Pops, I know it in my bones.'

We stay still for a few seconds.

'Ready?' she asks eventually. 'Walk with me. We're fine.'

She doesn't wait for me to agree, and we walk – slowly, carefully – until, bit by bit, visibility begins to clear.

In different circumstances, we'd be high-fiving each other; celebrating bagging a Munro. We would be high and giddy on nature.

Not today, though.

Instead, we concentrate as we cross the bare and stony plateau.

I grip Junie's hand.

Keep going and keep focused.

But *Easy from here* may have been an exaggeration.

The light fades as the snow eases and we see the cairn on the summit, the ice thicker up here, thankful for the spikes on our boots.

Junie frowns as she looks at her watch. We've taken a little longer than planned, thanks to the weather.

But she doesn't need to tell me to speed up. As we turn the bend, the sharp decline makes accidental trail runners of us both and suddenly, the worry is not getting lost but not being able to make it back down without a snapped ankle.

'Be careful!' shouts Junie from behind me.

But I can't answer her back, and she gives up speaking too. The sleet circles us like a predator.

Even mid-gallop, I see Junie make eye contact with any other hardy winter hikers – slipping their wet hoods down and shaking their heads like dogs after the blizzard – who are alone and roughly Poppy's height.

Making sure.

Our first day on the mountains has nearly come to an end though, and there is no sign of Poppy.

One foot.

In front of the other.

Nearly on flat ground again now, snow passed, skies clearing.

Keep going and keep focused.

But I am distracted, thinking of Emlyn, of Junie. Of those divided loyalties. Of what I really want.

Until I see something that makes me scream the mountain down.

COLDER

'What the bloody hell was that?' I ask Junie, shaken. 'Behind that tree. Jesus.'

Junie laughs hard, like she did when she was taking the piss out of Emlyn earlier.

'You're serious? Come on, you must remember. I've not been up here for years now, Rubes, and even *I* remember.'

I keep walking, to get away from whatever I have just spotted. It's easier now. The clouds have opened like curtains. The decline's eased. We can stop holding our breath.

'Not even the legends?' Junie presses. 'The Highland tiger?'

Oh. *That.*

I have a flashback. A teenage sleepover, stories whispered from sleeping bags in the dark about the *cat sidhe*, guardian of the other-world, a supernatural large black cat with a white spot on its chest.

Highland tiger is a nickname. The wildcats – closely related to the lynx, released back into the Cairngorms after a programme to save them from extinction – roam free here, especially on the edge of woodland and near villages. And we are back down now, on the periphery of civilisation.

'There's no creature more powerful,' Junie whispers into my ear, as we walk. I picture us telling each other these stories, torches shining on our faces, GCSE drama skills at the ready. 'No creature more ferocious.'

'Stop it.'

Junie starts laughing again, despite the cold wind blowing into my face, a waterproof fastened around it as tightly as it will go. 'It's coming for you. You're dinner now, Rubes.'

'It's not funny.'

'It is *quite* funny. That you didn't remember is funny. How long has it been since you've been up a mountain? You *live* here.'

But I am not listening.

Instead, I am staring behind me, my eyes on the spot where the wildcat appeared. But it has long gone now. Of course it is. It will have found whatever it was after – a vole or a rabbit, most likely – and retreated.

They're shy, wildcats. Solitary.

Just like our own.

◆ ◆ ◆

In the morning, as we arrive with sunrise for day two of our search and put on our head torches, we see another walker up ahead of us, alone and pushing into the wind but with a phone out, typing.

Junie rolls her eyes.

'It might be a map, to be fair,' I say, knowing how much Junie rages about people who walk through landscapes like this and stare instead at their tiny rectangle of phone. People who take themselves out of the real world, the realest world there is, surely – mountains and lochs, hares as big as labradors and majestic flocks of snow bunting – to be absorbed by their screen.

But I have stopped thinking about that.

Because. *Because.*

Junie holds a walking pole in her hand loosely. Lets it drop.

And we stare.

This woman has her back to us as she heads upwards. Her face is still ducked low at her phone, and is almost hidden in her waterproof jacket: the wind just as brutal as it was yesterday.

'Come on,' says Junie, picking up her pole. And we walk at speed, to catch this woman up. It's impossible to tell what colour her hair is or even to make out her build: she is slightly too far away. She is shrouded in layers, as we are. As any sane person would be in this weather.

But there is something about the angle of her face. Something about her movement.

My heart rate quickens.

The weather falls away.

It is easy to catch up with this woman. She is moving slowly: that'll be the phone.

We get closer.

But then we pass her, and it's clear: she is too short to be Poppy.

I realise I've been holding my breath.

'Morning,' says Junie.

'Morning,' says the woman who – now we are close – we can see is in her fifties. She slips her phone back into her pocket.

We walk ahead.

'Next one,' says Junie. 'She could always be the next one.'

I don't reply.

As we walk, I think about Seren, asking about bad Auntie Poppy, and how this will always be a part of our family folklore, whatever happens now. It will roll with us, change shape like a snowball, but it will forever hang around, zipping from generation to generation to generation.

Did you hear about the Winter sisters?

I tried to close the door but there was no point because it will always fall open.

The question is where does the story go next? Where do I *want* it to go next?

When my phone rings, I ignore it – we're onto the next mountain and I am on too tight a cliff edge, balancing like a dancer – but when the call ends, it beeps.

I sigh as I make my way around the bend. As soon as I can, I sit down on a knoll. Take my phone out to see who left a voicemail.

Emlyn.

'Call me,' he says. 'Urgent.'

Adrenalin charges through me. My body has known crises before. It senses them before they happen. And it is ready now, and charged.

I tap on his name to call.

Before it connects though, a text flashes up and confirms my worst fear.

It's Seren.

I stand still in an exposed spot where the reception holds. The wind flies around me, circling. And my fingers tremble as I hit the call button.

THE SUSPECT

THE CARIBBEAN

'Oh my God.'

The suspect looks around. She appears confused. Blinks, like the lights have just been turned back on.

'Oh my God. Oh my God.'

Her dad walks in through the side gate whistling Phil Collins' '*You Can't Hurry Love*'. She hears the clink of what she would guess are bottles of rum, carried in a thin plastic bag.

When he sees his daughter, she is staring down at the woman who would have been her stepmum, but who is now floating in the infinity pool.

Dead.

The suspect's father cries out, of course. Gets into the pool. Tries to drag his fiancée out before he realises it's too late.

And when the suspect runs inside to the kitchen and he goes after her, it starts the next set of events in motion.

'What have you done?'

He grabs her roughly by her slim shoulders.

'*What the hell* have you done?'

The movement is too fast, too careless, when there is a knife right there and she grabs it. Looks down; seems to enjoy its might. It lolls in her hand; she holds a weapon comfortably. In her bag is her Swiss army knife. Weeks before, she took her yard-long ice axe with her into the mountains.

The knife goes straight into her dad's aorta and she watches him bleed out.

Ok, *watches* is a little strong. She does try to stem the bleeding but it is like trying to put the snow back in place after an avalanche.

Her father is dead in less than five minutes.

Afterwards, she goes calmly, straight to the airport.

Her favourite Stephen King novels are found afterwards; violent quotes highlighted in orange. People from school post on social media: she was an oddball, not many mates. It doesn't really surprise them.

They all say: It's who she always was.

HOTTER

'Finally,' Emlyn snaps when he answers. Then his voice softens slightly. 'How's it going out there? Have you found—'

'No,' I say, frustrated. Why is he wasting time? 'Nothing. Is Seren ok, though? What's happened?'

'She's . . . well, she's fine, I guess.' He pauses. 'Mostly fine.'

Mostly fine? After that message?

He sighs. 'But she does want to tell you about something that happened to her yesterday on the trip. She's only just told me. It's . . . Oh Jesus, Ruby, it's effed up. Have you got a few minutes to talk to her?'

Yesterday – Friday – was Seren's class school trip to the Highland Wildlife Park. I got back after her bedtime from day one of our search and Emlyn and I were still barely speaking. I had forgotten about the trip.

'Of course.' I don't wait for an answer. 'Put her on.'

There's a rustle. Words I can't hear. And then that voice.

'Hi, Mum.'

But the voice isn't right. It's sitting on the edge of tears.

I speak close to the phone. Turn to try and block out the wind that's as bad today as it was on yesterday's route. 'What's wrong, chick? What happened on the trip? Daddy said something happened?'

She lets go of the sob. 'I got told off. On the school trip. I'm sorry.'

The relief. 'Oh. Well, that's ok! What happened? We all get told off sometimes.' That's a lie: I didn't. The old me was the world's biggest goody two-shoes.

'We were all hooting at the owls. It was funny.' She does a hoot.

'Ok. Great owl.' I laugh. 'That doesn't sound bad.'

'I should have stayed there, with my friends. But I thought I saw the lynx that we'd been waiting for over the other side, so I walked over there and it wasn't far and I could still see my teacher and . . .'

I picture it. Seren, wild and loose and tiny in the wildlife park. All those strangers milling around. No parents. The stuff of nightmares happening next. 'Still, chick. You know the importance of staying together on school trips. Did you have a partner?'

'Yeah. It was Dylan K.'

'Ok, well, really you should have stayed with Dylan K and the teacher was right to tell you, but it's happened now, so don't—'

'No, Mum.' She is impatient. '*That's* not what I got told off for.'

Junie sits down on a rock and takes out one of her endless pots of nuts from her rucksack. I mouth *Seren* at her and she nods.

She puts a handful of nuts into her mouth, takes an OS map out and starts examining elevation points. She may have moved to England, but this place is in-built in her. She is way more adept at navigating us through this terrain, in low visibility and a brutal wind, than I am. She even pushed for us to camp before I told her that I was scared my tent would blow away like a cagoule. And also, that I might freeze to death.

Eventually she conceded that it would be a 'little hard going' in February and we should search until as late as we could, then go back each night to mine to sleep.

'What did you get told off for then?' I ask Seren.

Junie looks up and laughs. And I smile myself, relaxing now. Whatever this is, it's manageable.

'Seren? What was it, chick?'

My hand reaches round for the water in my backpack.

Then she speaks.

'I got told off because of the lady.'

HOTTER

'The lady?'

I take my hand away from the bottle of water I was about to grab from my backpack.

'What lady?'

Junie's head, down on the OS map as she sits on the rock, snaps upwards. It's not the words, I know, but something she hears in my tone.

'I was watching for the lynx, and the lady said hi,' says Seren. 'And I know I shouldn't talk to strangers but—'

'No,' I say sharply. 'You shouldn't. You *know* that.'

'Sorry, Mum.'

But then, another thought. Another question.

'Seren. What did she look like? The lady . . . what did she look like?'

Junie's eyes are on mine now and I can see her chest falling and rising too fast even though she doesn't know the context and is only hearing one side of the conversation. But she's getting the gist.

She watches me. The map dangles, unimportant now, from her gloved fingers.

'Well, that was the only reason I spoke to her,' says my daughter, sobs swallowed again now but still, I can tell, on the precipice of tears. 'I know not to speak to strangers, I'm not stupid. But she was so nice and she . . . she . . . I spoke to her because she looked just like *you*, Mummy.'

HOTTER

There are only two people in the world who look just like me.

Tall and lanky with faces that mirror our body shape. Fair hair – barring Junie's recent dubious dye job – and brown eyes.

One is sitting opposite me. The other has been on the run for seven years.

'Did she say what her name was?' I ask, trying to keep my tone light. 'This lady?'

I need to keep my voice steady; try not to alarm my daughter more than I have already. But I *am* alarmed. I am alarmed in every corner of my body.

Don't rush her.

I have to let her tell me, without panicking. That's the best way to get a clear picture too. She's only seven years old.

'Seren?' I say gently. 'The woman – did she tell you her name?'

'No.'

'Ok, chick.' My heart breaks. The confirmation had felt so close. Just one word, that's all we needed. *Poppy.*

I take a deep breath. Try to work out the best question to ask next, to get as much information as I can before it is swallowed into the recesses of a child's mind, filed below the plot twists of *Dog Man* and her favourite six colouring pens. But while I am thinking, my daughter speaks again.

'She didn't say *her* name,' she says. 'But she knew mine.'

HOTTER

'She knew your name? Are you sure?'

Junie looks at me, mouthing: *What's going on?*

But I shake my head. I can't give anything else my attention, I just need to understand what Seren is telling me.

'How do you know that this lady knew your name?'

I am kicking myself for being all the way up here. I wish desperately that I was face to face with my daughter. I wish I could pull Seren onto my lap. I wish I didn't have to angle my phone so that the wind doesn't wail down it and distract her.

I wish a wash of sleet hadn't started sliding down from a heavy sky. I wish I wasn't bone-tired. I barely slept last night thinking about being up here again today; about what I actually wanted. What I would do, if we did find her. I lay awake, veering back and forth with my usual conflict: desperate to find Poppy; terrified of what will happen if we do.

Suddenly there are no views down to the snowy corrie, no swooping birds of prey, no awe at this place. It all just feels barren, a never-ending moonscape far from civilisation. Because all I want is home and a sofa and a blanket. Seren.

I repeat it. 'Seren? How do you know she knew your name?'

Through the phone, my daughter giggles. 'Because she said "Hi, Seren", silly.'

I should be lecturing her, properly now, about speaking to strangers. I should be horrified that she did that, despite all the unsubtle lecture-y fiction I've read to her since she was a toddler and all the warnings I've given about unknown men in parks.

But I suspect Emlyn has already done that.

And I just need to know.

'Tell me the whole story again, chick. Where exactly were you when this happened?'

She pauses, no giggles now, and I know she has heard my sharpness. My anxiety. 'She was just, um, standing next to me, Mum. We were watching to see if the lynx would appear, I *told* you that. People were saying it had come out.'

'And then she said "Hi, Seren"?'

Another pause. 'Yeah.'

'You're sure she said that? With your name?'

'Yes.'

'Ok. Then what did you say?'

'I . . . I said hi back.' There's a wobble in her voice. 'I know I'm not supposed to. But she looked like you and I saw my teacher coming over, and the lady told me to tell you something, and after that . . . she just walked away, *really* fast, like almost a run, she was quite zoomy, and she disappeared into lots of people and I couldn't see her any more.' She pauses. 'Can I go and read *Dog Man* now?'

I swallow.

'In a minute, chick. First . . . this is important. What did she say to tell me?'

'Erm . . .'

'*Tell me*, Seren,' I snap.

Junie frowns at me. Shakes her head.

'Sorry, chick. I didn't mean to sound— Just . . . It might be important. I need to know what message P— this lady gave you for me.'

Seren's voice comes out worried again. Edgy. 'She said . . . she just said to tell my mum that she loved her.'

A strangled noise tries to climb from my throat but I choke it down.

Be a parent. Stop putting this on Seren. Grow up.

'Well, that's nice!' I say, attempting light. 'Anything else?'

'Nope. Just that. Then she left and I got told off by Mrs Halliday for speaking to adults I didn't know and Dylan K said I was a rubbish partner and he's going with Ziya next time and then I got a bit upset.'

Then her voice comes again, hesitant through the phone. 'Who was she, Mum? Who was the lady?' A pause. 'Is she a baddie?'

And I shake my head, and I speak through tears.

'No, she's not a baddie,' I choke out, to my confused little girl.

In the background, though, it's whirring. We are halfway up the mountain. I feel so far away. But once we get back to the car park, the Highland Wildlife Park is only a half-hour drive away.

And unlike all the miles we've covered on the massif, we know Poppy was there. *Right there.*

'Ruby?' comes Emlyn's voice.

'Yeah. Hi. I'm here.'

He pauses. I hear him sending Seren off to get a snack. Then he is back on the line.

'Rubes, I think I've been understanding about all of this because I know it's something Junie needs to do,' he says. 'And I know it's tricky for you. But for *our* family, for me, you and Seren, you *have* to stop. This TV show is about to be a living hell for us, to be honest. This whole thing is a living hell. This is getting too close for comfort. And now it looks like Poppy is stalking our dau—'

'She's not *stalking* her!'

'What is it, Ruby, if it's not stalking?' he snaps. 'She must have known they were going to be at the wildlife park. That can't have been a coincidence. And she waited until she was away from her teachers then targeted her. That is not ok.'

'She didn't harm her. She just told her she loves me.'

'Is that not harmful, Ruby?' His voice is raised. 'Our daughter. I realise you're not here so you can't see her face but you must have heard it, how confused she was? She doesn't *get* this. Any of it. How could she? *I* don't get it to be honest. I don't get the theory here, all this time later, I don't get why any part of you would think it's a good idea if Poppy comes back. She's in hiding *for a reason*, Ruby.'

He sighs.

'Do you want her to come back and upend everything? Think about that. *Think* about what that would mean.'

I do. Constantly.

And it terrifies me.

HOTTER

'What's going on?' Junie fires at me the second I end the call.

I explain.

'Poppy was *there*?' she says in disbelief. 'With Seren?'

She stares at me for a few seconds, before she snaps into action.

'Ok, let's relook at the route,' she says, taking the map out of her side pocket again. 'If she was there . . . near Kingussie . . . I think the best thing to do might be to call it a day for now. Light's fading anyway . . . Then tomorrow, we head over there and do a long, thorough route, cover as much ground as we can? I'll work out the best way tonight.'

I nod, terror rising and rising.

This is too close. Too real.

I realise something then: the mountains was a long shot. I did it for Junie, but I never expected to find Poppy up here. Not really.

Now though, with a newer, fresher sighting . . . What if we do? What if, after all these years, we actually find our sister?

'Let's go,' says Junie, sounding focused.

We head back down the mountain, following Poppy's trail.

One foot.

In front of the other.

We walk fast but in silence for a long time, Junie navigating, until she speaks.

'Do you think she knows about it?'

'What?'

'*Hotter/Colder.* Do you think Poppy knows it starts tonight?'

I wince. Junie still wants me to watch the TV show with her when we get back home – that's the main reason she came up to Scotland. But how can I?

'Imagine,' says Junie. She stands still, hands on her hips and looks around her. She turns 360 degrees. 'She's probably watching it tonight too. The same show, at the same time, somewhere so close to us.'

Then she stands there and she shouts it, into the wind, into the sleet, into the mountains. At the top of her lungs, from the top of the world.

Desperate. Longing.

'POPPY!' she shouts. 'POPPPPPPPPPYYYYYYYY!'

THE SUSPECT

THE CARIBBEAN

The suspect walks through airport security.

Nothing happens.

She sinks three straight mini vodkas on the plane.

Nothing happens.

She finally sleeps. Fitful. She wakes.

Nothing happens.

She exits the plane and notices, as she walks down the aeroplane stairs, the tiniest trace of blood on her trainers.

Nothing happens.

She goes through passport control.

Still, nothing happens.

She checks the time. Nineteen hours since her dad died.

She goes to an ATM. Takes out as much cash as she can. She gets on a Piccadilly Line tube, heading east.

And then, the suspect disappears.

COLDER

Just one problem. That's not what happened in real life.

The suspect is not a real person; she is a character from *Hotter/ Colder*, the TV show about my family that I am watching now with Junie on my sofa, showered and in our pyjamas after our brutal day of searching in the icy mountains.

I relented, of course.

Knowing the show is there, lurking inside my TV, was like being an alcoholic trying to ignore vodka.

Emlyn is disgusted that I am giving it the time of day, and has gone to the gym, door slammed behind him.

Junie and I have sat through the credits – a cool graphic of tall, blonde women lined up on sunbeds, set to a faux-Europop soundtrack, that we watched while Junie towel-dried her hair and smeared orange dye onto my towels and I tried not to look pissed off.

Now, we are into episode one, the characters arriving on holiday. The names they are using in the show are different to ours, of course, but barely. The sisters are called the *Frosts*. It's set on another island, but still in the Caribbean.

'Are they serious?' I murmur. *'Frost?'*

'I told you,' Junie says quietly. This is the episode she has already seen. 'I did try to warn you.'

But I had ignored her. Told her to stop. Left the room when she talked about it.

Now, I realise why she thought we needed to get ahead of it. Anyone who remembered the case would see two minutes of this and know it was based on us. And that's a lot of people. Female murderers (especially young and pretty ones) are rare. They're intriguing. They're pored over.

It would only take a few minutes on Google to find *Hotter/Colder*'s origin story. To see a picture of the real-life Daisy Frost, Poppy Winter, who'd had so much written about her.

'Is that supposed to be me?' I whisper, when an irritating character called Summer Frost – subtle – marinates chicken. Tells everyone in a sing-song that dinner will be up in fifteen. She is American; all of them are.

'Mmm-hmm,' says Junie, with a scowl. 'And that's Emlyn.'

Summer's fiancé, Oliver Smith, kisses her on the cheek as she puts the chicken onto the sizzling plancha. Then he goes to sit next to the third sister, the eldest one, Flora Frost.

'And that's you?'

'That's me.' She grimaces.

'Junie,' I whisper, turning to her when we finish the first episode. 'This is so bad.'

But we are settled in for a marathon – all six half-hour episodes – and as they go on, it gets steadily worse. Watching ourselves – or some version – represented so inaccurately is hell. But what they do to Poppy's character is the worst.

'They're saying Poppy had a *coke* addiction?' Junie says, eyes wide – she was only given a preview of episode one. 'What the fuck?'

I shake my head, bewildered. I can't take any of this in.

When we have watched all six episodes, I look at social media. The show is huge.

And our names are being linked to it regularly.

I think of the school gate. The small community. How quickly – once the show is being talked about and the story becomes current again – will someone connect the dots, and realise that Seren's mum Ruby Jones is one of the Winter sisters? And Emlyn – *God*, Emlyn is going to be furious.

'I'm scared, Junie,' I tell her.

As well as showing Poppy killing my dad and Robin – violently, frenetically in the final episode as I cried and Junie raged – the other awful thing this will do is put our family back in the limelight.

It is stark and irrefutable: this show will make hiding so much harder for my sister.

And for us.

It's not just people I know. Now it's broadcast, it will bring them all out of the woodwork: the conspiracy theorists, the true crime obsessives.

'I know,' Junie says. 'I'm scared too.'

I stand up and walk to the front door. Check that it is locked.

◆ ◆ ◆

'It's ok,' says Junie, glancing at me above the laptop she is poring over now, as I walk back into the room. My chest rises and falls, too hard. 'Those posts that link the show to Poppy will fall away, they aren't being shared by anyone with a big following.'

But I can hear it: she is trying to convince herself.

'I'm sorry,' Junie says. 'Sorry that I pressured you to watch.'

I shake my head. 'I would have watched anyway, in the end.'

'But now you have those images, in your head, as though they're what happened, and you shouldn't have that.' Her voice cracks.

I look up. 'No, I don't,' I say, without thinking. 'Because they're not what happened. They're not my images.'

And Junie looks at me oddly then. Just the hint. Just the hint of a question.

◆ ◆ ◆

By the next day, the show is number one on Netflix in the UK and the US.

People talk online about *Hotter/Colder* in the same obsessed tones they used about *Bake Off* or *The Traitors*. Our pain is entertainment.

The images roll through my brain now; Junie was right that they would.

The actress playing Poppy – *Daisy* – holding a knife. Poppy – *no, Daisy* – covered in blood.

I shake my head. Try to fling the images loose.

But they are too sticky.

Still, we carry on the search, as planned.

In the car park. Junie looks at the map.

'Right,' she says. 'Let's go.'

I nod.

'It's rocky, this way,' she says, glancing behind at me, moving slowly. 'You ok with that?'

'Yep. Whatever you think.'

How can I say anything else? If anything, the show has made Junie more determined than ever to find Poppy. To figure out the truth, and clear her name. I know Junie was up late with her maps in the spare bedroom, working out the best way to cover the most ground in this area. Turning her original route planning on its head. Poppy will be long gone from the Highland Wildlife Park, of course. But it makes sense to head to that area. It's the most we have to go on.

We step across a stream and Junie stands with one walking boot up on a rock, fastening her lace.

'Is there any chance Emlyn would have told the police?' she asks me. 'About what happened at the wildlife park?'

I recoil. 'No. Of course he wouldn't.'

'Are you sure? If he's worried about Seren?'

'I am 100 per cent sure.' I sound defensive.

Junie says nothing. But she does it again: looks at me with the hint of a frown. I avoid her eyes.

We go up. Up. As we know – or think we know – that Poppy will. She always did. Some things don't change; the fundamentals of a person. What you do when you're frightened. Where you go when you want to hide.

Junie will always be most relaxed on a stage, pretending to be someone else. My mum would always choose warm climates. Poppy will head up a mountain. Some things stay with you through the life shifts. They would still be there if you went into witness protection.

We sit down to eat, and balance on rocks in silence, both of us in zombie mode, eyes on our phones.

Who are you then, Ruby? I think, as I scroll mindlessly. What are your fundamentals?

I used to run. I used to organise. I think about snapping at Seren on the phone, about forgetting her school trip, the eye rolls from the teachers. What the hell has happened to me?

Then, from the other side of the stream, Junie stands and holds her phone out.

Her face is set like clay. 'Look at this.'

It's a LinkedIn page, a TV producer. There's a postgrad degree in Broadcast Journalism; various TV credits.

I don't get it. 'What am I looking at?' I ask, eyes up to Junie. 'Who is he?'

'He . . .' She points to the page. 'Produced *Hotter/Colder*. I've been delving into it since they sent me episode one. It kept niggling me the level of detail they had. Not about the murders or Poppy being a bloody *coke addict* – bullshit – but the granular stuff about our lives, minutiae from the villa. I knew it came from somewhere.'

She's right. There were small details in that show that they couldn't have known, not without hearing it from someone who was there. What we had for dinner. Music we listened to.

This guy hasn't posted for a year or so, but Junie points to the last post he did, when he announced that he'd got a new job at a big network.

'Look,' she pushes, and there is a quiver in her voice. 'This is what I— Look at that comment.'

> Great stuff, mate. Always knew you'd be the successful one in our year! We should get a beer.

I frown. 'So what?'

'Look at the person who wrote that comment.'

'Lewis Young?'

'Except it's not Lewis Young, is it?' she says. 'Look at the profile picture.'

I click on the thumbnail.

And there he is.

Floppy hair. Movie-star face. Lines around the eyes.

The person who wrote the comment isn't Lewis Young. It's Lewis Williams.

Poppy's ex, and the man Junie has been trying to track down for the last seven years, convinced that he is the suspect we need; the man who really did it. Convinced that he is the person who – somehow, *somehow* – framed our little sister for murder.

COLDER

'I knew he was hiding something!' says Junie, voice vibrating with fury. 'I knew it.'

'But how would *he* know that stuff?' I ask, still staring at Lewis's picture. 'He wasn't even on the holiday.'

'No. But Poppy saw him while we were away – that night at Bleu, on the *yacht* – and she was his girlfriend.' Junie sounds impatient. 'She would have told him what we did, places we went, what we had for dinner. There might have been music in the background of videos. She would have shown him pictures. Enough to cobble together quite a lot of colour, I reckon, especially when you add what's in the public domain from Robin's Instagram.'

'*Why* though?'

'Same reason most people do most things?' She rubs her thumb against her forefinger.

We start walking again. Sleet is coming down.

'What if that's not all he did?' she says.

The sleet falls heavier; ices my cheeks. I look up.

'You know I've always wondered,' she says. 'And if it *was* him, Rubes, this could be his way of making sure people still think it's Poppy, by suggesting to his TV producer mate that this would make a good show then getting to be the main source on this thing. To totally control the narrative.'

I look at her. What do I say to that?

But Junie doesn't need me to answer. She is already typing furiously. Perhaps direct to Lewis Young on LinkedIn. Perhaps to her Saint Aurélie police contact. Perhaps to her journo mate Francesca, so she can give another interview to a magazine or newspaper and update them on this development.

'Junie . . .' I start, from where I am burrowed in my all-weather coat. But I need to go carefully; as she types, she is wide-eyed and convinced.

'I know,' she says. 'If it *was* him, he was home and dry. It's seven years later, yada yada. So you're thinking, why would he go to TV producers . . . why come out of the woodwork?'

That's not what I was thinking.

'But maybe, maybe.' And I can tell she is working out theories as she goes, veering from one to another. 'Maybe they were making the show anyway? And he got wind of it, somehow, through his mate and he thought . . . well, if he got in there, he *could* control that narrative.'

She finishes typing, and we start to walk again. It's impossible to stay still in this weather; the temperatures have dropped and the wind is getting in our faces like the most pissed-off adversary.

'Don't *you* ever think about who else it could have been?' Junie asks me as we barrel forward, heads down, along what has turned into a steep, narrow path. She turns and frowns at me. 'You never say it. Never speculate.'

I dip my head low. In the early days, she used to ask me this all the time. Suspects. Theories. Could it have been an intruder? A burglary gone wrong? The guy who ran the local shop told us there were some prominent gangs on the inland parts of the island. What about the odd starey guy with the long grey hair who was staying at the villa over the road – was he ever interviewed? And Lewis, of course – she has never stopped being suspicious of Lewis.

'I always wondered if Dad and Robin hurt each other,' says Junie, when I offer up nothing. 'Then maybe Poppy walked in or something . . . and she panicked?'

We've been here before. 'Forensics ruled that out. Remember? Said it wouldn't have been possible without a third party.'

'People get things wrong.' She shrugs. 'Happens all the time. Especially if they're being paid off.' She is stomping now, fuelled with her rage.

I stumble slightly, and she grabs my arm. Pushes on. 'A thief who panicked?' she says. Old ground, trodden as often as this path. 'Poppy is there. Gets in the way. They try to frame her. Threaten her.'

'Mmm-hmm.' I concentrate on the rocky earth and don't reply, however much I want to. How can I?

'There is one other theory,' Junie says, letting me pull in front of her. 'One that always used to . . . it used to bug me. But I couldn't say it. Not then.'

We are picking our way across ice-covered scree now, tentative and slow.

'But you can now?' I ask over my shoulder.

'Yeah,' I hear from behind me. 'I reckon I can now.'

'Ok,' I say, tentatively.

'Well, there were six of us staying in that villa,' Junie says. 'Two are dead, one is accused. Two of the others are . . . well, us. That leaves one more.'

And then I stop walking. Turn slowly and stare right at her, my feet balancing precariously on the uneven and frozen ground beneath us. And I wait.

She says it loudly. Clearly. Like she's been building up to it for a very long time. 'You know really, don't you? You know I'm talking about Emlyn.'

And with those words, my knees go from under me.

HOTTER

'Junie!' I say, stumbling again on the scree. My ankle. I wince. 'Junie! Of course it wasn't Emlyn! He's my husband.'

Fuck, fuck, fuck.

She locks her eyes on mine. 'Sometimes you . . .' She trails off.

'Sometimes I what?'

'Sometimes I . . . Oh, I don't know. You're not curious enough or . . . something and . . . I don't know. I wonder . . .'

'You wonder what?'

She takes a deep breath. 'I wonder if there's a reason for that. Sometimes I'm not sure you even *want* to find her. Not like I do. Not with that desperation. And I wonder why that could be, and my mind . . . I wonder if Poppy coming back is not a totally good thing for you. If it drops Emlyn in it somehow. If he saw something, or he did it, and you know but because he's Seren's dad and your husband you . . .'

'No.' I am shaking my head. 'God, Junie. No.'

But my stomach is flipping, over, over.

◆ ◆ ◆

I start moving again. It's not a good idea to stand still on this surface, with this wind raging at you, anyway. It's icy too. My ankle argues, but I need to get off the scree.

I wonder if Junie waited for now, when we need to have our eyes on the ground, to say this to me. If she picked a moment when she didn't have to look me in the eye.

'He never had an alibi,' she continues. 'He was at the volcano, at the sulphur springs with you on the fifteenth, sure – no-one questions that. But on the *sixteenth*, he was just hiking that nature trail alone. I always thought that was mad that that was accepted as fact. Was there any CCTV? Any witnesses? Anything at all that proved it?'

All these years later.

I am on the floor now, scurrying like a rodent. My hands are down on the rocks in a scramble. My neck cricks as I turn to Junie, who is still standing. Slowly, I come up too. Look at my sister, half an inch taller than me.

'I *am* desperate to find her. It's just . . .'

'Just what, Rubes?'

I sigh. 'If you really think Emlyn did it on that day,' I say slowly, 'when he was meant to be at the nature trail, then that would mean Dad was killed on the sixteenth. Forensics said it was the day before.'

She scoffs. Scuffs her boot on the floor. 'If they were telling the truth.'

Not this again.

'Well, something isn't right,' she says, to my silence. 'Someone knows something. And lots of Aurélians talk about the corruption in that police force. So . . . I don't know. I don't think that's conclusive.'

'Why would they cover up for Emlyn though?' I laugh, grasping at ways to persuade her. 'He's not one of their own. He's not some top dog in Caribbean government or something! He's a bloke from Llandudno.'

She looks up. 'I don't have all the answers yet. But there was this moment . . .' She watches me closely. 'Do you remember it? Emlyn was talking to the police officers before they questioned him, outside the station and it was . . .' Her voice gets more confident. Surer. 'It was shifty as hell actually, Rubes.'

I feel like I'm going to cry.

'You're not going to say this to anyone else, are you?' I hear the panic in my voice. 'Emlyn is . . . he's a good man, Junie. I know he can be a dick, I know. And he's . . . he's not perfect. But he's Seren's daddy. He's my husband.'

'Exactly.' My sister purses her lips. 'See. So maybe you would . . .'

'Why is this coming out now anyway?' I can hear how panicked I sound. 'It's been seven years and you've never— Why didn't you ever say this to me before?'

'Because I thought surely the police looked at him and must have ruled him out and also he was . . . you know, you were *pregnant with his baby*. You were about to marry him.'

She drops her voice, quieter. 'I might have lost you. Lost my niece or nephew. I couldn't face that. And I had zero actual evidence.'

'You still don't!'

She sighs. 'No. But maybe it's time to let someone look into it, at least. As a possibility. And I don't think the police ever did. I think they had their evidence with Poppy and they accepted it, and they never looked at other options. But there'll be new people on the force now. They might be willing to take a fresh look at things.'

'This is ridiculous.' I can hear it in my voice: panic.

'He wanted to declare her *dead*, Ruby!' She is shrill now. 'Is that not weird? Why would he want that? Does it get rid of any danger that she'll be found? If everyone stops looking for her?'

Jesus.

'Are you even happy with him, really?' she pushes. 'Be honest with yourself when you answer this, Rubes. I've seen you together. Is there anything about Emlyn that worries you?'

I bristle. Step across more scree. It feels like it goes on forever.

'Something very traumatic happened to me and I struggle to leave it behind,' I say, trying to slow my breathing. 'But he wants me to, and it gnaws at us. Is that detailed enough for you, or would you like transcripts of the fucking heartbreaking, broken, week-long rows we have sometimes, Junie? Do you need more detail on my messy, but actually mostly happy, marriage?'

She doesn't answer. We get to the bottom of the scree and exhale and without talking, we know we're pausing. We sit down on twin boulders.

Then after a minute of getting her breath back, Junie speaks again. 'Ok, last shot. You're married to him. Know him better than anyone. *Could* he do something like that?'

'Of course not!' I scowl at her. 'I had a child with him, Junie. I wouldn't have— No, of course he couldn't.'

Junie has always said that finding Poppy is one thing, but she can only come home, only live fully, if we hand the police another suspect. My stomach swirls, as Junie probes and probes to try and pin this one down: on my husband.

'I guess the question you need to ask yourself is . . . Is Emlyn more likely, more *capable*, of this than Poppy?' asks Junie, more gently now. 'Maybe you need to open your mind to the possibility, at least.'

She offers me one of her endless pots of nuts. I shake my head.

When she's finished eating, she stands and puts a hand out to me. Helps me up.

'I thought you were convinced it was Lewis,' I say.

She sighs. 'I'm not *convinced* of anything. But I am suspicious of a lot of things, and a lot of people. And Emlyn is one of them.'

Emlyn.

As we start to walk, my mind goes over things. After Seren was born, Emlyn – at my hospital bed, as I devoured cold buttered toast and stared at the new human in the cot – told me we needed to draw a line. To move on. To prioritise our daughter, who didn't deserve to have this define her family.

I nodded. He was right, and I tried. I tried very hard.

'She loves this walk,' says Junie a few minutes later, changing the subject. And I have that pang that I often do, ugly envy of those two and their closeness. Even now. Even after all these years. Even after everything.

I am the middle sister who should – by sibling positioning rights – have been equally close to both of them. But the space between them and me only widened when I met Emlyn, and I knew deep down that they didn't love him. I knew they had in-jokes about him. *Mr Vanilla.*

I put him first. It's odd that we do it, isn't it? Put romance top of the pecking order, when it's the most precarious relationship. Parents die, husbands leave. Sisters stay until the end.

'Did you two walk it a lot?' I ask. We are back on a flatter, wider, less ankle-breaky path now. There's a satisfaction in stepping off the scree onto the solid crunch of iced grass.

'Yeah. It was a good one from her place in Kingussie. Not far. We called it our break-up lap.' Junie smiles. 'Mostly before I moved to Edinburgh but we did it the odd time after I came back too. Whenever we got dumped, or we dumped someone . . .

up we came.' She grins. 'Won't surprise you that we were here pretty often.'

My sisters' love lives was something they bonded over. They talked to each other, way more than they talked to me, about blokes they were dating. Shitbags who ghosted them; fuckwits who lied about their wives.

In that second, I see it flash over Junie's face, that bewilderment again. *How could Poppy not have told me she was in a relationship?* Even seven years later, I know it's something that she struggles with. Because it opens up something else too. *If she didn't tell me that, what else didn't she tell me?*

Junie points back up the mountain. 'We skied down it a lot too.'

'But there are no lifts.'

Junie laughs. 'No, Rubes. But we managed.'

I feel myself flush red. Boring middle sister, the rule follower. No wonder they liked each other more.

Poppy's favourite kind of skiing was backcountry and off-piste; she was in the mountains as soon as the snow came. She worked a few seasons on Cairn Gorm, operating the lifts and fitting people with equipment. She'd talked about training as a ski instructor.

The lives present themselves again: *maybe she did.*

'There's a bothy there,' says Junie, snapping me out of the thoughts as we walk along a stream, on the flat now, a few minutes later as the sleet comes down more heavily. 'We can stop. Eat. Shelter for a few minutes.' Then she pauses. 'Oh God, flashback.'

I turn to her. 'What?'

'I've just realised which bothy it is! I used to come here when we were teenagers, drinking with Ruth and Robbie and those guys. *Voddy in the bothy.* It was a thing. But there was this guy who ran it back then – terrifying, slept upstairs. Hated everyone. Then this one time, he found the booze and—'

She trails off. 'Anyway, long story. It was much more wholesome when I did this walk with Poppy.'

'You never asked me.'

She looks at me. Sad smile. The slope starts to steepen. It keeps you guessing, this terrain. You get used to something and it shifts. Nothing stays the same.

As we walk, it comes down with more intent: thin rain that's got a hankering to be ice.

'We did ask you,' says Junie eventually. She's in front of me, the track too narrow now for us to walk alongside each other. 'But you had your own life. You were a grown-up. It was always like that, and good for you, you seemed to do it all, all those different friendship groups, that packed social life.'

She stops and pulls her hood up around her face. 'It was hard to get a booking with you.'

I can't speak for a second. That person she just described is unrecognisable to me. I haven't spent time with a friend in months.

'Not now,' I say, pulling my own hood up too, as the sleet comes down with more determination. 'Now, there's a lot of availability.'

She nods. 'But you'll get there again. It's who you are.' She pauses. 'Poppy found that stuff harder.'

It's true; Poppy found a lot of things hard. 'It wasn't who she was,' I say quietly, not even sure Junie can hear me. 'Small talk, being with big groups of people. It wasn't her.'

One foot.

In front of the other.

I wince at the ice that is landing on every exposed part of my face. My cheeks sting.

Junie walks with a long stride, then stops. She takes her backpack off and starts to dig into a pocket.

'What are you doing?' I shout over the weather, irritated. 'Come on! This is grim.'

She takes out her binoculars.

'There's lots of people taking that path over there,' she says, indicating an edge that is just about visible. 'I just want to . . .'

She doesn't need to finish the sentence. I know. She wants to make sure one of them isn't Poppy. That we don't slip into the bothy and miss her, when she's that close. I stand with my head bowed, waiting. Eventually she takes the binoculars from her eyes and shakes her head.

And I hide it: a tiny exhale of relief.

Still on the way to the bothy, we pass another group. Exchange pleasantries. *Afternoon. Could do with this sleet stopping, hey. Well, you don't come to Scotland for the weather etc. etc.*

They tell us that they're winter Munro-baggers. They've come all the way from Canada; they're aiming for six this week.

Canadian, except . . . I still scan their faces. She could have joined them to blend in. There could be contact lenses that change eye colour, different hair, weight gain. It's been long enough that anything could be different now. Maybe she does live in Canada.

If Poppy is here though, she isn't in a group. She isn't with people, talking, showing her face, taking risks. She is in the mountains alone; that human wildcat, solitary and focused. We will have to spot her from a distance. Make sure we don't scare her.

Keep her tame.

Ten minutes later, we finally make it inside for our food break. We pull our hoods off and sit down on makeshift rucksack pillows.

'Thank God for that,' Junie says, with a sigh. She adjusts the spikes on her boots and pulls a granola bar out of her backpack. 'It feels harder today.'

I nod in agreement. 'Hunger's not helping,' I say, unzipping my coat on the bed frame. 'What have we got?'

Today, the snack standard's dropped. Tupperware full of broken crackers and peanut butter. Squished bananas that have been in bags since yesterday. Too-sweet granola bars.

We shovel in Junie's never-ending bags of nuts and seeds, like two lanky squirrels. Junie takes out her camping stove and makes us each a cup of coffee and I pass her the last square of chocolate.

Something hangs between us, though.

Emlyn.

When we've eaten, I lean my head back against a hard stone wall that's as comforting as a soft duvet, compared to outside. At least, for now, we have shelter.

I give Junie a watered-down smile. I like walking – we've done it our whole lives – but I am not as hardy as my sisters. Doing it with this wind, in the sleet and these below-zero temperatures, is gruelling. Especially when I don't even want to—

I shake my head. No. No point thinking like that. There is no choice. Junie would do this, whether I came or I didn't. It's far better to stay close.

I reach down to my boots. My feet burn. The idea of walking in only socks would appeal, if it weren't for the ice underfoot. If it weren't for terrain I'm scared of. Black runs. Corries that attract avalanches. Precipices at every turn. This is not a soft place. There is also the fact that if I take my walking boots off, I don't think I'll get them on again over a scrum of blisters.

'She'd love this,' says Junie and I laugh.

'Yeah.' I wince. 'She would, the absolute nut job.'

And we give ourselves that moment to think of Poppy, as she really is, simple and complex and ours, before she became everybody else's. A wanted woman, a myth, a TV character. *Daisy Frost.*

'Maybe the freedom suits her.'

Junie frowns at me.

Then she shakes her head. 'No. It doesn't,' she says, sounding irritated. 'Poppy liked to escape but then she liked to come home. It doesn't suit her.'

I feel my skin prickle. Picture Seren peering out from under her glasses in her cosy spot. Junie's right. Imagine not being able to come home.

'Hey, we have reception again,' says Junie, holding her phone up to the sky.

I reach around to my bag. Dig out my phone which is plugged into a battery pack. But it pings before I get a chance.

The wave comes again.

Panic.

Guilt.

What now?

But it's not Seren.

Instead, it's a text from a number I don't know.

Thought you'd like to see this. Hope all's well. I think about her often. PS I'm so sorry about the TV show. I can't believe they've done that xxx

There are photos attached to the message.

Forty or fifty of them.

They look like pieces of paper, with messy handwriting all over them.

Messy handwriting, that belongs to Poppy.

HOTTER

Junie snatches my phone off me.

Zooms in on the first photo.

'Did Poppy ever tell you what she was working on in Saint Aurélie?' she asks, without looking up at me.

'You know she didn't. We talked about it at the time. How secretive she was about it.'

And then, when Poppy disappeared, she took her laptop with her. Whatever she was working on wasn't in the cloud.

'We presumed it was one of those novellas she wrote with no punctuation though, like usual?' says Junie. She's still looking at my phone, squinting. 'God, I think I need reading glasses,' she mutters.

'They didn't have *no* punctuation . . .'

Junie was always ribbing Poppy about this: begging her to write a *proper book*. But still Poppy let her read her words, because she trusted her judgement. It was another thing I was left out of. 'It's a stylistic—'

'All right, Sally bloody Rooney, I *know*. I do read. I'm being facetious.' She interrupts me and I bristle. 'Anyway. The point is—'

But it's dawning on me now and I interrupt her in return, taking the phone back. 'This is it? This is what she was working on? But this is—'

Poppy's handwriting still wriggles in and out as I try to swallow it whole. It's not a book. But it's research. Prep. The words jump out. Names. *Brooke Shields. Christie Brinkley.* Places. *New York. Cape Town.*

'This is about Mum,' I murmur. 'It's notes about Mum's life. Before us. Old modelling days.'

'Who sent it?' Junie asks.

'Shannon.'

Lovely, sweet Shannon. Poppy didn't have many friends, but living with someone was the best way for her to make them. Slow and steady. Accidental. Not the awkward version of herself that she became when anything was formal.

Shannon didn't find a replacement housemate for months after what happened, even though she had to cover the extra rent, and mutual friends – Shannon had been a good conductor for Poppy and introduced her to her circles – had turned their backs on Poppy.

They didn't want to be linked with someone who had done *that.* Olivia Menzies-Clark even gave an interview about Poppy to a tabloid.

I shudder, remembering.

Not Shannon, though. She was loyal.

'Shannon's still in the house but with her boyfriend,' I tell Junie, reading the second message that immediately follows. 'They're about to move out . . . she's having a baby . . . they're relocating back near family in Dundee. She says they were having a big sort-out when they packed. Came across this in the loft.'

I go back to the photos. All of them are the same. Notes and scribbles that make no sense to me. I scroll again and pause. 'Hey,' I say, frowning. 'Any idea who Eliza is?'

Junie looks at me, sharp. 'What?'

I pass her the phone. 'See there. It's annotated. "Ask Eliza".' I scroll down. 'And again, there. "Ask Eliza". And there. Loads more times. Who's Eliza?'

Junie is frowning, as though trying to bring something to mind. 'Eliza was . . . well, the only Eliza I know of was Mum's best friend.'

'Mum didn't have—'

'Friends?' Junie smiles. 'No, she didn't. Not when we knew her. But she had them before. She wasn't just our mum, Rubes.'

I picture myself standing alone at the school gate. Climbing into bed at 8 p.m. on Friday nights. I remember that woman Junie described before, the one with a rolling social life and plans for Friday night. My stomach dips.

'How did they know each other?'

'Modelling days.' She takes her phone out of her pocket and googles. 'Here.' She waves a photo in my face. 'She did Revlon with Mum. Levi's too.'

Oh.

'It's just 'cause I'm the eldest,' Junie says, kindly, seeing my face. 'I knew more about that life. Mum kept in touch with some old friends for a while.

'But then it got hard, no social media, barely even any phones back then. Eliza was still sipping cocktails at the Groucho on a Friday night in her miniskirts while Mum was . . . well, I suppose she was changing our nappies. They drifted.'

'But if I didn't know that, about Eliza or whoever, then *Poppy* wouldn't have known about her either.'

Junie looks at my phone. Shrugs. 'Well, she obviously did.' She zooms in on a photo again. 'And what's even odder, it sounds like she *knew* Eliza. Look – this bit has got "get more info from Eliza". As though they've already been talking.'

We sit on the bunk frame in the bothy, the wind picking up now outside, both trying to play catch-up. Where does this fit into everything? *Does* it fit in? Or is this unrelated; a distraction we should discard to get on with finding our sister?

'You know what I think?' Junie says, as she stares at one of the photos. 'I think Poppy was writing a biography. Mum's biography.'

Then she takes out her own phone and starts typing.

I think about it. Yeah. A biography would make sense.

'Right, I've messaged Eliza,' Junie says, a few seconds later. 'Facebook's good for something. She's still in London by the looks of it. So maybe if we don't have any luck up here, we go down and see her.'

I frown. 'Why?'

She shrugs. 'I don't know. But there's no doubt that Pops was weird about that writing, and it was right before what happened . . . Maybe this biography or whatever it was had an impact on something . . . Put something in motion?'

Junie's voice drops lower. 'And if we're honest, Rubes, Poppy *wasn't* acting normally, was she? In the run-up. We both know that, whatever we said to the police. I know she didn't do it. Obviously I know that. But maybe something was going on with her. Something that led to something else.' She shakes her head. 'I don't know. But it's something to try.'

I swallow. Nod.

Then the old, heavy door of the wild brick bothy creaks open, and someone else walks in. I scream but it doesn't matter. It wouldn't matter if both of us screamed at the top of our lungs. Because as the wind swirls outside and the sleet blurs vision, we are too remote, too isolated, for anyone to hear us.

Why d'you think the wildcats come here?

COLDER

'Jesus Christ,' says Junie, bending over double in the bothy, whose roof is barely higher than our heads. 'A warning would have been good. Not sure there's a defib round these parts.'

There is no apology.

Instead, the police officer's eyes flash between us, suspicious.

'What are you two doing here?' he asks. He's in uniform and walking boots. I have never seen him before.

Before I answer, he takes out a warrant.

I check it, then nod. 'We're out for a walk,' I say. I nod towards our rucksacks.

A frown. 'Pretty chilly for that?'

I shrug. 'We grew up here, we're used to it.' I nod towards the spikes on my boots. 'We have good kit.'

The officer's eyes are everywhere, and suddenly I am alert. 'Are you looking for something?' I ask, watching him.

'Some*one*, actually.' He nods. 'There's been an Interpol red notice issued on a murder suspect for seven years. But this week we've had reports of a sighting in the area, so we have a high presence of officers covering ground locally.' He looks closely at us. 'Both of you match the description. Can I get your names?'

Junie sits down now on the hard floor, resigned. She points to her face. 'June Winter.' She watches his face register the name then she points at me. 'Ruby Winter.' She turns to him. 'That's why we match the descriptions, because we're her sisters.' She looks up at him. 'I presume you're looking for Poppy Winter?'

The officer doesn't answer but I see surprise fly across his face at our knowledge, and he looks at us both, closely.

'Are you out here to meet up with her?' he says, his voice changing now. 'Is that what this is?'

'Sure,' says Junie, gesturing to the bed frame and the bare floor. 'It's our favourite sisters' brunch spot. Super cosy. Pops goes wild for the avo toast.'

He ignores her snark.

'This would be a good place, if someone wanted to hide,' he says. The eye contact is intense. 'No-one else around.'

Junie raises an eyebrow. '*You're* around. We saw some Munro-baggers from Canada. One bothy we walked past had five people, a guitar and a sodding ceilidh.'

'So you're not planning to meet the suspect? You're just *on a walk*?'

He looks outside, where the sleet is coming down again on a diagonal, and raises an eyebrow.

I try to keep my voice steady. 'My sister came to visit me.' I gesture at Junie. 'She lives in Liverpool. We like walking. My husband's got my daughter for the weekend so we can have some sisters' bonding time. Good for the soul, you know. Plenty of fresh air, exercise, get back into nature.' I pause. 'We both try to look after our mental health, since what happened. Which I'm sure you know all about.'

'And how's that going?' He cocks an eyebrow at me, like I'm being sarcastic when actually, it's true. I'm just missing one key part.

Junie answers. 'It was going well, until about ten minutes ago.'

He looks annoyed.

Then my phone rings, loudly and piercing.

A number I don't know.

'You'd better get that,' says the officer, eyes moving pointedly to my phone. 'Could be important.'

And the room swirls.

With the TV show on the horizon, Poppy has edged closer. She even spoke to Seren.

And now, I have an instinct.

It's her.

But at that very moment, there is also a police officer standing in front of me. Watching as I answer the phone.

COLDER

'Hello?'

The officer is staring at me.

Junie is staring at me.

My heart is a samba drumbeat.

There is no reply.

I say it again. 'Hello?'

It's her, it's her, it's her.

I am so sure. So relieved. So scared.

The police officer doesn't take his eyes off me.

'Hello?' I ask a third time.

Still, no-one answers.

'Is there anyone there?' I ask, trying to keep my voice even.

And then, I hear a breath. A pinched sound. Something emitted from a throat. Whoever is there, there is someone. This is not AI; this is not a machine. This is a human, whose lungs fill with breath.

I press the phone closer to my ear.

I am desperate to say the words: *Is that you?*

But the officer's eyes are still on me, Junie's too. I think she's read my facial expression. Is starting to realise what is happening.

Then I hear it again, that breath.

Seven years, and I can't even tell her that I love her. I can't even say the thousand other things I need to say; the ones that are so long overdue.

But I can't say them now.

I watch the police officer, typing on his phone. Glancing up at me as he does it.

The longer I stay on this call, the more chance they have of tracing it. Of finding her. He might be calling it in now.

In my head, I hear Emlyn's voice. 'Please think about me. Me and Seren.'

And I have no choice.

I touch my phone, and I end the call.

HOTTER

ONE WEEK LATER

Opposite me on a packed train to King's Cross, Junie's mouth is forming silent words. She spins a pen around in her right hand. Looks at me expectantly and gestures to my ear.

I take out an AirPod and pause my podcast. Parenting is my topic of choice these days. There's no more true crime. 'Say that again?'

'Eleven across, former New York City mayor Ed?'

I shrug. She taps her pen on her chin for a few seconds, then leans down to fill in letters. KOCH.

'And done,' she says, contented, and flips the book closed.

I put my earphones back in and press play. Try to tidy up, sweeping the debris of falafel wraps and coffee cups and Twixes, a deluge between us, into a brown paper bag.

Junie checks the time on the phone that's plugged into the socket next to her, and I look too. Twenty minutes until we arrive into King's Cross.

Eliza didn't reply to Junie's Facebook message, but when we got back from the third day of our mountain pilgrimage without finding our sister, we decided to take a punt on a visit anyway.

Online privacy wasn't Eliza's strong point; we easily figured out which London apartment building she lived in from her posts.

'That'll do,' said Junie. 'We can figure the rest out from there.'

It's been a week since I took that phone call in the bothy. A week of trying to call the number back, over and over, even though I told Junie I didn't think it was Poppy. Messaging it privately. Googling it.

This number has not been recognised.

I should be pleased.

The police took the number from me as well, of course. If I was right and it was Poppy on the other end of that call, then the best thing she could have done – for her and all of us – is throw that phone into a loch, then run. Far from the last place where the phone pinged. Because the police will have *that* information now too.

'Any rubbish?' asks a woman in an LNER train company uniform.

'Thanks.' I throw the paper bag in and look at it in disgust. Most of that is mine. Junie came prepared with her Tupperware full of bloody nuts, as usual.

I used to be healthy too. I used to run 5K every day. All these things I used to do. All the things I used to be, before.

Looking out of the window I blink hard to stop the tears from falling as I catch a glimpse of a football stadium through the terraced houses, sprawling industrial estates and then we start to see tube stations; underground trains lined up neatly next to each other like boxes.

'Nearly there,' I mumble to Junie, taking out my AirPods.

'The next station will be London King's Cross. London King's Cross, our final stop for this train. All change, please.'

The train pulls into the platform and someone hits me in the face with a backpack as they swing it onto their shoulder. I wince. Put a belated protective hand up to my nose.

We didn't want to wait a week until we came to see Eliza. But first we were waiting for her to get back to us, then – once we'd decided to take a punt and come anyway – we had to wait for Emlyn to come back from north Wales. He had left as soon as we came back.

We stand up now. Grab our own bags, and clamber out of our carriage. I get a wheely case to the back of my left calf as we walk down platform six to the main concourse.

'This way,' says Junie, as we see a sign to the underground.

'Only one stop,' she says a few minutes later as the tube doors close. 'Not worth sitting down, Rubes.'

But I wobble, as the train starts to move.

Junie is way more comfortable with London than I am. She went to drama school here, at LAMDA, and did a lot of jobs in the city too. Stayed in digs here on and off for years.

At our tube stop, Junie and I step off a ridiculously long escalator. Then another. We swipe our bank cards on the barriers and head out of the exit. I blink into bright sunshine as Junie looks at her phone – currently talking to her, giving instructions – and walks straight ahead. I follow her lead.

'I thought you'd know your way around,' I say.

She pulls a face. 'I was a south Londoner. North's basically another city.'

She looks around. The street we are in outside Angel tube station is hectic; buzzing. We head past a flower seller's stall painted yellow with daffodils and then an old Victorian pub, a plethora of drinkers with their hands wrapped around pint glasses on the pavement, even though we're still in February. But I unbutton my coat: London February is different to Scotland February.

Then, across a road and into a passageway filled with antique shops and bijou restaurants with chalkboards outside advertising triple-cooked chips and octopus.

Old and new, the kind of place which makes your eyes go in every direction, which peps you up with every step. A man walks past me in Crocs and bright red socks, a young Irish terrier pulling at a lead.

When we come out of the passageway, Junie's phone starts speaking to us again. 'Cross the road in fifty yards,' it says.

'We look like such tourists,' I mutter. 'Can't you turn that thing down?'

Across the road, there is a tiny cocktail bar. A guy comes out of Tesco Express clutching two bottles of white wine and a chocolate fudge cake, then climbs onto a bike without any sort of bag and steers with one hand while somehow holding the whole lot. I stare after him before we weave across the road between barely moving traffic.

'Right,' Junie says, glancing at her phone and stopping. 'This is it.'

We look up. Four floors, a fairly modern building, tiny balconies on all the flats. As far from my world of mountains and space as you could get.

On the outside of Eliza's building is a thick metal gate, where you can see through to mailboxes and a courtyard and across to a swanky-looking gym.

'Oh, bugger,' says Junie, shaking the gate. Locked.

We stare at it, like we can bust it open with mind control. Then someone speaks through a tannoy. 'Can I help you?'

'Oh! Yeah. I'm trying to get hold of someone who lives in one of the flats,' says Junie, into the speaker.

'Which number?' says the deep voice that I presume belongs to the concierge, who can see us through a camera somewhere.

My eyes fly about. 'I can't buzz you up without checking with the resident but I can call up for you and ask. What's your name?'

'Junie Winter. Sorry – the resident is Eliza Jacques. I . . . I don't know which flat number though, she just said to come here and she'd let us in.' *Lie.*

There is a pause. 'Eliza? Did you say Eliza?'

'That's right.'

He buzzes and the gate opens. His voice comes through the intercom again. 'Come to the desk, we're just through the courtyard.'

When we get there, a guy with a warm smile and a shining bald head is surrounded by Amazon Prime boxes and bunches of bright flowers. He has a laptop in front of him in a tiny gap between them, and is staring at it intently. Then he sees us and looks up. He comes out from behind the flowers, explorer emerging from a tiny rainforest.

'Hi, girls. I'm Tony. Concierge. It was for Eliza Jacques? In Flat 15?'

He seems to have forgotten that we said we don't know which flat she lives in (noted: seems like a nice guy but don't put him in charge of your security).

I nod. 'Yeah. That's it. She's a friend of our mum's.'

He nods. 'Ah, ok. Well . . . I hope you haven't come a long way.' He frowns. 'Because Eliza moved out.'

Junie's voice is high-pitched. 'What? When?'

He thinks. 'Only a few days. Less than a week ago.'

Less than a week ago.

'Did she not mention it?' asks Tony, frowning. 'When you made your plans?'

We say nothing. Exchange a glance. Eliza never got back to us. We always knew coming here was a gamble. But we thought the worst-case scenario was that she'd be away for a few days. That we'd have to wait it out in London, or come back. The anticlimax is a punch to the gut.

Then Junie rallies. 'Oh, she didn't but it's fine,' she answers, coming to. 'We're down to be tourists anyway. The flower market. Natural History. And I've been keen to get to Do Ho Suh. We'll probably grab theatre tickets this evening.'

Tony's eyes light up. 'Do Ho Suh is quite something,' he says. 'Enjoy.'

Junie looks at me, knowing I have no idea what they are on about.

'Thanks so much for your help, Tony,' she says. We turn and walk back towards the courtyard.

Then we hear his voice.

'Wait!' he says, and when I turn he is watching us closely, brow furrowed again, deep lines across his forehead. 'Are you two by any chance connected to the other girl who used to come here?'

I freeze.

He rubs his bald head. 'I don't take that much notice of other guests' visitors but Eliza was older than most of the residents, you know, so I kept an eye out for her. And this girl came a lot. Never knew her name.' He looks at us both closely. 'But you two look like her.'

I swallow hard. 'I think you might mean our sister.'

He smiles. 'Ah. That makes sense, yep. What a likeness.'

'Do you know what she came here for?' asks Junie. 'Our sister, I mean. Did she ever say?'

It's the first time the concierge looks suspicious. 'She didn't tell you?'

When we don't answer, he carries on: 'Not a clue, I'm afraid. Just know I used to buzz her up sometimes. She'd turn up with a backpack, stay a few days, then leave.'

She stayed here?

I think of Lewis, in the coffee shop that day in the Caribbean. *Man. Poppy Winter. More secrets than anyone I know.*

Seven years later, and they're still emerging.

Tony carries on. 'Nice girl, always said hi. She used to come a lot, years ago now. But then she stopped.'

My mind is racing. If he knew Poppy, he may have recognised her when she was in the news. But if he did, he doesn't let on. I guess even big news stories don't make it to everyone's feeds. You could have gone on holiday and missed the Winter sisters entirely. The news agenda moves on fast.

'Ok,' I say to Tony. 'Thanks for the help.'

We turn to go, but he speaks again.

'Except for that one time,' he says.

I swivel to face him. 'What?'

'Oh, just that one time she came more recently. It had been years and years since the last visit. She'd changed a lot. Hair was different, I think . . . But there was something about her body language. I still recognised her.'

'When was that?' says Junie, with urgency. 'When did she come more recently?'

I hold my breath.

He pops back behind the desk; starts to type something on the laptop. 'Oh, not long ago at all,' he says, distracted now, head back in his work. 'Not long before Eliza left.'

I blink.

Try to take this in.

Poppy came here not long before Eliza left.

Eliza only left a few days ago.

So perhaps she spoke to Seren, called me – I'm still sure it was her – and then she came to London to see our mum's old best friend.

I don't have any doubt now that Poppy is seeking out contact. That she is getting less careful. We are ahead of the police and we could find her first.

If we want to.

I look at Junie. I can't voice that to her, of course. She is focused entirely on finding Poppy. On making contact. And she has to think I want the same thing. Otherwise she will question me again.

And she will look again, at Emlyn.

COLDER

Junie slams her hand onto the brick wall of the tapas restaurant next door to Eliza's building, the smell of sizzling garlic drifting out of the open door, then winces. Her fingers are grazed.

'How can we keep getting so close, then missing her?'

But it's obvious to me. It's because Poppy – while tempted to make contact, to edge closer – still doesn't want to be found. And the thing I don't say: *maybe that's for a good reason.*

We walk towards the tube.

This time we don't meander down the pretty cobbled alley, but through the village green which has been taken over by an arts and crafts fair. Minimalist prints by local artists and expensive vegan blondies; homemade soy candles and spiky succulents. Twenty-somethings sit cross-legged on benches in bright leggings, drinking bubble tea in giant scarves.

'Let's head in there and get a drink,' I say, pointing to one of around three thousand coffee shops I've seen since our train pulled into London. 'We can't go home yet. I can't face that bloody train.'

'And I need caffeine.'

'And that,' I agree.

As we head inside, I try to play catch-up.

Poppy came to Scotland, craving proximity to home and the mountains and her niece, but then she was spotted. That was too much. She panicked and pivoted. Came down here to get lost but find some solace with someone she trusted. She clearly had a relationship with Eliza.

But where next?

In the coffee shop, we wait for our hot drinks and slabs of cake at a wobbly wooden table in a badly lit corner. Next to us, a couple giggles, tight together in beanies, watching a video of themselves doing karaoke the night before.

'I can't believe Eliza's moved out,' says Junie, casting an irritated glance at the couple and the phone. 'That can't be a coincidence, can it?'

I shrug. 'Could be. She's in her sixties. Might have gone into a retirement home, or moved to be nearer family. Relocated to the seaside or something. It's not an unusual time to want to get out of the city, is it?'

'We should have asked Tony,' says Junie, leaning back and rubbing her grazed finger.

'One Americano, one latte, and your cakes,' says the waiter.

'Oh. Thank you.'

'I think even Tony would have drawn the privacy line at passing on a forwarding address without permission.'

'I don't know,' she says, the creep of a smile through a mouthful. 'Tone was pretty free and easy with his info.'

I pick up a fork. 'Did you still want to go to that . . . thing you wanted to go to?'

The look she gives me is scathing. 'It's an exhibition at the Tate, Ruby,' she huffs. 'No. Not now. Let's just have these then find somewhere to crash for the night. Head back in the morning?'

◆ ◆ ◆

The next morning, we say goodbye at King's Cross. Junie stays on the tube to Euston; she isn't coming back to Scotland with me. She gets snippy when I suggest that she does.

Instead, she'll get a train to Liverpool – she has an audition coming up and needs to make her tape by the weekend. She says she doesn't have the right space at mine; needs her white background. Probably ideal to not have a seven-year-old running around too.

We agree to catch up tomorrow, and plan what we will do next.

On the journey home, I turn my parenting podcast off. I can't hear anything but my own thoughts anyway.

What the hell are you doing, chasing her around like this?

Emlyn's words run around my head.

Leave her be.

And he's right, isn't he?

It's late when I put my key in the door. Seren and Emlyn are asleep and without thinking about what I'm doing, I head for the bathroom cupboard.

Oblivion.

That's what I need.

Oblivion.

◆ ◆ ◆

The next morning, Seren charges straight into our room and throws herself on top of me, blinking before she's had chance to put her glasses on.

I am groggy from the sleeping pills and struggle to open my eyes.

'Hey, chick,' I mumble.

'Hi, Mum!' She snuggles into the warm gap between our bodies, and I curl myself around her.

'Coffee?' I murmur over her head to Emlyn, trying to function.

He rolls over and looks surprised. 'Sure.'

Seren runs straight downstairs, grabs a box of Lego and tips it onto the kitchen table. Pieces drop to the floor and scatter.

She starts to build, her entire focus on what she's doing. I watch her. Imagine being able to focus like that. Knowing what your aim was; having no doubt.

'How was London?' asks Emlyn, walking into the kitchen in his running kit as I fill the kettle.

He has no idea that the trip down south was anything to do with Poppy. If he had, he would have argued with me, like he did when we went to the mountains: *This has to stop, Ruby.* Instead, he just thinks it was a chance for me and Junie to re-bond.

'Whistlestop but nice,' I say, on a yawn. 'We saw the Do Ho Suh exhibition.'

'Junie feeling ok?'

I'd messaged him on the train to say we were coming back early because Junie was ill.

'Bit better now, I think.'

The kettle whistles and I fill our mugs. Emlyn picks up a certificate Seren won at gymnastics that's on the side. Idly reads. 'I heard the Do Ho Suh's amazing?' he says, eyes still on the certificate.

I nod. Murmur a yes. Hope he doesn't ask for any more detail about an exhibition I've never been to and know nothing about.

Then the knock at the door comes. And the fake exhibition trip is the least of my problems.

HOTTER

'Sorry to bother you. We want to ask you about another potential sighting of your sister,' says a police officer who I haven't dealt with before. Who has just introduced himself as DS Jack Sweeney, and is standing on my doorstep.

Next to me is Seren's discarded Smiggle rucksack, with the plethora of keyrings attached to it, mini Rubik's cubes and Lego and a little plastic SEREN that Emlyn brought back from Llandudno. There aren't may Serens in Scotland, but there are a tonne of them in Wales.

I pick up an empty salt and vinegar crisp packet.

Another sighting.

Emlyn ducks his head out to the hall when he hears the voice. 'All o—' he goes to ask.

Then he spots the police officer. His face clouds and he disappears back into the kitchen before I can speak.

I turn back to DS Sweeney. 'Where was the sighting?'

But then Emlyn appears in the hall with Seren.

The officer moves out of the way.

'I'm taking her out for a bit,' Emlyn says, clutching Seren's hand. 'I'm not having her here for this. Not after—'

Seren stares at the police officer from beneath her glasses. Her bottom lip wobbles.

'She's in her pyjamas!' I argue. 'You don't need to leave, you're being over the top, just keep her in the kitchen, this won't take—'

I move towards Seren but Emlyn moves her out of my reach.

When I turn, I see an expression on the officer's face that makes me feel it: deep, deep shame. I'm ashamed of us, pulling our daughter between us like we're in a game on *Gladiators*.

I step back. 'Ok,' I say, forcing a smile for Seren. 'I'll see you in a bit, chick. In time for pizza, hey?'

My hands dangle by my sides.

'Get in the car, chicken,' Emlyn says, pressing the key fob to open it, and as Seren runs over to it, he turns to me.

'You're normalising this stuff,' he hisses. 'Stalkers, police. She's getting so anxious, you can see it in *everything*. It's impacting school, friendships. Her mood.'

The police officer sighs. 'I'll be in the kitchen when you're ready,' he says. Not his first domestic.

I ignore him. Answer Emlyn. 'It's not . . . I haven't . . .'

He sighs. 'You haven't seen it because your head's somewhere else.'

He rubs at his chin, thumb and forefinger splayed. A habit I've seen so many times when he's upset.

'Think about what you're risking.' He looks, then, like he might cry. 'Can you think about me, Ruby? I know you think about Junie and Poppy and about how finding her would make you feel. But just once, can you think about *me*, and what you finding Poppy means for *me*? Because I am telling you something, what it means for me is pretty catastrophic.'

Then he turns away from me. But before he walks out, he speaks again, low.

'Not to mention what the hell it would do to Seren.'

Then he slams the door and I hear the car engine turn on. My family drives away.

◆ ◆ ◆

The police officer looks up at me, as I walk into the mess of our kitchen. 'Domestic done?' he says, smirking. 'Can we get on now?'

I sit down, without replying.

'Right, I'll get straight to it,' says DS Sweeney.

I nod. Spot Mr Owly, Seren's favourite teddy, on the floor, and fight back tears. How am I supposed to do the right thing by everyone? It started on that day seven years ago, and it's never let up since. Being pulled in two different directions; it's constant.

Sweeney eyeballs me. 'Have you travelled anywhere recently?'

The lie comes out easily. 'No. Why?'

He looks at a notebook. 'Not London?'

'Oh. Yes. Just to see an old friend of my mum's.'

'Not to meet Poppy?'

'No.'

'Like when one of our officers found you and your sister in the middle of the mountains having a balmy February walk last week? You weren't looking for your sister there either?'

'No.'

Silence.

'You've never met this woman before though, have you, this friend of your mum's?' he asks, never taking his eyes from mine. 'You've never been to visit her?'

Seren's face when she ran to the car.

'Why now, then?' Sweeney pushes.

I fixate on Mr Owly.

'Ruby?'

Looking at that tiny, grubby owl is making me feel panicked. Out of control. Trapped.

'I found out that Poppy knew Eliza,' I tell him. 'I thought she . . . I thought Poppy might have been there.'

He nods. 'And when you got there, you found out that you were right, that Poppy *had* been there,' he says. 'The same thing we found out, when we visited the apartment block and talked to the concierge yesterday.'

He waits for me to speak. I don't.

'We found out that Poppy Winter visited Eliza Jacques, stayed with her for three days, and then was seen leaving. According to an eyewitness who lives in the same building, the time she left is estimated to have been within twenty-four hours of Eliza leaving as well. And now – this is an interesting one – we can't get in contact with Eliza. No forwarding address. Phone disconnected.'

With that, I give him my full attention.

Eliza has disconnected her phone?

'She's a sixty-five-year-old woman,' I scoff. 'I'd say it's unlikely they're on the run in London robbing banks together.'

'Oh, I'm not saying that,' he says. 'Not at all. Because if they were on the run *in London*, there's no way that this latest sighting of Poppy would have come from where it did.'

I take the bait.

'Where was the sighting?' I ask, dread building.

Is Poppy back in Scotland?

He doesn't take his eyes from mine as he says the words, and I know he is watching my reaction carefully. To see if I am genuinely surprised, or if I have known my sister's movements all along.

But he must know that my shock is real when he says the next words and watches my face.

'The sighting was in Saint Aurélie, Ruby.'

HOTTER

'I think you should stay here,' says Emlyn, from the doorway of our living room later. 'When we go to Lanzarote tomorrow. I think you should stay here.'

The holiday was booked a few months ago and we're going with Emlyn's extended family, including the cousins that Seren adores who live in north Wales too, Osian and Gethin. A hotel with four pools and water slides.

I sit upright on the sofa. *'What?'*

'You said the police want to keep in touch with you about these sightings, and about Eliza. I don't want the police calling in to our hotel, Ruby. I want Seren to have a normal holiday.'

He glances towards the kitchen, where Seren is playing.

'You don't need to take her away from me,' I argue.

'You *lied* to me about London, Ruby! You *lied to me.*' He shakes his head.

Tears roll down my cheeks. Lower.

He sighs.

'It's difficult. When Junie wants to—'

I glance over at my phone, on the coffee table. I can see it lit up with a message. *Junie.*

'It's always about Junie, isn't it?' he says. 'Always. I'm sick of hearing her name.'

He sits down next to me. Lands hard. Rubs at his temples, where I notice for the first time that the hair is going grey.

'Look, it might not be a bad thing, anyway,' Emlyn says, that V of his fingers spreading across his chin again. 'With Rose not coming, you know, maybe this is . . .'

Emlyn's brother Gareth is going through a divorce. Gareth would probably rather that his kids didn't have to see Seren with her mum there, when their own mum, Rose, was at home.

I go to argue. I don't care if Rose isn't coming. I still want to be with Seren at the all-inclusive in the Canaries. Watching my girl cannonballing into the pool in her little green swimsuit. Dancing the Macarena in her Crocs at the mini-disco.

Or do I?

Because I know what that message from Junie is going to say. The same as the last one. I told her about the sighting, and she fired it back immediately:

I'm looking at plane tickets.

HOTTER

The plane tears down the runway, the roar and whoosh that feels like it happens simultaneously in the engine and in my midriff, and in minutes, we're above the clouds.

'Here we go again,' mutters Junie, taking a pot of nuts out of her bag and offering me one. I shake my head. 'This has to be it. Has to be.'

She takes her crossword puzzle book out of her rucksack, then shoves a wad of paper back inside the bag.

I've barely had time to think since I told Junie that I would come out to Saint Aurélie with her. Since we booked the flights, and I waved Emlyn and Seren off. It was better, I persuaded myself, that I went with Junie. Better than her finding Poppy alone. Better than it being the police.

As the seatbelt sign flicks off, I put down my copy of *Grazia* and close my eyes.

Why is Poppy in Saint Aurélie?

Eyes still closed, I try to order things.

What's there? *Who's* there?

I presume the police will know if Eliza is with Poppy from the flight logs, though I doubt they plan on telling us.

I turn to Junie but she's deep in thought. Tapping that pen on her chin and filling in her crossword, like usual. When she looks up, she turns to me. Speaks through a mouthful of nuts (also like usual).

I blame a lot of these habits on her living alone.

'I guess Poppy got herself a passport then,' she says. 'Documents. God, that means she could have been anywhere . . . literally *anywhere*, in the last seven years.'

I nod towards a woman on the other side of her. A warning: *keep your voice down.*

'She has headphones on,' Junie says, with a glance to her left. 'Chill out.'

'Didn't you *presume* she would have a passport?' I whisper back. 'And documents? How would she have managed for all this time otherwise?'

Junie shrugs. 'Cash in hand. Off-grid.'

I laugh. 'Maybe in the seventies or something but . . .' I trail off. 'It's 2025, Junie, that would be impossible.'

She frowns. 'How do you know?' She shakes her head. 'I just don't get how she would have sorted that. She doesn't have dodgy gang connections. It's not like she could hook herself up on the dark web.'

I squirm slightly in my chair.

'I guess you get resourceful, when you need to.'

And I wonder about myself then. Could I do it, if I needed to?

'I always thought that she stayed in the UK,' Junie says. 'I give sheep shearers a second look when I'm in the sticks anywhere. Bar staff.'

She stares at the back of the seat in front of us.

'Remember when I did all those island trips? Iona, Bute, Harris and Lewis . . . I was convinced she was on one of them. *Obsessed* with it. I just thought that's somewhere she could live happily. Be comfortable, without needing the whole set-up of a normal life. I guess it's what I would do.'

I never went with Junie on those early trips. I was pregnant, dealing with midwife appointments and heartburn and scans and then a baby, *a whole baby*, who needed me. Truthfully, I appreciated the excuse that Seren gave me.

'They're such small communities though,' I point out. 'I would have thought they were the hardest places to hide.'

Junie nods. 'Yeah. I realised that after a while. Once I walked into enough of those parochial pubs with everyone gawping at me because I hadn't had my christening there.'

That's when Junie started combing cities instead.

'Remember how long I spent in Glasgow that winter?'

I nod. Seren was a little older by then. Junie had combed homeless shelters and hostels with a photo. No posters. The only one who didn't want to shout loudly about her missing person, instead asking quietly and moving on, keeping her head down.

She wanted to find her, talk to her, figure it out. And then, only then – when they had the full story and another suspect – would it be ok to shout.

Junie would call me, defeated, when she got back to her hostel or cheap hotel late at night. 'Still nothing.'

'Tell you what's weird,' says Junie now, shaking her head. 'If she has a passport, she'll have a whole identity. The new name is probably more real to her than her old name now. What names did she always like, when she was a kid?'

'Britney?'

'Not sure she'd go for that now.'

In front of me on the plane, I hear a giggle that sounds like Seren and it's a jolt back to now. To reality.

I am going to the Caribbean – all those miles away – without my daughter.

And meanwhile, she isn't in her usual safe places either. She has never been on holiday without me before. Panic seizes hold of me. What am I doing? There are too many moving parts. Seren's plane home could crash; my plane could crash. Why have we gone in different directions?

I don't even want to be here. But how could I let Junie do this without me? What if she finds her? I need to be there.

I grab for my bag. *Bugger.* How could I have been so stupid? My pills are in the hold.

'What are you looking for?' asks Junie.

My breathing gets shallower. 'Nothing.'

But she is watching me closely.

I scratch at my skin, wriggle and squirm for the next twenty minutes, and I can feel Junie's eyes, still on me. Until the flight attendant comes and I order two vodkas.

I pour the first one out, neat over ice.

'I thought you didn't drink any more.'

'Everyone does it on the plane.'

'All right, Fun Bobby.'

I ignore her functioning alcoholic *Friends* reference. Drink the second vodka straight after the first and then fall quickly asleep. I only wake when Junie shakes me.

'Ruby,' she hisses. But I am groggy from the vodka and ignore her, keeping my eyes closed. *'Ruby,'* she says again, more urgently now.

The tone of her voice persuades me. 'What?'

She gestures to her lap. In it is a thick pile of printouts – the paper I'd seen in her rucksack earlier – and a yellow highlighter with the lid off.

'Look,' she says, her eyes like saucers, shaking a piece of paper at me. 'I've been reading this, all the notes that Shannon sent over that Poppy had made about Mum. The stuff you forwarded to me. That we think she was using to write Mum's biography.'

'We already read that.'

'Well, I wanted to go through it again. Properly, without squinting at my phone. Check there wasn't anything . . .'

She looks at me.

'There's something we missed, Rubes,' she whispers. 'There's something *huge* that we missed.'

I am barely awake, still blinking and reluctant. 'What do you mean? We read it all.'

'But we didn't see the importance. We didn't read between the lines.'

I look at her. No idea what she means.

'Mum's accident,' Junie says quietly, and I wince, like I always do when I hear mention of Mum's accident. That nightmare of that day. When we were all sat down, lined up on the sofa, as Dad told us that Mum had died hiking in the mountains on the day of the worst avalanche to hit the Cairngorms in a decade. Four lives were lost that day; devastatingly, our beautiful mother's was one of them.

'What about it?'

'According to Poppy's research for this project, Mum wasn't in the mountains that day.'

I sit up. A feeling of foreboding creeps across me. I shiver. OTT plane air con.

'She was at home, Rubes.' Junie pauses. 'She was at home, with Dad.'

'No, that's—'

'I'm telling you, Rubes. She was at home.'

And she lets the implication sink in, without needing to say another word.

HOTTER

I am wide awake now, pulling away my red neck pillow and sitting upright. Adrenalin floods my body. Well, adrenalin and vodka.

I glance at the woman on Junie's other side but her eyes are closed and her mouth is open and slack. Her headphones are still on too, her phone lolls in her lap.

Junie, though, wouldn't even notice if she was listening intently and making notes. My sister looks possessed, jabbing at the words on the sheets of paper.

I look at them again. They're images of Poppy's notes. Scrappy, messy. Tangents and unrelated thoughts. Zipping timelines and multiple question marks.

We had gone over it. Concluded that, yes, Poppy was writing a biography of Mum's life and Eliza had been helping her with it. But that was as far as it went. There was no link to what happened in Saint Aurélie. No big revelation that explained everything.

'Remember the parts Poppy got directly from Mum's diaries?' says Junie. 'I took the diaries after Mum died . . . But I was a teenager. I was too self-centred to bother reading much of it.' Her face flushes pink.

'How did Poppy get them, then?'

'I gave them to her,' she says. 'She was upset one day because she didn't have many memories of Mum. I thought it might help her feel . . . more connected or something.'

A flashback. Mum, scribbling in a notebook. Large Shiraz next to her; biro between her teeth, long legs tucked underneath her on the sofa.

'Look,' says Junie. *'Here.'*

She passes the paper over to me. Jabs at one line.

There is a date, underlined: 5 December 2005. The day Mum died.

'This bit Poppy's written out verbatim from Mum's diary.'

I peer more closely.

'Look . . . 4 December, Mum writes that she's been ill in bed all day. Flu. Real flu. She feels horrendous.'

A pause.

Junie looks at me. 'Ruby,' she says gently. She gestures. 'Look here. She says she was planning to stay in bed the next day too. On 5 December, she was planning to stay *in bed all day*.'

I stare at her.

'Maybe she felt better?'

'If you feel better the day after you have the flu, you might get up and move to the sofa. You don't head up a mountain, Ruby. Not at the best of times. And definitely not when there's a bloody avalanche forecast.'

I bite my lip. *Shit.*

'Tell me it wasn't always a weird story,' whispers Junie. 'Tell me it wasn't always a weird story that our mother went out hiking, *alone*, in that weather.

'The others who were out were young lads who'd ignored the warnings. Them, and remember – that one super-experienced climber who got caught out. But Mum . . . she didn't even like hiking, Rubes.'

I shake my head. 'That's not true. She had started to.' I remember her, showing us her new walking boots. Twirling around in a designer waterproof.

'Yes,' concurs Junie, with a nod. 'Ok, yeah, she had started going more. I even went with her a few times. But that was in June, July.' Junie smiles. 'She admitted it herself. She was fair-weather, she liked hiking when it involved a fancy picnic and a paddle in a stream.

'The idea that she went alone in December, when there had been such a huge dumping of snow . . . I even remember thinking afterwards, *that's odd*.'

'Then why didn't you say something at the time?'

She laughs. 'Say what? When your dad tells you your mum's died and you're seventeen, you don't query the details, do you? You don't accuse him of lying, or suggest that his story might be dodgy.'

I can hear my breathing. 'You think Dad was lying.'

Next to me, I feel rather than see her nod. 'More than that though, I think *Poppy* knew he was lying. That message, Rubes . . . the one with the date of Mum's death. I think she was trying to send us in the right direction. Make us realise what she had realised.'

My stomach lunges forward then, and when the flight attendant asks if we want drinks, I order two more vodkas, ignoring Junie's judgy stare.

And while I pour the first one into the small plastic cup, Junie speaks.

'And if Poppy knew he was lying . . .' Her voice cracks and I hear it. Heartbreak. And something else: terror. 'If Poppy knew he was lying about Mum's death . . . then she had a motive, Rubes.'

HOTTER

In Saint Aurélie, I whisper to Junie across the gap between our twin beds. 'Are you awake?'

The reply comes through the darkness straight away. 'Yes. Can we go?'

Junie and I landed at Rémy International Airport a few hours ago. We decided to sleep before we went looking for Poppy, but for me, sleep's been impossible. From Junie's wide-open eyes, it looks like she's the same.

Fifteen minutes later, we're in the rental car that we picked up at the airport. Junie is clutching a piece of paper with a list written on it: the cafés that we will go into to ask about Poppy. We have twelve on our list, all of them near the place where she was spotted.

Junie is distracted though, and I know what's on her mind. All this time, there is one thing she has never considered – the idea that Poppy is guilty – but now, a germ of a thought has been allowed in. *What if, what if.*

I watch her, and the guilt slams into me like a fist.

There are a couple of branches of Rituals – the nearest thing to Starbucks you get out here – but the rest of the cafés are the kind of cute indies that Poppy would immediately get comfy in; back-to-back Diet Cokes in place next to her, hand out to stroke any stray cats that meandered by.

Café after café after café.

We're on number five, Celeste's Fish Shack, when we get our first hit.

'Hey,' I say, the now familiar wafts of local coffee beans, fresh banana cake and cocoa hitting as soon as I get close. 'I think my old friend's been in here recently.' Non-threatening, big smile, following the same script I've followed in the others. 'She's about the same height as me, people say we look similar . . .'

The Aussie woman sweeping the floor doesn't notice the lack of name. Just looks me up and down, poker-straight black bob flicked to the left with irritation, and barks: 'You mean the girl who works here? Sarah?'

'Yep, Sarah,' I bluff. 'When's she in next?'

There's a beat, while she decides whether to answer me.

'Not until Friday,' she replies. 'She's casual staff. Just helps on busy days. We get rammed on Fridays, weekend starts early here before the street party.'

I nod. *Casual staff.* That sounds promising.

'Bingo,' I say, when I get in the car with Junie and turn the key. Junie offered to drive but she doesn't do it a lot, living in a city, whereas I've always found it soothing. It's quite likely about the control freak in me. I don't want anyone else being in charge.

'Sarah. Casual staff, in again on Friday.'

I know we're both thinking it. *Is that who Poppy is now? Sarah?*

Junie sucks in her breath. Nods. 'Sarah,' she mutters, trying it out. 'Can you imagine her being a Sarah?'

I shake my head. Of course I can't. But then I can't imagine her being anyone but a Poppy.

We drive to four more cafés but have no luck. We ignore the steam vents from the volcano and the spike of the mountains, as we drive through one of the island's largest towns.

We ignore hillside farms and the edge of the beautiful rainforest. This trip isn't about sightseeing. It isn't about beauty. It's only about finding our sister.

And then, in the final café on the list, a place called AJ's, we get our only other hit.

'Catriona, you mean?' says the manager Alain, a heavyset old boy with a slug of a goatee across his top lip. He speaks in a French accent.

I nod.

'Yeah. Catriona.'

A Scottish name.

'Keeps me in business, that girl, my most reliable regular. Lived here for years, she's an honorary Aurélian. In early every day for her cocoa tea, before she heads off to her work.'

Does that fit – living there for years – if she's been in the UK? But she might have gone back for a reason each time. To see Seren; to pick up Eliza. For short visits. Perhaps this has been her home all along.

I look back at this man, who is still smiling. He looks like he cares about her.

'Where does she work?' I can't help blurting out, but my question sets Alain on edge. Either he doesn't know where Catriona works or he thinks I'm asking too many questions.

He doesn't answer. And all I want to do is reassure him and say *thank you, thanks for looking after my sister. If you have been there for her and liked her and smiled at her when I couldn't, then thank you.*

But of course, I don't.

'Come in tomorrow if you want to catch Cat,' he says, and gets on with wiping down the surfaces.

Cat.

'But we're closing up now I'm afraid so I'll have to ask you to—'

'Oh, yes, of course, yes. Sorry. I'll pop in tomorrow.'

This time I try the name out when I get into the car. 'Could she be a Catriona?' I say to Junie. 'A *Cat*.'

Junie stares out of the window. Says the name herself. 'Way more Scottish,' she murmurs.

'That's what I thought.'

Cat or Sarah. Cat or Sarah.

God, are we close?

Closer than we have ever been?

My belly plummets.

We've been everywhere in a decent radius, and tomorrow and Friday, we come back out with two targets. Two cafés, AJ's and Celeste's Fish Shack, to meet two women, Cat and Sarah. One of whom could be our missing sister.

As I drive, I glance at Junie. For her, it's simple. All she wants is to find Poppy.

For me, it's always been far more complicated. It has always been about that question: who do I protect more?

◆ ◆ ◆

We have five days before we have to be back in the UK, to beat Emlyn and Seren back onto British soil, so that they never know I have been here. I loathe the level of deception. I loathe lying to my daughter and my husband.

In the morning, when I wake, there is a message from him. It's a picture of Seren with her goggles on, face beaming up as she leans on the edge of the pool.

I zoom in on the photo. She looks happy, she's with her dad. It's ok. It's all ok. Still, I feel twitchy, a sparking plug. Guilty, too. I know why Emlyn wants me to leave this alone, and I know he's right.

When I put the phone down, Junie is still flat out under her thin white sheet. I creep down for breakfast but she calls as I'm finishing my waffles.

'Why didn't you wake me?' she snaps. 'We need to go. Cat gets to the coffee shop early.'

'It won't be open yet, it's fine. But I'll come now. See you in the lobby.'

I sneak her out a croissant wrapped in a napkin and two bananas for later, and take a last gulp of my coffee. Three minutes later, Junie is eating the croissant in the car and I am telling her off for getting pastry on the seat.

'Someone's missing parenting,' she mutters.

'Someone's remembering it's a rental car,' I snipe back. I am on edge.

We pull up at AJ's.

'Together?' she asks, and I pause.

'Are we sure?' I say, trying. 'Are we sure that this is the right thing? What if she doesn't want to be—'

But Junie is watching me, frowning. 'Is this about Emlyn?' she snaps. 'For fuck's sake, we finally find something and you— Have you spoken to him? Is he putting this in your head?'

I shake my head. 'No,' I say. 'Forget it. You're right. Ok, let's go in.'

Alain is at the till as our eyes scan the place. But it's 7.15 a.m. and there's just one customer. An old guy in a linen waistcoat in the corner with an espresso and a newspaper and an ageing chocolate Labrador lolling under sandalled feet.

'Hey, welcome back,' Alain says. 'You were the one looking for Cat, right? What can I get you?'

'That was us. One Americano, one latte, please, the latte's a decaf.' As he turns to the machine, I try to keep my voice casual. 'No Cat yet?'

He looks at the clock. 'Give it twenty minutes.'

We sit at a table in the opposite corner to the old guy. It's not a big place, and the furniture is crammed in close together, a mishmash that makes it feel like you're in someone's living room.

The door opens. I watch Junie's body image mirror mine. Our cores stiffen, then sag.

Just a middle-aged man with long grey hair in board shorts, a greying white T-shirt with holes in and Birkenstocks.

Then only a minute later, the door goes again. A woman with long red poker-straight hair to her waist walks in. Crop top and shorts. Hot curves.

Also not my sister.

Alain smiles at her, though.

'Hey, Cat,' he says.

◆ ◆ ◆

The next day me and Junie head down to breakfast together but neither of us eats much. Half a pancake sits abandoned on my plate. Junie stirs a bowl of granola round and round and round.

After a few minutes, she looks up. 'Shall we just go? Even if we're too early, at least we're doing something.' She groans. 'I can't cope with this waiting.'

I can't cope either.

But not with the waiting.

It's the guilt I can't cope with. The guilt when I think about telling Emlyn where I am; what I'm doing. What I'm risking.

'Ready?' says Junie.

I nod.

We down the last of our coffees and head out to the rental car.

'Tell me which way,' I say to Junie, as I pull out of the car park and am immediately overtaken by a driver in a sports car with the roof down going way too fast. I slam my hand on the horn.

But I'm starting to get used to it again; the way people drive here, speeding, the hills. Except for every now and again when the thoughts creep in and I feel fear take over. *You can't die; what about Seren?*

And then, the world overwhelms me again. I glance at the back seat where I put my bag, but I can't take my pills, not in front of Junie.

Junie turns a Haim song up on the radio. Hums along. She is feeling positive, I can tell. She knows we are close, and she's giddy with it.

I feel sick.

Cat, I suppose, was a punt. She could always have decided to skip the cocoa tea yesterday, make it at home to save cash. It was luck that she turned up. Every day can't mean *every single day*, even for the most committed coffee shop regular.

Sarah, though. Sarah's going to work and getting paid. We'd have to get unlucky for her not to be there.

If it isn't her, though, maybe that is my out. Maybe Junie will accept it then, that we looked and we failed, and now it's time to leave Poppy alone.

Though of course I know that's not true. Junie will never leave it.

'Swing a right, Rubes,' she says. 'Then we should be there.'

But as we pull up outside AJ's, we realise something.

We aren't the only ones.

'Oh, fuck,' murmurs Junie next to me.

I clutch the steering wheel tight.

Because outside the café, there is a police car.

'The Winter sisters,' says Dana Henry, her hair shorter, and more lines on her face than the last time we saw her, as I slow the car to a standstill. But it's definitely her, the detective who turned up on the beach on that catastrophic day seven years ago.

She leans down to my open window. Cocks an eyebrow. 'Fancy seeing you guys here. What do you think then? Shall we pop in and get a coffee?'

PART THREE: POPPY

COLDER

THE DAY BEFORE

'Did you watch it?' asks the dark-haired man at table seven in a Glasgow accent that makes me tune in. I always notice the Scots. 'Did you watch *Hotter/Colder*?'

A fork clatters from my hand down onto the tiled floor.

I have been wiping down the table next to theirs, table eight. It's just been vacated by two adults who couldn't aim ketchup at a plate. I forgave them because they had the island's cutest puppy.

Getting a job was easy on this island – there are so many tourists, who need so many chips.

I look up now, take these people in.

The man pushes a fringe in need of a trim out of nearly black eyes. He has black stud earrings, and every centimetre of his doesn't-miss-a-gym-session arms is covered in tats. The girl with him, petite and in her early twenties in a tiny bikini top and shorts, has a baseball cap covering a blonde bob. A pink flip-flop dangles from shiny toenails that have had a recent pedi.

'Bit dark for me,' she says. Her own accent is bland; London commuter belt and a good school.

He looks up in surprise. 'Oh, really?'

'She kills her own *father*, Liam.'

I think someone is asking for coffee from the table behind me but they have faded into the background with the rest of the world.

'I've fallen down a rabbit hole with the backstory too,' this guy – Liam? – says, not noticing me. 'You know it's based on a real story? The sisters are Scottish, grew up in the mountains near my auntie. Posh East Coasters. Apparently one of them went to the drama classes that my twatty cousin went to and he was *duologue partners* with her which might be why I'm such a weirdo creep about it.'

The man leans back in his chair and laughs, as I stand up.

Then Monique from the kitchen shouts at me – table seven's order is ready, why am I just *standing* there? – and I jump. When I come back with their drinks, Liam is still trying to sell the TV show to his friend.

'One café au lait,' I say, putting down his drink. Trying to make sure my barely alive accent is completely dead. 'And one black.'

'Thanks,' he says, without looking at me again.

'Then we've got a blondie to share with the extra plate and fork.'

The girl says thank you but Liam barely registers me.

'Hey, careful!'

Then suddenly he is looking right at me.

I have knocked my shaking hand into his too-full coffee and spilled some of it onto the wooden table.

But I can't speak. Can't reply to him. Can't find a *sorry* or an *I'll get you a napkin*. I just stand there.

'Hello?' Liam looks at me like I'm moronic. 'I said, *can we get a napkin*?'

'Of course.' I snap into action. 'Of course. Sorry. I'll get it now . . . And there's sugar on the side,' I murmur, head down. 'Let me take this for you as well.'

Two dirty cups and a crumb-strewn plate left by the last customers tremble between my fingers like tables in an earthquake.

'Something's not right though,' the guy says, stirring his drink, frowning, analysing this show like data when I return with the napkins and mop up the coffee pond. 'To be that violent, when she seems so *normal*.' He turns to me. 'Thank you.'

I nod and turn away. Wipe down the table behind them, still listening. Everything is shaking now, not just my hands.

So normal.

I almost laugh.

The girl opposite him shrugs. 'Most murderers don't go around wearing T-shirts saying *I'm a Murderer*. It's just because she's pretty. People lose their shit over pretty psychos.'

'True,' he says. 'Look at Candy.' He does a motion, like he's stabbing someone frenetically with an axe.

And then, while he's still air stabbing, the guy looks up and right at me. I freeze. He frowns and holds the eye contact. Keeps looking and looking and looking at me. Stabbing and stabbing and stabbing. I don't look away.

I choke out the words, 'Let me know if you need anything else.'

Then I walk fast out the back and down the side passage next to the café.

I've seen it, of course. I watched all the episodes of *Hotter/Colder* in one go, in London, with a cold beer in my hand. And I shook with fear. All those people, seeing me – or some version of me – being so violent. How would I ever come back from that?

Then I thought about my sisters, watching it. How it would feel for them. And once that thought crept in, I couldn't stay away. The phone call, the wildlife park . . . The TV show was the moon; it looked the same for them wherever they were, as it did for me, wherever I was, and I felt a pull like the tide.

Now, I lean against a graffitied wall and take my phone out of my back pocket.

My phone contract, of course, like everything else, is set up in my new name.

Higham.

Sarah Higham.

HOTTER

Celeste's Fish Shack's side passage is a grim space, filled with broken plastic chairs and an old air-con unit and God knows what other crap, and I sink right into it, leaning against the wall.

The signal is always rubbish here. I wave my phone around in front of me and think. What happens when a TV show is based on a real story? I remember it with *Baby Reindeer*; interest is ignited. People are curious. They search to see who the people are behind it. How different they look to the actors. How much artistic licence was taken.

They look to see what happened next.

They hunt.

Before the TV show, we were a seven-year-old news story. Now, we are current. Any one of the millions of people who googled after watching *Hotter/Colder* knows what I look like. And any one of them could spot me. On a street, on a plane. On table seven at Celeste's Fish Shack.

I glance towards the café door.

Lean against the wall and try to breathe. Try to be rational.

I've changed so much, surely, in seven years that I *can't* be recognisable. My hair is in a home-dyed brown bob. All the piercings in my ears and the ring through my nose are gone. I leave my hair down to cover my tattoo. In winter – when I'm not in the

Caribbean at least – it's roll necks and scarves. There's the contact lenses, green instead of my own eye colour, brown. And, of course, I am older. God, I am so much older. I am thirty-two but I look forty. As well as many other things, murder accusations aren't great for your complexion.

Still, if someone is *obsessed* with the case . . .

I need to go back in. Monique will be fuming; there will be sandwiches waiting to go out and moaning customers. She'll be wondering where the hell I've gone.

But I can't move.

Whether Liam recognised me or not, it won't be long before someone does.

The TV show has erased the time passed. It's put me right back to square one, as fresh in people's minds as when I was international headline news in 2018.

And what have I done in the middle of that?

I could laugh, it's so ridiculous.

I have come back to Saint Aurélie. To the place where I peeled myself off my dad's body in the kitchen and walked out of the villa that day covered head to toe in his blood. Carrying that neon green breadknife.

After I had said goodbye to his killer.

HOTTER

I have no choice but to go back to work. I put my phone away.

I'll draw attention to myself if I walk out mid-shift. Plus, I need the cash. It's not just my complexion that's taken a hit; I wouldn't say seven years on the run has been a strong financial move either.

Back inside, I look around. The guy who watched the show, Liam, has left with his mate. Most people have left. Bengy, who waits tables here too, is on his break, scrolling on his phone and eating a prawn sandwich in the corner. It's always quiet around now, the lull that comes after people stop ordering lunch; before they start ordering rum cocktails.

'Oh, *now* she comes back,' says Monique, sticking her head out from the kitchen. 'When everyone's buggered off home anyway.'

I grab the mop and bucket.

'Where have you been?'

'Bad stomach,' I mutter. 'Sorry.'

I get started on the floor.

Then I hear another voice.

'Sarah.'

I look up to see my boss, Aussie Donna, who's just arrived for her shift.

I respond automatically to *Sarah* these days. It took a while after Lewis first set me up with the new identity. After he sent someone to meet me in London and give me everything I needed, for a fee. Since *bam*: as easy as changing my hair colour, I had a new name. I was Sarah Higham.

Now, Donna is eyeballing me. 'Just to let you know, someone was in here yesterday looking for you.'

Here we go.

I feel the muscles in my jaw tense.

'Oh. Ok.'

Drips of sweat form in my armpits and I picture it: an imagined egg timer, the last grains of sand slipping through it.

Time's up, Poppy.

I hold my breath. 'What did . . . what did they look like?'

It was the police, surely.

Donna smiles and tucks her hair behind her ears. 'Sorry, babe, sad to report it wasn't a hot guy. It was a woman. Scottish. Maybe an old mate or something? She was a similar age to you.' She shrugs. 'Dunno. I was a bit harassed at the time and she didn't leave a name.'

A woman.

A Scottish woman.

Donna goes to walk away but then she turns. 'I told her you weren't in until tomorrow.'

'Why?' Donna knew I was in today.

But she shrugs again. 'Dunno, really. Had a vibe. She was suddenly too nosy, and I just thought I'd . . . buy you some time, in case. I've had people I've wanted to hide from. Times I've wanted to cut ties. It's how I ended up a billion miles from home, truth be told.' Her sparky eyes focus on mine. 'I had a hunch as soon as I met you that you might be the same.'

It's Sarah who nods, not me.

Sarah who says thanks.

Sarah who carries on mopping the floor.

Sarah who can brazen these things out.

I, on the other hand, watch my hand shake as it grips the mop too tightly. As my mind races.

The woman could have been one of my sisters.

If the woman does come back tomorrow, I could see *one of my sisters.*

But if I do that, I will bring them into this. I will implicate them in a choice *I* made that night. And isn't that what stopped me going through with any of it in the end? From speaking on the phone. From knocking at their door.

There is also the possibility that it wasn't Ruby or Junie at all. That this is some sort of trap; a way for the police to draw me out.

Sarah might be brazen. But as I push the mop back and forth and back and forth and back and forth, I know that I am not. *I* am terrified. *I* am terrified of people finding me. But I am mostly terrified of people knowing the truth. And of them realising that the story of the Winter sisters is so much worse, so much messier, than they ever could have imagined.

COLDER

Half an hour later, I put the mop in the cupboard and take my apron off. 'I'm finishing up, Dons,' I say. 'See you tomorrow, I'm on earlies.'

'Great,' she replies. A distracted smile as she writes the evening specials in chalk on the board.

Baked catch of the day with lime and garlic. Seafood bisque.

'Thanks for today, Sarah.'

If my sisters did come in, do they now know that's the name I go by?

I still avoid authority any time I can, even with the documents. I've managed to swerve hospitals and the police.

I have relationships but I always hold something back. They tell me they love me; I think: *How can you love me? You don't even know who I am. What I've done.*

I always thought I would have a plethora of pets by now, but that's too much of a commitment too. I make do with the strays.

I know I will never get married. Never have a child.

I accept that.

After a while, I started to turn when someone shouted *Sarah*. I've trained myself not to turn or respond when someone shouts *Poppy*, but still when I hear it, my brain responds.

Me.

That's me.

Coming back to Saint Aurélie – via Oslo to bury the connection – is the first time in seven years that I've been on a plane. Flying always felt like an unnecessary risk. The idea of being on a plane made me feel trapped and exposed. If someone recognised me in row D in the middle of a twelve-hour flight, there was no getting away.

When I came out here, I stood in the security queue at Heathrow, putting my Sarah Higham phone in the tray, convinced my whole body was giving me away, screaming GUILTY GUILTY GUILTY from its Poppy Winter pores.

Waiting for an alarm. A flurry of activity.

Nothing happened.

But it doesn't mean nothing will.

I grab my bag and leave Celeste's out of the back door, walking fast down the beach in my flip-flops past the men and women at surfing school.

A young woman crashes off her board and slips under a beast of a wave. When she comes out of the water, she makes eye contact. I look away quickly.

Over the years, I've started to relax. Now I'm back in the earliest, darkest days, when everyone is a threat. When eye contact is dangerous. When every human interaction could be *it*.

Since the TV show, I've itched with the need to be back in contact. But that isn't fair. If I see them, they'll protect me. And I won't risk jail for my sisters. Ruby's a mum.

Seren. That girl, with her spindly limbs and her pink glasses and some sort of graphic novel with a dog on the front clutched tight in her tiny hand. What was that funny thing she said to me? *Oh biscuits.*

Nope. Not sending your mum to jail.

The best thing I can do for Ruby and Juno is to leave them alone. Even if they've come out here to find me. Even if they believe finding me will be a good thing.

I know better.

I stand up, dust white sand from the back of my shorts, and walk up to the boardwalk where I locked my bike up this morning. I jump on and start the long, steep ride home.

As I turn to my left, I catch the eye of that surfer again, her brown curls shaken out of a ponytail now, as she walks along the beach with her board under her arm. I swear she frowns at me.

Has *she* watched the show?

I turn my face away and soon afterwards my bike, off the cycle path and onto the road and from there I start the proper climb; at a good forty-five degrees. My thighs burn.

On the winding island road now, a driver, roof down with Harry Styles blaring, drives past and looks at me. I duck my head and pedal faster.

My breath is short. Ragged. I reach the top of the hill and pause, folded over my handlebars and panting.

Then off I go again, along the main road and the rough track now, with its potholes and bumps. I've done this route every day this week.

Suddenly, I am flung in the air again, almost coming off my bike.

I put my head down and cycle harder, and the old feeling comes back. *You're being hunted. Leave.*

Except this time, I remind myself, I don't need to leave. Because I have a place to hide, and someone who is willing to keep me hidden.

I put my head down and cycle harder. I just need to get back there. Back to my mum's house.

COLDER

Eliza and my mum bought Frangipani Cottage together in the mid-eighties, when they were on the island shooting a Levi's commercial. Calling it a cottage is a downplay; it's a sprawling one-storey labyrinth.

I call Frangipani Cottage my mum's house, but they owned it together. Now that my mum is dead, it belongs to Eliza.

'Imagine if that was your house' was their favourite game wherever they went in the world. As part of the earliest crop of supermodels, they went to a lot of places. And they did a lot of imagining.

That lighthouse in South Wales: *imagine if that was your house.*

That beach hut in Thailand: *imagine if that was your house.*

And then, driving into the rainforest on Saint Aurélie: *imagine if that was your house.*

That day, according to Eliza's version of events, 'the game went a bit far'. In the least surprising news for anyone who's ever met Eliza, it happened after some rum punch. But buying Frangipani Cottage was a boozy decision superior to most. It became a lifelong bolthole.

When I arrive at the bolthole, Eliza is waiting for me.

She is waiting for me on the huge, sprawling veranda, as I push my bike, sweat pouring down my back, round the side of the house.

She is waiting as she always waits, with a rum cocktail clinking with ice cubes in her hand and her long slim legs wrapped and snaked around each other. Her toes are painted bright orange; her eyes are closed.

'Oh, hello, my darling,' she says, opening them and smiling, those crinkles around her eyes. But then she sees my face. 'Oh! Oh no, Pops. What's wrong?'

I know how I must look. Especially to her – glam as ever in her linen palazzo pants and ivory silk blouse. That wide-brimmed sunhat that she usually uses for gardening on her balcony in London has been repurposed now; something to snooze under in the Caribbean golden hour.

And here I am, with hair that smells of chips, coffee, people. With sweat dripping into my eyes. Exhausted.

I've cycled forty minutes from the beach and all the way up the steep, winding incline. Across the potholes.

Most houses are built up into the hillside, on the Caribbean Sea's side of the island, so that you have a view of the water. Here, though, we are inland, on the edge of the rainforest that makes up 70 per cent of the island. Miraculously, when so much of Saint Aurélie is a tourist hotbed now, huge swathes of this part are still undeveloped and wild. People really like to swim.

'Pops, come on,' she whispers to me. 'Come on. Is it the show?'

She has watched *Hotter/Colder* too, of course. With me, at her flat in London. Clutching my hand the whole time. Swearing at the screen and trying to persuade me to turn it off. But I was determined to watch the whole thing. It is always better to know.

'Come on,' she repeats, ushering me into the wicker chair opposite hers when I don't answer. 'Sit,' she says, pulling her chair closer. 'Tell me everything.'

I tell her about the woman who came to Celeste's, looking for me. I tell her how I am desperate to go back tomorrow, how it could be Rubes or Juno, but how I know that I can't do that. I tell her about Liam.

'It's all because of this damn show,' she says, her facial expression darkening now. 'Those *leeches*, making money off your pain. What a godawful, scumbag of a thing to do.' She's been repeating a version of that since we watched it. 'But your sisters . . . here . . . Oh gosh, darling. I do wish you would see your sisters. Are you sure there's no—'

The shake of my head ends her sentence.

'But there must be a way,' she says, quieter. She reaches a hand behind my neck and touches my tattoo. 'Your mother would— You can't go your whole life without your sisters.'

What's the alternative though? Risking *their* freedom? *Their* safety?

It's not something I'm willing to do.

We sit in silence for a minute, until she walks inside. When she comes back, she hands me a short, pale drink and I sip it without asking what it is and then splutter. Cough like a fifteen-year-old trying cheap vodka, even though whatever this is will be high-end and expensive.

'Eeesh, that's strong.'

'In a crisis, Pops, you want a weak drink as much as you want a weak man, remember it.' She pokes a finger in my direction, the one with the little signet ring on it that belonged to her late husband Raymond. Then she slips her sunglasses back onto her face. 'You're safe here, ok? Remember it. You're home.'

Home.

I feel my breathing slow. Sip my possibly pure ethanol and stare ahead. The huge swimming pool is as still as a house, like it is holding its breath. The palm leaves droop like tentacles.

Everything here is calm.

It is home.

I am ok.

'Could you eat?' she asks eventually. 'I shopped today. I could cook?'

'Bloody hell, things are bad.'

'I mean I could fix you a salad, cheeky girl.' But she is smiling.

I reach out and grab her hand. 'You're fine. But thank you. I'm just glad to have this place. Am I ok to stay? Are you sure, even with this . . . I'm just not sure what the hell I would do oth—'

She squeezes my fingers. 'You have it. Forever. Or for as long as you need.' She holds my eye contact. *'Home.'*

She couldn't bear that I hadn't had a feeling of home, for all those years. The thought of it made tears spring in her eyes.

She remembered that feeling from her modelling days, she said. Impermanence was a state that caused a chaotic mind. Humans needed roots.

I look at Eliza with her bare feet up on the leg of the table; limbs of a twenty-two-year-old, still. But she's lost weight, and she was already skinny. I feel bad – it's probably the stress of leaving her home, of keeping me hidden.

'Did you ever think about selling this place?' I ask her, looking around. 'After Mum . . .'

She considers. 'Gosh, I did when Soho House Aurélie opened in 2022 and prices went through the roof.' She laughs, putting down her drink. She coughs and winces. 'That was a game-changer. Then carnival launched and celebrities started getting spotted here – influencers and all that business – and *Condé Nast* put us on their list of ten most beautiful destinations and suddenly . . . that year, we landed on the map. Certainly thought about it then too.'

She chuckles.

Now, we sit on the veranda looking out at the mango, lime and cherry – *sour* cherry, I learnt that the hard way – trees. It's been nearly two weeks since I turned up in London. Since Eliza suggested we come here. The nightly whistle of a thousand tree frogs has faded from raucous chorus to barely noticed background noise.

Home.

'But no, never seriously. Frangipani is not for sale. It's too precious.'

I nod. The smells mingle. Frangipani, of course, and the rich cocoa which grows at the farm nearby.

'Gosh, your mum loved that smell.' Eliza laughs now, as the scent drifts over. She inhales the air. 'Those agents could tell us to eat another bloody salad all they wanted but they couldn't stop us *smelling* chocolate. Here we could do it all day long. We felt like rebels.'

She touches her top lip, where there is a tiny bead of sweat. Sits up and tops up my rum cocktail from a shaker.

'Can I ask you a question?' I ask.

She spreads her arms wide. 'Anything, my darling.'

'Why did my dad bring us to Saint Aurélie on holiday?' I pause. Look around. 'He knew about this place, didn't he? He'd have seen it in Mum's will, at least, even if he didn't know about it before that. And that's too much to be a coincidence.

'Did he come here, do you think?' I press. 'While we were on the island?'

Eliza doesn't answer. Instead, she stares straight ahead at the swimming pool. A bright yellow lilo bobs in the centre, abandoned now until tomorrow. Eliza likes to float around on that lilo like a teenager, long skinny legs hanging off the end and still in that humungous hat, sipping a glass of champagne or a strong rum punch while Madonna plays from the speaker on the veranda.

'I don't know, my darling,' she says. 'But I wouldn't be surprised if he did, yes.' Something flickers across her face then. Disgust?

Then she turns to me. 'You really don't think there's a safe way for you to see your sisters?'

I shake my head. 'No.'

She sighs. Stares into the middle distance, a frown across her face that I don't see often. Her face is always bright. Open. Now, for a brief second, it closes in on itself.

Then she stands, abruptly, and her expression returns to normal. 'I'm exhausted, darling. I'm going to head to bed. Lock up, will you?'

'Of course.'

She kisses me on the cheek. 'Goodnight, goodnight,' she whispers, and her palm nestles and stays in my hair, despite its stench of chips. 'Love you, my darling. It will all be ok.'

I close my eyes. Revel in it. The reassurance, the words, but mostly that rare thing, now. *Touch.*

Eliza has never asked me the question, the one that must have crossed her mind over the years. *Did you do it?* Even though she would have more right than most to ask. Even though I am staying in her home, and there are knives in the drawer, and we watched that TV show together and she must have seen that CCTV image of me, coated in blood, the neon green visible under my sleeve.

She must have wondered.

Something catches in my throat.

'Love you too, Eliza.' I grab her soft hand as she heads to bed. 'And thanks.'

I sleep for twelve hours, and wake up more rested than I've been since the murders. Something about being mothered. Something about *home.*

I feel safe.

It doesn't last.

COLDER

After I hung up on Ruby, I got rid of that phone straight away. And I ran.

Her reaction had made it obvious: the police were still tracking her phone, even after all this time. She couldn't speak to me. Couldn't say the one word she wanted to: *Poppy?*

On the train to London the next day, I berated myself. It was stupid to bring my sister into things, after all this time. Implicating her. Messing with her life. What was I doing? I had *known* that.

But the TV show had started something. I couldn't get rid of an urge to contact *someone* who knew me. So when I got off the train at King's Cross, I walked into a shop and bought another burner. Then I called Eliza.

The police wouldn't be tracking Eliza's calls. They probably didn't even know Eliza existed. My notes on Mum's biography were only on my laptop, which was long gone into a Saint Aurélie public bin. My cloud storage had reached its limit a year ago; I'd always been too skint to pay for more. There was a box of messy notes and research at home but it was God knows where in the loft; Shannon's terrified of spiders, she'd never dream of stepping foot in there.

I had met Eliza about a year before my world was flipped on its head like a table in a bar fight. Not long before I met Lewis. She told me she'd been Mum's best friend, back in the day. They'd kept in touch, but less as the years went on. Eliza had just joined social media, and decided to look us up. She had seen us all at Mum's funeral but wanted to let us be with our family. She'd paid her respects and left.

'But didn't you know my dad?'

'No,' she said. And a curtain was pulled across the subject. That was the end of that conversation.

'Your profile picture . . . you look exactly like her,' Eliza wrote to me. 'Gosh, my darling, I adored her. We were such good friends. So very close. I'd love to meet you? Share some memories.'

The next day, I got a train to London. We went to the sort of old-school brasserie that I would come to know was peak Eliza. Classic and classy. We ate rare fillet steak and thick-cut chips and bread and butter that was unrecognisable from any bread and butter I'd known. We drank small measures of Barolo from giant glasses that sat on starched white linen.

Eliza ordered side dishes freely and generously, filling up the table with bowls of broccoli and buttery carrots. Afterwards, she ordered tiny petits fours for us to share. She never ended a meal without something sweet. Oh, and coffee. *Always* coffee.

I had booked a Travelodge for that first trip but when I told Eliza, she pulled a face like she was allergic to the word *Travelodge* and insisted I stayed with her. I was happy because it meant more hours talking about my mum. Seeing her too, in Eliza's neat and ordered photo albums. Mum with huge purple shoulder pads in a private dining room at Claridge's in 1986. At the Chanel show at Paris Fashion Week in 1987. At a party at Kensington Roof Gardens thrown by someone whose name Eliza had lost over time, smiling at the camera with a little sunburn on her nose, Eliza next to her holding a slim cigarette between her fingers. I touched the old, faded photos like they were diamonds.

I started visiting Eliza every few months. I didn't tell Junie and Ruby. I'm not sure I can explain why, other than that they'd had more of Mum than I had. This part was just mine.

'You tell me you're a writer,' Eliza said on my second visit. We were in her apartment, drinking tea and eating fancy shortbread biscuits that I let sit on my tongue and melt. 'I have a suggestion for you. How about you write a biography?'

'I'm only in my twenties,' I said hesitantly – *what was she on about?* 'And my life isn't—'

'Not an *auto*biography. I meant your mum's biography, you daftie!' she exclaimed, laughing from her belly. 'Gosh, an autobiography at your age, my darling, imagine. You're a child!' My face coloured – what an idiot I was. 'No, I meant you should write *Maria's* story for her. I have so much material for research.' She tapped the cover of a photo album. 'Here.' Then her head. 'And my gosh, *much* juicier stuff up here.'

She winked at me. The rest of her face wore the life experience of a woman in her sixties but that smile was twenty-three and pure mischief. 'It would make *one hell* of a read. We had a wild old time, me and Maria back in the day. Smoking Vogues back to back instead of eating dinner. Free Dom Perignon every night if we wanted it. Private jets. We never went anywhere unless it was VIP.'

She tilted her head at me.

'Do you know that Cindy Crawford was nearly your godmother? But Maria thought she might be too busy to do a good job, so she picked your dad's sister Beryl.'

I stared at her, trying to work out if she was serious. 'But I think it would be nice for you too, Poppy,' she said. 'You were far too young, still a baby, when she passed. This would be a way for you to get to know her.'

My mum's story was my next writing project.

I pored over the photos. I researched. I delved. I collected notes. Alongside it, Eliza told me her stories.

That's when it began really.

When I began to loathe my own dad.

HOTTER

In Saint Aurélie, I am in my pyjamas, watching Eliza pour me coffee while she whistles 'True Blue' – you can't live with Eliza without having Madonna songs running through your brain at most times – when there is a knock on the front door.

Eliza looks up from the coffee pot and frowns.

Frangipani Cottage has one and a half acres around it. We are in the rainforest; more likely to be visited by parrots than people.

I look at her, panic flying across my face. 'Eliza,' I say. 'Eliza, what—'

She turns down the speaker and hands me my coffee. Her movements are slow and careful. Eliza doesn't do chaos or panic.

'Don't worry,' she says. That hand goes to my hair again. 'Don't worry.'

Still, I lurk in the corner of the kitchen, primed and out of sight, while Eliza goes to the front door.

That feeling comes again.

Hunted.

A sense that I will be ripped apart limb by limb if someone finds me. They have all seen those pictures. The CCTV. They have seen the version of me from the TV show, wild and violent. Why *wouldn't* they come for me?

I hear Eliza's voice. And a man's, too. But they are muffled and I can't make out the words. I clutch my hot mug close.

Is it local police, or did the guy from the café – Liam – follow me? I think of the way he looked at me. He could have recognised me, reported me to the UK force, high on the power of being a true crime amateur detective; of finally solving the mystery of the real-life Daisy Frost.

I put my coffee down. And I get ready to move, fast.

What have I done, trying to make a home? Drinking rum cocktails by the pool as though I am living it up on a fancy holiday. What have I done, thinking I can relax?

Idiot.

I glance across the room. Think. Can I get to where my Sarah Higham passport is, in my bedroom, without whoever is at the front door seeing me? Can I get to the back door and out?

But then I hear a click. The door is closed.

'Just an old guy who got lost,' says Eliza lightly, as she comes back into the room and turns the music back up. 'La Isla Bonita'. 'Running out of fuel and panicking he'd get lost in the rainforest, bless him. Wanted directions to a petrol station.'

Then she turns and sees me.

'Oh, my love.'

While she's been at the door, I've shrunk. Now I'm hunched in the corner, barefoot, like a threatened animal.

'Come over here, my darling. Come on. You can relax.'

She holds out a hand and I take it.

Eliza and I sit down at the table. The coffee is lukewarm now. Still, my shaking hands cling to it like a comforter.

That night I fall asleep and dream such vivid dreams, of Linda Evangelista with her arm around my mum and eighties jeans commercials and giant bars of chocolate, until I wake up and realise I have slept solidly again, this time for ten hours. It's 9.30 a.m.

I walk into the living room to ask Eliza if she wants coffee. It will be her second or third; she's an early riser and a coffee fiend.

Except this morning, the pot is cold. Eliza's huge sunhat is on the table.

I frown.

'Eliza?'

I put the coffee pot on and head outside onto the veranda, to see if she's already swimming or lazing on her lilo, speaker playing her Madonna songs low so as not to wake me up.

But there is no music. The pool is still.

'Eliza!' I yell.

There is no reply.

I do a lap outside in case she's watering some plants or pottering over by the fruit trees but there is nothing.

I am about to go to her bedroom – thoughts flying around my head about a heart attack in the night – when I notice it. There, on the table on the veranda, weighed down by an empty tin of local Saint Aurélian cocoa. A note. I slide it out from under the tin.

The feeling's a familiar one. Dread.

Why would Eliza leave me a note? If she was going somewhere, she would have told me last night. We don't do impromptu; she knows I can't cope with impromptu. And anyway, where would she go?

My eyes scan the note.

Oh God.

Oh God.

Oh God.

No.

Dread was the right feeling.

Because on the note that she has left on her veranda at Frangipani Cottage, Eliza says she has gone to the police station.

She has gone to the police station to confess to my dad's murder.

HOTTER

I hold the note limp in my hand, like it's not the most important item of paper I will ever see but something as prosaic as a shopping list.

And then I feel it.

A flood, a wash, a *deluge* of adrenalin courses through my body.

I can't stop it. I can't stop any of it.

She's gone. Eliza, who has become a surrogate mother figure to me. *Eliza* has gone to confess to the murders.

And what does that mean?

It means that Eliza is now the one who faces a jail sentence, or possibly worse. A bleak Google deep dive taught me a long time ago that while it's not been – God, unfortunate word choice – *executed* for decades, Saint Aurélie still has the death penalty. Even without that though . . . Eliza is sixty-five. She likes Liberty hand cream and good champagne. How will she manage in a foreign prison cell? Jesus Christ, in *any* prison cell?

I go back inside, pick up my phone and call her.

Then I hear it.

She's left her phone here, in her bedroom.

Shit.

I walk to the front room and look out of the window. The black convertible BMW that she drives around the island with the top down, is gone.

She is serious. She's done it.

She's gone to the police station.

My brain tells me to run. Run. *Run.*

Because the second that Eliza goes to them, the police will be on their way here, to her home. Which means that after seven years, after all of that hiding, all of that running, it's about to happen.

They're about to find me.

I jump up, used to moving fast.

I pull on shorts and a T-shirt. Shove my passport and my wallet into a bag. There is no time for anything else. I don't know what time Eliza went out but she gets up early; it could have been hours ago. The police could be here any second.

I put my phone in my back pocket and pull on my trainers. I can plan where I am going when I'm on the move but for now, I only need to focus on one thing. I can't be here.

Then the knock comes.

'Poppy Winter?' shouts the voice.

And after all this time, it's over.

HOTTER

The door is unlocked. They push it open and come in.

Two officers. Both women.

They step into the hall and look through to the kitchen at me.

I sit at the table, holding one pink trainer in my hand, the other already on my foot.

Hunted. Trapped.

And they stare at me as they say my name again. My real one. 'Poppy Winter?'

And instead of running – I could, perhaps, if I went out of the back door in one shoe and headed for the rainforest – I only nod, because I am computing something.

If Eliza has confessed, then the police I've been terrified of for so many years . . . they aren't a threat to me any more. Because while there will be questions about why I was on CCTV with my dad's blood all over me and the murder weapon in my hand, they no longer think I'm a murderer.

Does that mean I am – an impossible concept to get my head around after this long – *free?*

'Yes,' I say, voice vibrating. 'I'm Poppy Winter.'

Saying my real name feels alien now; hot chilli on my tongue.

'Would you be able to come with us to the station?'

The words are reasonable; the tone is gentle. The officer who speaks then introduces herself as Superintendent Dana Henry. She even *smiles* at me.

I nod.

'Well, I've heard a lot about you over the years, Poppy,' she says, in that warm voice again. 'Good to finally meet you.'

She doesn't grab me, handcuff me or arrest me.

Which must mean I'm right. I am free.

And despite how long I've wanted this, dreamt of it, it's hard to feel happy. Because *Eliza. Eliza.*

I slip on my other trainer. Tie my lace with shaking hands.

In the car, the two officers chat to other each in the Creole that's used on the island; colloquial and light, laidback chat between colleagues.

I stare out of the window, trying to play catch-up.

Eliza?

Eliza *confessed to murder?*

Luxurious hotel complexes roll past. The overwater bungalows that the honeymooners go back to for the night after they eat fresh lobster on the beach and sip champagne. It's what the island is most well known for. Well, that and my dad's brutal murder.

Beaches, beaches, beaches, beaches, beaches. The tourist ones – hectic and buzzing – and then the ones that the locals prefer, without the expensive restaurants and the gift shops but surrounded by green, tucked away and minding their own business. A child whose hair flies out behind him like a mane runs with a body board in neon yellow swim shorts and throws himself onto the surf.

Free.

After everything, the time, the pain, the distance, the running, the panicking, the near-misses, the hiding, I thought the crescendo would be big and loud.

In reality, it's muted. Low key. Its soundtrack is 'Shake It Off' by Taylor Swift on the car radio and a discussion, as the officers flip into English now, about which is the best route to take to the station, and whether the West Coast highway will be rammed at this time of day. The crescendo is mundane; a trip to the shop to buy onions.

◆ ◆ ◆

In a stark, overly air-conned room at the police station in Jamestown, Saint Aurélie's capital, Dana explains that while I could technically be arrested for absconding and possessing false documents, since I am no longer wanted for murder, the DPP – Director of Public Prosecutions – has decided to drop all charges.

'Eliza has explained the CCTV, the blood,' she says, eyes on mine.

I am still. Waiting.

'How you arrived after she had done it and hugged your dad,' she continues. 'How she shoved the murder weapon at you to get rid of it in a panic.'

I stare at her.

'Which means you're free,' she says, smiling at me.

'And Eliza?'

Her face contracts. 'We will try Ms Jacques. But obviously, given the situation . . .'

'Situation?'

The police officer looks up from her notes, a flash of surprise across her face. 'The situation with Ms Jacques' health?'

Eliza's sixty-five but her health is good. She swims length after length of that pool every day, before she resumes her spot on the lilo, legs dangling, hands vogueing at me as I walk past, humming to herself. She puts the top down on her sports car and floors that thing round mountain roads like she's Lewis Hamilton.

She is well. I tell them.

'What do you mean?' I ask. 'Eliza is really well.'

That look, again.

Then back at me, with a sympathy-tilt of the head. 'Poppy, Ms Jacques has told us, and doctors' notes have confirmed: she has been diagnosed with lung cancer. It's advanced. At most, she only has six months.'

HOTTER

The cough.

The weight loss.

She was breathless, wasn't she, when she walked even short distances?

How had I not realised?

I missed it all. Like I missed the fact that she was about to confess to murdering my dad. I wasn't paying enough attention.

In the corridor, I put my hands on the wall, palms first, and brace, remembering things she had said. Retrospectively connecting the dots.

There must be a way. You can't go your whole life without your sisters.

Was this the way?

And I am so busy thinking about Eliza that I don't see them.

I don't see my two sisters, standing at the other end of the police station corridor with their backs to me. The girls who are part of me, who look like my triplets. The women I would move mountains for.

'Is she here?' I hear Junie say, and I peel my hands off the wall and turn.

I stand still, just for one second, and take them in.

And then, after seven years, I say their names. Desperately. Loudly. And finally, without fear.

◆ ◆ ◆

Juno is the first of us to pull out of the knot of sisters that stand, clinging to each other and sobbing and unable to form words, in that corridor in the police station in Jamestown.

A stark space. Bright lighting. Chewing gum on the walls. A dubious stain on the floor. In the middle of that, love.

'Are you ok?' Juno asks, pulling away from me, peering at me closely. 'Are you— I've looked everywhere. Oh my God, I promise you, I tried— Are you all right? Have you been safe? We knew you didn't do it, we obviously knew. And the TV show. All of it. Where did you— And it's—'

There is too much to cover. It overwhelms all of us.

All I can do is stare at them.

'I don't get any of this,' Junie says, fingertips rubbing her temple, and I hear her and I see her and I think: *Yep, still Juno.*

Ruby, though. Ruby is different. Smaller, somehow.

She says less.

And I get it. Because I know that I am changed too. Warier. More suspicious. Cynical. My old impulsiveness is there but it is buried away now. It has to be. I think five steps ahead always, like life is a game of chess.

I am doing it now.

'Did Eliza really do it?' Juno carries on, lowering her voice as she glances past me up the corridor.

Eliza must be in one of these rooms, being questioned somewhere well away from us.

'How did she even meet Dad and Robin?' Juno doesn't wait for answers. 'I thought it was Lewis, I even thought it was *Emlyn* . . .'

She looks guiltily at Ruby. 'But never Eliza. And how did— Why did you run, Pops, if it was Eliza who did it? That's not fair, it's not—'

Her voice contains every emotion on human record.

Over her shoulder as I grasp her, I glance at Ruby. She is on the floor now, back to the wall.

I'm sorry, she mouths.

Think, Poppy.

I remember what the police told me.

'I panicked,' I tell Juno, pulling back. 'I took that breadknife from Eliza, I didn't even think, I know that's stupid but I had walked in in the middle of it and I had Dad's DNA all over me. I hadn't slept in days, I was almost delirious and then . . . Then I saw them release that CCTV and I panicked even more. I knew that everyone thought I did it and I was – I was terrified I was going to prison.'

'Seven years though?' Junie says. 'You could have— You could have *explained*! Eliza – I mean, I don't know her but she wouldn't have *wanted* you to take the blame, surely? She would have wanted to confess herself, rather than that? Why didn't she confess earlier?'

'It gets hard,' I say, eyes still on Ruby. 'It gets hard to undo things.'

Ruby looks back at me, so many things communicated in that stare.

So many secrets.

And so many lies.

COLDER

ONE YEAR LATER, CAIRNGORMS, SCOTLAND

'Macchiato,' says Juno, wading slowly towards us in chunky, wide snow boots and a thick padded black coat through a field of fresh snow.

She puts a takeaway cup into my double-gloved hands. I take a large swig straight away and strip off a layer of my tongue. Wince.

Juno hands the next drink to Ruby. 'And hot chocolate.'

Juno takes her puppy, Bodhi, from Ruby's arms and swaps him for the drink. I lean over to Bodhi and nuzzle into his soft head. He's the best comforter, and I need comfort. Eliza's funeral was only one week ago. She spent the rest of her life on bail at her home in Saint Aurélie; the trial, in the end, was delayed for medical reasons for long enough that Eliza's death came first. Even if she did outlast any forecast.

I stayed in the background at her funeral, with my sisters, unsure how people would greet us. Whether they would blame us for the way Eliza spent her final months. But when I spoke to Roland, who called himself Eliza's 'gentleman friend', he laughed heartily at that suggestion.

'House arrest in the Caribbean with her pool and good coffee and a fridge full of champagne?' he said. 'We couldn't have gifted the old girl a better last hurrah.'

Later, Junie and I vogued with Roland at the wake, which was held in a beautiful Victorian pub down a residential side road off Upper Street. Eliza had arranged it herself; she'd specifically requested that they served champagne and played Madonna.

'My best boy,' I say now, in the ridiculous voice I always speak to Bodhi in. 'Who's my best boy?'

As I pull away and try again with the lava drink, Seren whizzes with below-zero fear down a hill in front of me, face first on a sledge. Ruby sucks in her breath.

'No idea where this daredevil streak comes from,' she says, shaking her head. 'She used to prefer the sofa and a blanket.'

Juno's eyes flick to me. 'That's deffo a Poppy Winter influence.'

I smile. It *is* true that Seren and I spent six hours on the mountains together yesterday when I gave her a ski lesson and that it was me, in the end, who had to bribe her with chips so she would let me go home and thaw out. The girl doesn't tire. She also bankrupts you in snacks.

It's also true that every time I see her, depending on the season, we swim across the loch or hike to spot the mountain hares or ski and that Seren is up for it *all.* It's true that we're content in each other's company. That she makes me laugh, more than I realised a kid could.

It's true that Seren is my new favourite person, and that I love her even more than Bodhi – though she is banned from telling him that – and it makes my insides hurt that I missed so much of her when she was a baby, a toddler; that there will always be that gap.

I am changed, forever. But sometimes I think being with Seren brings me back to the old version of me more than anything else does.

'Bloody hell,' says Ruby, putting her hand out into the air. 'Is that *more* coming down?'

The UK has had more snowfall this winter than it's seen in two decades, and our mountains are the epicentre. Families are cancelling pricey trips to the Alps; throwing kit into the car and driving north from Cornwall or Kent to Scottish ski resorts instead. Every hotel in the area is booked up and mega bucks.

Even at the crematorium in East Finchley for Eliza's funeral last week, there was a weighty layer of snow on the ground. I had a hot water bottle up my coat.

Meanwhile in Saint Aurélie, they have had their own extremes. A category five hurricane hit the island last week, ripping roofs from buildings and uprooting trees. Party boat The Parrot – where Faith, the housekeeper at Green Fig, told us her son worked making cocktails – was pulled from its moorings and thrown like it was a soft toy against unforgiving rocks. It is destroyed.

Frangipani Cottage only had minimal damage, saved by its inland location and the wind-break of the rainforest. Thankfully. Because those acres, that swimming pool, that bright yellow lilo, the sour fruit of the cherry tree and the veranda: it's all ours now.

The note attached to Eliza's will said only this: *For the girls. Use it whenever you feel the need to retreat. Or to drink strong cocktails and sniff chocolate. Just like your beautiful mother did xxx*

We all use it for what we need.

Ruby is planning to go there on a make-or-break holiday with Emlyn this year. The jury is out on whether we want them to make or break; Ruby loves him, Juno and I still find him insufferably tedious.

Juno goes to Saint Aurélie whenever she can between jobs to prep for auditions and learn lines and – I imagine – to get her puzzle book soggy as she floats around on the lilo.

I like the solitude. I am grieving one of the only people who ever got me. My surrogate mum. I grieve Eliza much more than I grieved my dad. Blood's hit and miss. I go to Frangipani to sit quietly and listen to the tree frogs and to think about her, and what she did. I go to swim and to snorkel around the reefs on the south side of the island, and I go to barely see another person. But mostly I go to try to process what happened to me. To get my head around how I lost seven years of my life.

And how no-one else was to blame for that but me.

HOTTER

'Are you watching me?' shouts Seren, as she sits at the top of the hill inside her sledge.

'Of course we're watching you!' I yell back at her. 'You're a bona fide sledging legend! Olympics incoming!'

'Not sure they do sledging at the Olympics,' mutters Ruby. Then she groans, watching her daughter, as she pushes herself off the ledge and starts to hurtle downwards. 'That nut job won't even put a hat on. How is she not freezing?'

'Doesn't that remind you of someone?' Juno says to Ruby, laughing. Then she turns to me. 'Mum used to go mad at us for letting you run around in the snow without a coat when we took you out. But you wouldn't listen.'

Ruby can't watch as Seren speeds up, faster and faster down the hill. I, on the other hand, cheer her on. I only stopped sledging myself to grab this drink.

Then suddenly, Seren is off her sledge, sobbing in the snow, long and spindly limbs everywhere, classic Winter. 'Mum!'

'I'm coming! Hold on!' Ruby trips and falls in the thick snow carpet. 'Just a few seconds!'

I watch my sister, skidding and sliding down the hill and through the falling snow too, towards her daughter.

Maybe one day I'll have that. Things are possible, now. I'm at least getting a menagerie of animals.

I've come up to Scotland with Juno and Bodhi to visit Ruby and Seren for the weekend. To make the most of this mega dumping of snow.

But the rest of the time I live with them in Liverpool. Juno's been there, when I've cried for Eliza. When I've cried because I don't know who I am now. Not the Poppy who was on the run, always waiting for something and ready to flee, but not the impulsive wild child from before either. Poppy 3.0, undefined. What do I do?

'You write that bloody biography,' says Juno. 'That's what you do.'

Ruby offered me her spare room, but I knew it would cause issues with Emlyn. I'm a tall, human reminder of what happened and he doesn't want that. Emlyn likes order. Becoming a part of the chaos that landed on the Winter family is something he wants to put behind him as much as he can.

I've accepted, though, that I can't do that. I need to fold the chaos into my story. It's too much of a behemoth to hide away.

Eliza told the police that she killed my dad after an argument over the ownership of Frangipani Cottage and him trying to make a claim for it.

He wanted to sell to developers who were searching for land on Saint Aurélie that they could build on. Inland – this beautiful area by the rainforest – was being looked at as an option, as free coastal space was now a rarity.

Eliza turned up at the villa to confront him about it.

She told the police that she had heard stories over the years; enough to make her suspect that my dad was controlling of her dear friend, my mum. Wasn't that backed up by what she saw at the house – Robin's body, floating in the swimming pool? More violence, from a man she had always suspected was an alcoholic and an abuser.

And now he was coming for their sanctuary, the one that had meant so much to two independent women in the eighties? She didn't bloody think so.

Some online commentators think it's convenient that Eliza confessed to murder when she was dying and wouldn't spend any custodial time in prison anyway.

And of course, they're right.

Eliza didn't kill anyone.

JUNIE

SIZZLING

Seren's little pink glasses lie abandoned for the day on the table. She went to sleep fast after her day of sledging on the mountain. Ruby – with a grey towel on her head and in her navy fleece pyjamas and dressing gown – lights a fancy candle and puts a bottle of M&S Pinot Noir on her kitchen table. She unscrews the lid with a little *crack* and moves Seren's glasses gently onto a shelf behind her.

I look up from my puzzle book, chewed blue biro dangling from between my fingers, as she goes to the cupboard and takes out three wine glasses.

Ruby sits next to Poppy, who puts down the paperback she is reading. *Blue Sisters by Coco Mellors* is now splayed out on its front, like it's sunbathing. The blind is open: outside, lit up by the moon, I can see the snow still coming down.

'We need to talk to you,' my sister says in that old-Ruby way; that I'm-the-boss-of-you way.

We?

She glances at Poppy. Poppy nods.

I look between them. This alliance is not a common one.

'Riiiight,' I say, slowly. *What's going on?*

Poppy is fidgeting, as usual, and is in her pyjamas too, no make-up, her knees pulled up and into her chest. For a second, a wave of nostalgia sweeps over me. Across the candlelight, they look like my little sisters as kids, waiting for a bleary-eyed Mum to scoop our porridge out of the pan for breakfast as I got out the bowls.

The Rowse honey in the centre of us on the huge wooden kitchen table. Mum shouting ignored instructions for us not to dollop on too much. *Do you* want *to lose a tooth? Remember what the dentist said!*

But then I see it. Whatever this is, it's big.

The two of them are sitting across from me like they're on a job interview panel, with the weirdest expressions on their almost-identical faces. One of Poppy's hands leaves her knees; wanders up to where her tattoo is. She presses and prods the skin.

I move my puzzle book to the side. Suddenly, there is not enough saliva in my mouth.

Ruby pours me a large glass of wine. Passes it over.

'I'm ok, I don't want—' But I stop. It doesn't matter. I drag my teeth across my bottom lip. A little sweat is gathering in my armpit. 'Go on then. Tell me. Whatever this is, get on with it.'

Poppy looks at Ruby.

'Eliza didn't kill Dad,' she says.

I stare at her. 'But she confessed.'

'She lied.'

I laugh. 'Of course she didn't.'

After all these years, we have our answer. We finally know the truth. God, the relief that has come from that. And now they're trying to tell me that's not right? To take us back to the beginning?

I meet Poppy's eye contact, but she looks away.

Why would Eliza lie?

'Poppy.' I hear my voice, and it sounds like a warning.

No. *No.* After all these years, she can't be about to tell me that . . .

'Poppy,' I say again but this time it sounds like *please.* Like I am begging on my knees.

I have never asked her. Never needed to. Now, though, I ask her straight. 'Was it you?'

She shakes her head but doesn't look surprised – or upset – at the question. 'No. It wasn't me.'

'Then why did you end up with the blood on you? If Eliza's story wasn't— Why did you run? What did—'

Past theories flash across my mind:

Lewis. Emlyn. The Caribbean police force, the corruption.

But then there is a tiny sound, barely a whisper, from across the table.

'It might be easier,' says Ruby. 'If I explain.'

'Why?' I snap at Ruby but my eyes are still on Poppy. I want *Poppy's* story. *Poppy's* explanation. Typical Ruby, inserting herself into everything. 'You weren't even there.'

But there is another noise then, that comes from Ruby's throat. A sob, almost a choking sound.

It forces my eyes towards her.

'Yes,' she says, looking straight down onto the kitchen table. 'Yes, I was.'

SIZZLING

'No,' I say slowly. 'You *weren't* there. You were at the volcano with Emlyn.'

She shakes her head, the towel wrapped around her hair coming looser. Left, right. *No.*

I hold my chest.

Watch her.

I can see that she is scared of my face; scared of my reaction.

She should be.

I have never felt rage like this. Never felt any emotion like this. Not when Poppy disappeared, not when Dad died. None of it was like this. The betrayal is like a saw, and it is slicing me open down the middle.

I know Ruby's movements that day like I know my own. We have been over them with the police, in the station, in the hotel. With the family liaison officer. With each other, a thousand times. With *Lewis*. Up mountains and at 30,000 feet.

And every time, my sister – the only sister I had left – was lying to me.

'I started feeling sick on the way to the volcano,' Ruby says, quietly. 'I made Emlyn turn around. We went back to the house.'

That day had been Emlyn's thirtieth birthday. The plan was for him and Ruby to head to the drive-in volcano, where you could see the view from the top of the mountain then bathe in mud that was supposed to fix all ills. Bad backs, arthritis, eczema. The saddest sadness.

'Fingers crossed it can fix being a knobhead,' I had whispered to Poppy at the dinner table the night before, Ruby off fetching a salad. Poppy had laughed so hard, nose buried in her wine glass, that she snorted.

After the volcano, Ruby and Emlyn had gone to stay at one of the fanciest hotels on the island, The Pike, with its award-winning architecture and open view out to sea.

Hadn't they?

At Ruby's table, my hand is still clutched to my chest. 'So you didn't go to The Pike? Or the volcano?' But she had told me about the mud bath, described it in detail.

'You didn't even tell *the police* that you went back to the villa.' I can hear it in my voice: fear. 'Why did you lie to the police, Ruby?'

My middle sister, who follows rules.

It's obvious though, isn't it?

There is only one explanation for why Ruby would break the rules.

She would only do it for Seren.

Which means I was right.

Emlyn.

I come back to that thought I have had so many times. That *Ruby* persuaded me away from. That Ruby made me feel so guilty for even considering.

Emlyn.

The man who never wanted us to look for Poppy. The man who wanted us to declare her dead and move on.

All this time, Ruby has been covering for Emlyn.

'Emlyn went back to the villa with you then,' I say, a quiver in my voice. 'Right. Now this makes sense.'

I feel my whole body start to shake. The man so inane that we call him *Mr Vanilla* is the reason that my sister went on the run for seven years. My dad's killer, destroyer of my family.

I will kill him.

I could, I realise. I could kill him. I always presumed I wasn't capable of murder but I know in that second: that's not true.

Before Ruby can answer, I speak again.

'It was him,' I say, feeling like I may walk round the table and pull her up by her throat. 'And *you* covered up for him. Even though it meant your own *sister* took the blame. You fucking *coward*, Ruby.'

My voice shakes with rage, and for the first time in my life I am fearful of my own emotions. Of what I could do.

But Ruby is shaking her head. Crying. Muttering the word *no* over and over and over.

'Stop lying, Ruby,' I snarl at her.

'I'm not lying,' she says. 'It wasn't Emlyn who killed Dad, Junie, I swear to you.'

I scoff. 'Who the fuck was it then?'

And Ruby finally meets my eye contact, and says it. Just one word, that changes the world.

'Me.'

RUBY

BOILING

Junie is clutching her chest, gasping for air, and I look at Poppy in terror.

'Should I call an ambulance?' I ask her.

'Give her a minute,' my little sister says. She is next to Junie, hands on her arm. 'Juno? Just breathe. Breathe.'

Finally, Junie speaks. 'Tell me,' she says, still short of breath, as pale as if she'd fainted. 'I want to know. Tell me all of it.'

I look at Poppy. *Shit. Have we done the right thing?*

We've talked about it, both of us having a gut instinct that it's time. Eliza is gone. It's over. But maybe we should have died with this secret.

'*Tell* me.'

And I nod. Flush red. 'Ok,' I say quickly. 'It wasn't Emlyn. He didn't want us to search and he didn't want Poppy to come back because he was worried about *me* being exposed, not him.

'He was worried about Seren, about her having a mum in prison.' I wince. 'He was worried about her knowing I had killed my dad. He wasn't being selfish, Junie, even if I got mad at him at times, he was just . . . he was trying to protect me. Trying to protect our family.'

She doesn't say anything.

'Emlyn didn't even come back into the villa with me that day,' I carry on. 'He offered to, but I was so sick, I wanted to be on my own, and it was his birthday. I told him to drop me back at Green Fig, then go and do what we had planned. I said I'd let him know later if I was still ok for the hotel.'

As soon as I got back to the villa, I ran upstairs to our en suite and retched over the toilet bowl. *Those bloody prawns.* I could taste the paprika I had chucked all over them the night before. The cayenne. In the bowl in front of me, there were tiny gross globules of thick mayonnaise.

At least I was alone.

Dad and Robin were at the chaotic food market in town. They would come back later, loaded down with huge coconuts and mangoes and fresh spices that made Sainsbury's look like it sold dust. With a big bottle of local rum for cocktails and bags full of juicy limes. Dad would have bought Robin more jewellery, more trinkets.

Poppy wasn't at the villa either: she must have gone to Adeline's; the café by the beach where they didn't get pissed off that she nursed two Diet Cokes all day and took up a whole table while she wrote.

While I lay on the floor in the en suite, thinking those things, two things happened.

One: I realised that the tampons I'd packed were still in my case. My period had been due to arrive as we did but not one had been used.

Two: I heard my dad and Robin come home. They were arguing.

'It's an ego trip, Fraze!' Robin yelled, the first words that were audible from downstairs. 'You don't even like hot countries. You'd never use it. I'm sick to *death* of hearing about this thing. Can't we just enjoy the holiday? I don't want to go there again, ok, I *do not want to.*'

'It's mine.'

An exasperated sigh. 'It's not *yours*. It was *hers*.'

I crawled to a seating position. Leaned against the bathtub. I couldn't cope with people now, and definitely not shouty people. But I was curious too. What were they arguing about? Who is *her*?

I would have to figure that out later though. Right now, I had no brain space for anything else. Because I was trying to process something.

'It was morning sickness,' I tell Junie, now, at my kitchen table. 'Not the prawns.'

Pregnant, despite the endometriosis I'd been diagnosed with as a teenager, after the twelfth or thirteenth time I'd been sent home from school with period pain that made me weep.

Pregnant, despite my low ovarian reserve and despite never using contraception, and this never happening before. Despite the bleak prognosis from the doctors.

Poppy nods at a photo of Seren in her school uniform on the wall. 'I mean, there's kind of a spoiler.' She tries to smile.

Junie flinches at the sarcasm and looks at us both. 'You do realise you're breaking my fucking heart,' she says.

I look down at the table, ashamed.

'Keep going,' says Junie, cold as a Winter should be. 'I need it all now.'

As I processed the pregnancy, Robin shouted something inaudible but when Dad replied on a yell, his words were clear. 'Because I wanted them to be here when we get married, for God's sake!'

And then something quieter but clear from Robin. 'But I don't want to marry you.'

From my dad, loaded with disbelief but with flaming rage too: 'What did you just say?'

By the time my next bout of nausea was over, Robin and my dad were arguing in a higher pitch. More desperate. She was crying.

I sat up slowly and tried to make out words but all I could hear was chaos. Rage. Something clanged loudly against what I would guess was a wall. There was a scream. And then, silence.

I waited.

Nothing.

Should I go out? Leave them to it?

I leaned my ear against the wall.

But then the nausea landed again and all thoughts of my dad and Robin faded. I lurched towards the toilet.

Afterwards, I sat against the sink, a low whimper coming from my throat. And I tried to process things. Morning sickness was a good sign. I had a dim memory of Ridiculously Fecund Ellen at work telling me that. A good job, if that was true. With my endo, this was likely a one-shot situation.

I stood up slowly, holding the lip of the marble sink. I needed to get my phone from my bag downstairs. Had to tell Emlyn.

I slid the lock back on the bathroom door. I was consumed suddenly with the need to eat every carb in sight, like I had a student hangover. The message to Emlyn would have to wait. All I could think was: *bread*. Dad never went to the market without picking up fresh baguettes. As guaranteed as his bottles of rum.

Outside the bathroom though, the air was off, the silence louder than the abated screams.

'Dad?' I tried, from the top of the stairs.

I walked down and through to the huge open-plan kitchen. I was standing next to the island now, those four stools lined up underneath it, tall wooden soldiers. Underneath, there was a squashed strawberry and a piece of grated carrot. The housekeeper wasn't due back until late tomorrow; I was the only other person who tidied. But I was too distracted to feel my usual irritation.

On top of the island, the baguettes *were* there in their paper bags, pointy ends hanging out, but the nausea had come back. My appetite had disappeared again.

Everything was still, including me.

My voice came out differently. 'Robin? Dad?'

Nothing.

Something was off.

'Hello?'

Especially with the rampaging noise of earlier. This quiet was too sharp a turn.

And it was then that I spotted her. Through the open glass bifold doors that led out to the terrace and beyond that, to the long, meandering swimming pool we'd spent most of the last ten days lazing around in.

She was next to the inflatable pink sprinkled doughnut; at first I thought she was swimming. Something about that jarred though, and I quickly realised why.

Had I ever seen Robin – who wore make-up like a mask and *did not* like to get it messed up – even floating on the doughnut in the pool, let alone submerging her face like she was doing a front crawl? Doing anything more than walking across the steps on tiptoes with her manicured fingernails in the air like she was surrendering?

Never.

She wasn't doing a front crawl this time, either.

It would have been quite hard for her to do a front crawl. What with her being dead.

◆ ◆ ◆

At my kitchen table now, Junie puts her wine glass down. There is a tiny trace of tannin on her top lip. Her eyes are wild.

I look at Poppy and see it on her face too: a fear that this is too much, that this will be unbearable. That I have broken Junie, and she won't forgive me.

There's no choice now, though.

I need to carry on.

Not with Netflix's narrative, or Eliza's. But finally, with the real one.

I was about to run to Robin when I heard my dad's voice.

'Don't bother, Rubes. It's too late.' He was sitting with one leg crossing his knee, on a beige armchair in the corner of the kitchen.

When I spun round, my arm knocked against a baguette. 'But it might not be . . . She could . . .'

'It's. Too. Late,' he said, pronouncing every syllable. He had a glass of red wine in his hand; his eyes were a little dazed. *'Leave her.'*

He stood and put the wine down on a worktop. Then he picked up a baguette from the island and took it out of its paper bag. Reached for the bread knife and sawed himself a slice.

What was he doing?

I turned away in disgust and headed towards the bifolds. But he put the breadknife down, reached out and yanked me backwards.

'No.'

Then he went back to his snack. Took out another knife and carefully buttered his thin oval of bread.

I watched him, confused. Why was he acting like this? Why would he not want me to go to her? Unless. *Unless.*

'Have you called someone?' I asked, eyes on him. 'Have you called an ambulance, Dad?'

He raised an eyebrow and half smiled. 'Ambulances aren't for dead people, Ruby.'

Then he put down his butter knife and walked past me, still eating the bread. With his other hand, he calmly turned the lock of the bifold door and stood in front of it, barefoot with his chest puffed out like a nightclub bouncer.

'How did she—' I tried. But I stopped.

My brain was hissing: *You know the answer. But if you don't want to hear it, then don't ask.*

Instead we stayed silent, fixed to our spots. Actors before the curtain goes up.

My dad finished chewing. He leaned his head back, stretching or despairing, I'm not sure which. I trained my eyes on his Adam's apple. When his face came back down, he looked like his soul had fled. 'She pissed me off,' he said, eyes cold.

And I was shaking my head by then, crying quietly, *no, no, no*, but a little part was saying *This is who you are. It's who you've always been.*

The part whose earliest memory had fallen into full view by then. Screeching car tyres as Dad's Land Rover pulled into the drive of our family home, deep in the mountains. The radio alarm next to my bed had said 1.35 a.m. The door opened and then, as the clock flicked to 1.36 a.m., I had heard my mum's scream pierce a hole in the air.

There were other memories, of course. Other images.

The raging burn up my mum's forearm that was the same shape as the iron. I'd started my period the day before and I saw it as she made me a hot water bottle. Her eyes followed mine. She slowly pulled down the sleeve of her turquoise jumper. Neither of us said a word.

A few days before she died, when I picked up the upstairs landline to call a schoolfriend and heard Mum whisper on the phone to someone – Eliza, even? – that she was leaving Dad. When I put the phone down in a panic. Told no-one. And then so soon after, she was dead anyway.

I thought about what I had heard Robin say. *I don't want to marry you.*

'It was because she was leaving you,' I said to my dad in Saint Aurélie. 'Same as Mum. She was leaving you, and you couldn't handle it. *Again.*'

'What did you just say?'

His eyes looked different to normal, and I regretted what I had said instantly. But I couldn't think about that. This – talking, arguing, remembering – was all wasting valuable seconds. Minutes, even. God knows how long it had been since Robin . . .

Behind him, I saw a flinch of movement. It could have just been the breeze moving Robin's body. But what if it wasn't? What if she could be saved?

I went to push past him.

'Ow!'

He grabbed me, hard on the sides of my arms, pincering firmly enough to bruise. I thought about that burn. 'I'm your father,' he hissed, 'and I'm telling you, *no*.'

Control and control and control.

'You're my father and you're telling me no?' The laugh was nervous but sounded mocking. 'Are you kidding me?'

And he slapped me then, hard across the face. The shock was intense. I was still reeling when he did it again.

Another flashback, then. My dad, hitting me so hard on the leg that it came up in a huge ugly bruise. The next day at school, friends laughed at me for wearing tights. It was the last day of term, twenty-four degrees at lunchtime. Sweat pooled behind my knees.

In the kitchen in the Caribbean, I went to hit back but I was inexpert, flailing hands landing on my dad's face and chest, before he grabbed my wrists and held them tight.

'You're leaving a woman to die,' I said.

And the thought was even more lucid: *Was she even the first?*

I was fifteen when Mum died. The adults told me how it happened and I, of course, accepted it. Sobbed my heart out under my duvet. Decided I would never believe in God again. Went running for hours, loud Kelly Clarkson on my iPod, trying to drown out the noise in my head. *My mum, gone.* I never told anyone that I had heard her planning to leave him. Now that she was dead, how could I sully the image of their glamorous marriage; her the supermodel, him the tall, brooding businessman?

I never, ever questioned the story of how she died. Why would I?

Then, though . . .

Mum's body – along with that of a twenty-seven-year-old man named Lorenzo Conti, a winter hiking enthusiast from the Dolomites – was never found. She had been hiking in sub-zero conditions, alone. Wanted to clear her head. Was struggling with 'her nerves'.

According, of course, to Dad.

In Saint Aurélie, I thought about something else: the way I'd caught Poppy looking at Dad, often, on that holiday. Loathing.

Thoughts swirled. I couldn't quite make the dots connect, but there was something. Something dark. A question Poppy had asked me a few months earlier: 'Were Mum and Dad happy, before she died?' I had told her a solid *yes*, despite what I had heard on that phone call. I didn't want to taint her memories.

I shoved past Dad to go to Robin. He stopped me again.

I was only a few inches shorter than him but he weighed twice what I did, and despite his age – he was sixty-six – he was at the gym three times a week. A few months ago, he'd done the Great North Run in just over two hours.

The part I go over, in the early hours, when I reach for the pills, when I chase oblivion, is the different way life would have swung if I'd never come back to the villa that day.

As Dad's age-spotted hands landed on my arms again to stop me going to Robin, something else came into sharp focus: *the baby.*

My baby would be an adult one day. They might need someone to help them. They would deserve that.

And then, as I moved my arm, I felt it, its handle at my right elbow.

The breadknife with the neon green handle that had just been used to saw off the end of that baguette but which I also used then to shock my own dad. To snap him out of his rage, and get him to back off, so that I could try and help Robin.

But he panicked. I saw that fly across his face. He thought I was going to use it.

And when he lunged forward to grab the breadknife from me, and he was near to my belly, my baby, I panicked too. And I *did* use it.

Afterwards, I found out that the breadknife hit his aorta. That's what caused him to bleed out so fast. Why it was so impossible to stop the flow.

Eight years later, in my kitchen, tears stream down my face.

'I did it,' I repeat.

I can't look at Junie.

'I'm sorry,' I whisper, facing the table. 'I'm sorry.'

And my shoulders shake with the release and the guilt that I have never learnt to co-exist with. That taunts me every second.

After my sobs, though, comes silence. It might last for thirty seconds. It may go on for five minutes. I am not sure any of us know.

We just wait. We wait until Junie, who I have kept in the dark for so long, who I have lied to so many times, is ready.

'Are you a fucking psychopath?' she says finally.

I pull backwards, away from her. Take a sharp intake of breath.

The worst thing is how calm she sounds.

'Honestly, I think you must be, to lie to my face like that, so many times,' she says. 'You're my *sister.*' She stares at me, eyes wide and unbelieving. 'And that's before we even get on to why the fuck you let our *little* sister take the blame for what *you* did for seven years. It would have been longer, too. Only Eliza helped with that. Not you.' She is spitting the words at me now. 'You fucking *coward.*'

But before either of us can speak, Junie shoves her chair backwards, stands up and flings open the back door.

'I can't breathe,' I hear her say.

I watch her from behind. Hunched over, hands on her knees. Reeling. Because of me.

'Do we go after her?' I ask Poppy, still hearing it. *Are you a fucking psychopath?*

Poppy shakes her head. Even after all that time away, she knows Junie better than me.

'Give her a minute,' she says.

But then Junie reappears.

'It's not even the part where you killed our dad, though that is a pretty fucking huge thing,' she says, framed in the doorway. I shake with the cold air that blows in, but Junie is in a T-shirt and doesn't seem to notice.

'But you didn't tell me and you lied to me constantly, *every fucking day*, Ruby!' She is shouting, uncontrolled. 'Everything we have been through together. You have broken my heart. You have ripped me apart.'

A coldness runs through my body that, now, is not to do with the door being open. But about a fear. A terror. *She's lost to me. There is no coming back from this. And she's Junie.*

'It was my fault,' Poppy says, desperately, eyes on us both. 'Before I went, I told Ruby not to tell you. I thought . . . I thought it was the right thing. That otherwise you were implicated and then you could get in trouble yourself.'

'So fucking WHAT?' shouts Junie. 'Do you think that would have mattered to me? You're my sisters.'

Then I see Junie process something, and when she speaks again, it is quieter and more deliberate. She is looking at Poppy.

'What do you mean, *you* told her not to tell me before you went?'

'I'm sorry, Ju—' I start.

'I don't care,' she spits, glowering at me. 'Don't you bother saying sorry, don't you bother saying anything to me.' She turns to Poppy. '*You* just tell me why you took the blame. I presume that's what this is? You made it look like you did it, with the CCTV? To make it seem like it was you to the police?'

Poppy nods, small and sheepish.

'But why?'

Poppy glances at the photo of Seren.

'Oh,' says Junie, realising. 'Oh.'

POPPY

BURNING

Junie's anger is electric. The room sparks with it.

I reach with a shaking hand for my wine glass but stop myself.

No.

My dad was an alcoholic. The kind of alcoholic who would make you feel ludicrous if you suggested it, of course. He didn't drink at 9 a.m. He held down a job, and he looked smart. But if there was alcohol around, he drank it compulsively and fast. We lived in the middle of nowhere and there were no taxis, but being designated driver didn't make a difference. We often climbed into the Defender when I knew Dad was over the limit.

I push my glass away, with difficulty. Addiction can be genetic *and it* is up to me now, to work out who I want to be. It is not him.

'I came back from Adeline's and I found Ruby staring at Robin's body in the pool,' I tell Junie. 'I screamed at her to help me get her out but . . .'

I glance at Ruby.

'She didn't move. Shock, maybe. I don't know.'

I was in the water quickly, doing a front crawl towards Robin.

I'd been confused. Why was Ruby even there? She was supposed to be at the volcano for Emlyn's birthday.

Then she said, from the side of the pool: 'I'm pregnant.'

Treading water in my long-sleeved, billowing sundress, I looked up at her.

Now?

She was telling me this now?

In any other world, I would have been euphoric. But there was a dead woman in front of us. It wasn't the fucking moment.

I reached Robin, and tried to heave her out but it was like weightlifting an *elephant*. How was she this heavy? Those bare bum cheeks; that tiny frame.

'Jesus Christ, *help* me, Ruby!' I panted.

She still stood there.

I finally stopped trying to heave Robin's body out of the pool when I registered that Ruby was covered in blood. And when she said something else. 'Dad's dead, too.'

At the kitchen table, a noise comes out of Junie's throat, like she is hearing that news for the first time.

I remember climbing out of the water and sitting on the end of a thickly padded grey sunbed cushion. Sun beating down on my wet arms as I got my breath back. As I took in those words. *Dad's dead, too.*

Then Ruby told me, staccato, everything that had happened. How Dad came for her. What she did to him.

At first, I couldn't speak. We stayed there, in that uncomfortable tableau, Robin floating next to the inflatable doughnut, Ruby staring ahead. Me, dripping onto the sunbed.

She couldn't mean this. This couldn't be real.

'Wasn't there a chance it was self-defence?' Juno asks now. 'If she—'

Ruby shakes her head. Winces. 'Poppy asked that, at the time. But I knew how many times I'd—'

Ruby had glanced towards the villa kitchen, where she'd told me Dad's body was. 'Wait until you see him,' she'd said. 'No-one would call that self-defence.'

Then, with barely blinking eyes, she'd finally looked at me. 'He hurt Mum, didn't he? And you found out.'

And I didn't know how she'd worked it out. But I was pretty sure she was right. Researching Mum's biography had led me to the same conclusion. Mum hadn't been in the mountains on the day of the avalanche; she had been at home with the flu.

Safe, then. Except that I know it now, as an adult. Sometimes your home can be more dangerous than any icy mountain. Even when the forecast says *avalanche*.

My mum had been ill in bed. She was a sitting duck.

There were plenty of hints in the diaries. Never explicit: I think Mum was too scared to even write it in there. But there was enough to pick up on, once you were looking for it. Eliza said Mum had been the same with her. Comments she'd made. Hints she'd dropped. Bruises she had tried to cover. Enough to make Eliza suspect that her friend's marriage was not a happy one.

I look up at Juno. 'Carry on,' she mutters.

'I remember Ruby telling me that if she had a girl, she would call her Seren,' I say. 'Seren Maria.'

Ruby is crying, audibly. She looks at Juno, eyes pleading for something. 'I knew they wouldn't even let me hold her, Junie, if they knew what I'd done. It was never meant to . . . but after everything I had—'

Ruby had been told there was near-zero chance of her getting pregnant, with the severity of her endometriosis plus her extremely low ovarian reserve. She had a perfect storm of fertility blockers.

But somehow. *Somehow.*

I was too selfish – aged twenty-five – to spend my life in a Caribbean jail cell. But I was not too selfish to know that Ruby's child couldn't grow up without a mum. I had struggled from the age of twelve without mine. I was not too selfish to know that Ruby couldn't be taken away from her baby because of a split-second decision.

So I made my own split-second decision.

I scanned mentally through the week's movements at Green Fig. The housekeeper wasn't due until late tomorrow; Junie even later. I had a long window.

'Tell Emlyn to come back and get you,' I had said to Ruby. She was still standing next to the pool. I walked to her. Put my hands on her bare shoulders. Shook her, ever so slightly. 'Do all the things you'd planned to do today. Make sure people see you doing them. Speak to people. Then go and meet Junie tomorrow, like you were going to anyway.'

There was a beat before I added: 'Don't tell her anything. Don't tell *anyone* anything.'

'I have to tell Emlyn,' she said, eyes wide. 'I can't get in the car now and not—'

'Fine,' I accepted. 'But just him.'

At the kitchen table, Junie snorts. '*Emlyn* knows? You could tell Emlyn but not me? Oh, this gets better and better.'

She stands up and walks to the patio doors. Kicks the glass, hard. Slams the heel of her hand into the wall. And then, she starts to cry.

'I did *everything* for you,' she says through her tears as she turns to me. 'I shouted your innocence from the rooftops. I never stopped looking. I put my life on hold because in the end, *everything* came down to what I could do to prove you didn't do it.' She wipes the back of her hand across her nose. 'I spent everything I had. I couldn't bear the idea that the world thought that about you. I would have done anything to find another suspect. To make everyone see you like I did.'

My head is bowed low.

'It was bad enough when I thought it was just Lewis, that you couldn't trust me with your relationship. But this. My fucking *heart*, Poppy.'

I duck my head even lower. Shake with silent sobs.

Ruby says *sorry, sorry, sorry*.

But I don't. Because I wouldn't mean it.

My mum used to wince when she saw me throw myself down a mountain on a snowboard or face first on a sledge: *my Pops, no fear.* She would kiss my face all over and squeeze me tighter at bedtime and whisper that I had a special one-of-a-kind spark, a magic, a power, a *charge*. That she loved how I didn't overthink things. That I threw myself in; that I *lived*.

Teachers at school viewed it differently. Junie and Ruby were academic. I came through third with an expectation set out that was never met. School reports used words like *impulsive, impetuous, wilful, distracted*.

My dad said it was simpler: I was just naughty.

At the villa that day, in those minutes when we were alone with the bodies, Ruby showered and changed. I took her other clothes from her. 'I'll get rid of those,' I told her.

And I went into the kitchen.

Well, she wasn't exaggerating: she hadn't stopped at one defensive stab wound. I winced, looking at the blood, the body. Something in Ruby had snapped like a stick of rock.

I closed my eyes as I hugged my dad but the hug was functional; I needed to make sure that my DNA was all over his body. By then, it was the only reason I would have hugged him.

When Emlyn pulled into the drive, I walked with Ruby to the left side gate of the villa where there were no cameras, and as Emlyn opened the passenger door, I shoved her into the Suzuki. 'Go,' I told a bewildered Emlyn. 'She'll explain. Go.'

I watched them drive away, hoping that Mr Vanilla would step up – for once – and give Ruby an alibi. She was having his child, for God's sake.

When the Suzuki disappeared from view, I looked around. We were isolated at Green Fig; there wasn't a person for miles. No-one else knew Ruby had come back here this morning. No-one had seen her drive away.

I got a change of clothes, then I picked up that breadknife with the neon green handle – if anyone queried why Ruby's DNA was on it, that would be easily explainable. She prepped every meal we ate.

I walked out of the other side gate, the one that I knew had the camera trained on it, making sure the breadknife was visible. Then I got changed quickly behind a mango tree and left my clothes in a bundle there. I drove to the airport in Dad and Robin's sports car.

Impulsive. No fear. A death wish.

I hoped that the police would apply Occam's Razor: the most obvious solution is the right one.

I was on CCTV holding a blood-smeared knife. I have a bad relationship with my dad. My DNA was on the body. Robin's too, from when I tried to heave her out of that swimming pool. I guessed they would either blame my dad for Robin's death, or think I killed them both.

And now, I'd run. Who runs? Guilty people.

But here is another truth, an uncomfortable one. You know who also runs? Women who are unhappy. Women who have just had an enforced break from the copious amounts of cocaine that their boyfriend, Lewis, who didn't roam around the world because he was a *free spirit* but because he was a drug dealer, supplied to them.

I had been trying to get away from Lewis for a long time. Every time, I was pulled back. Back and back and back and back and back.

Lewis didn't want to meet my family. I didn't want him to meet my family. *Hey, here's my drug dealer boyfriend.*

But he still turned up on Saint Aurélie on my family holiday, to make sure I didn't leave him for good. That four thousand miles wasn't far enough for me to finally break the cycle.

Surprise! Michelin-star dinner booked. Yacht ready and waiting. And of course, my first line of coke since I'd been here. Then my second. Third.

Once I was back in, I couldn't see how I would ever be out.

I worry about becoming addicted to alcohol because I am an addict, just like my dad. Ruby too, perhaps: she told me about the pills.

Juno and Ruby know this part. Ruby has known since the night of the murders, at the hotel when Emlyn told her about a row he'd had with me a few days before, after he found me doing a line in the villa kitchen. When I came back, Juno asked how I'd got a new identity without any dodgy contacts. I told her about Lewis then.

You know who also runs? Women who are trying to leave something behind. Women who are desperate.

That was a part of it. I needed to break the cycle.

On Saint Aurélie that day, I made a snap decision that severed my life into two parts. I covered for Ruby for seven years, at first roaming those anonymous places that cities do so well – hostels and backstreets and libraries and parks – before I felt confident that I could live more fully. That I could start again, with that new identity.

Sarah.

I settled into the cheapest studio apartment I could find on the north edge of Glasgow. I got a job in the sweating kitchen of an edgy coffee shop. I didn't make friends. I was quiet. I went to Loch Lomond in my boots and I walked. I bought a second-hand laptop and I wrote – poetry, oddly enough. It helped that I was never sociable anyway; I lived a solitary life with ease.

Now, in Ruby's kitchen, Juno looks at me.

'You can ask anything. Whenever. I want to help. Explain.'

My eldest sister takes a long, deep gulp of her wine. Then she looks at me.

'You sent me a message that day,' she says, frowning. 'But you deleted it before I read it. What did it say? I was so pissed off with myself for not reading it. That bugged me.'

I nod. 'Yeah, I remember. I sent it just before I threw my phone into the sea, with Ruby's clothes.' My voice cracks. 'It just said I loved you. That's all.'

'Why delete it then?'

I shrug. 'Panicked? I thought if I sent *anything* to you, the police might link you to things. Think it was some sort of code.' I shake my head. 'I don't know. It felt safer for it to be gone. Even though I realised afterwards that the police could probably recall it anyway.'

'Did you send Lewis that message with the date of mum's death on it too?' Juno asks, putting her glass back down.

I nod.

I *hated* contacting Lewis – about that and, later, for the new identity. But his was the only number apart from my sisters' that I knew by heart.

'I'd been researching Mum's biography and I was suspicious about her death. About things not lining up.

'Then Ruby said something that day, at the villa. She was suspicious too. She had overheard Mum make this phone call, before she died. I couldn't send a proper message, spelling it out. But I thought that one would make you look into it more.'

I knew Ruby's phone would be tracked. Same with Juno's. But Lewis had a phone no-one knew about; a burner. I knew him well enough to know that he would take the message to them; would love inserting himself into things, thinking he had information. He wouldn't be able to help it.

I reach out to my side and squeeze Ruby's hand. 'I thought it might help ease some guilt. I don't know.'

Juno stares at us both. 'I wouldn't have said a word. You must know that?'

'That wasn't the point.'

You can get years in prison – seven in the Caribbean – for covering for a murderer. Enough mess had been made.

'I nearly told you,' Ruby says to Juno, her own tears torrential now. 'God, so many times, Junie.'

Next to me, Rubes wipes at her eyes, nose, with a tissue from the box on the table but it's a deluge.

'But Poppy was right, it would have been unfair. I didn't want you to have to hide something too.' She pauses. 'It doesn't do good things to your head.'

'Is that why you stopped speaking to me?'

Ruby nods, but it's overtaken her. She is crying too much to speak now.

'I tried really hard to stay close to you,' says Juno, pulling out a tissue of her own.

'It got too difficult.'

Juno stands up. Paces the room for a while, wine glass in her hand. But at least she isn't kicking things any more.

She turns to Ruby. 'We talked about Mum and the avalanche on the plane back to Saint Aurélie,' she says to Ruby. 'I said to you that it was weird. And you lied to me. *Again.*'

Ruby nods. 'I know. I'm sorry. I panicked. I didn't want to tell you the conversation I'd had with Poppy. Because it was when— It strayed too close. To that day and what happened. And I had tried so hard to keep you out of it.'

But Juno is not focused on that. 'Should we go to the police?' she says, frowning. 'If we really think that Dad did kill Mum, then said she was at the— That he saw the news and saw an opportunity to explain away something he'd snapped and done, is that what we— That he blamed it on the avalanche but really it was—'

Sentence after sentence, all too grim to finish.

'They could look for a body,' she says. 'We could have a proper burial.'

But Ruby immediately looks up and shakes her head, eyes wide and pleading.

'No. I know the body would mean something, but the odds of finding it are— I know I don't deserve to ask you anything, any favour, but please, Junie, not the police.'

I look at Ruby and know she feels the same as I do. She still lives in fear of the police. We don't want to invite them to our door. I hold my breath and wait.

'Ok. No police.'

I feel Ruby exhale.

'Why did you come to Saint Aurélie?' Juno asks, turning to me. 'You'd found out all this stuff about Dad. You hated his guts. So why come on the holiday?'

'I wanted to know why Dad was going to that island, of all places,' I say. 'I knew it couldn't be a coincidence, that Frangipani was there. I told Eliza I'd report back.'

Juno nods, and I can see a grain of the rage abating.

'To see if he could make a claim for it?' she asks. 'Sell it off to developers and make a shitload of cash?'

I nod. 'Yeah.' Then I think about Eliza and her chutzpah. 'Fat chance Eliza would have let that happen, even if he'd lived long enough to put it in place.'

I pause. 'Mostly though, I came because I wanted to go on holiday with you two.'

Something curls up inside my throat.

'I could even tolerate Dad for that.'

But we are still way off any smiles from Juno. Way off any bonding. Ruby and I decided together to tell her, knowing there would always be a piece missing otherwise and that we couldn't live like that. But fear runs through me: *will we ever get there?*

'I can't believe Emlyn was in on this,' Juno says, turning to Ruby. 'Of all people.'

She looks at me. 'I really thought it was him, you know. Emlyn.' She laughs, brittle, and turns to Ruby. 'When you held back, I thought it was because you were covering for him, because he was your husband and he'd asked you to. But the whole time it was . . .'

She trails off, shakes her head in disbelief. Slips her right hand into her mouth and bites her bare nails.

'I saw him speaking to the officers before they'd even got inside the station that day,' she says. 'God, I thought he was trying to get his story out as fast as he could because he'd—'

Ruby nods. 'I think he was trying to get his *alibi* out as fast as he could. To remember what I'd told him to say. It didn't come naturally to him, lying.'

Juno nods. 'No. I can imagine.'

'He loved her,' I say quietly. 'She was having his baby. I suppose that's the only thing that supersedes moral code.'

Ruby smiles, sadly. 'I still don't know if we'll make it. Sometimes I see him, staring at me in the kitchen when I'm boiling pasta for Seren or something and I can tell he's thinking: *You killed your own dad. And you made me complicit.*'

Her voice cracks. 'We struggle.'

At that moment, the best thing about Ruby's struggling marriage comes into the room, hair sticking up at funny angles, eyes blinking into the lamplight. 'I can't sleep,' says Seren Maria.

Ruby drains the dregs from her wine glass and stands. 'Come on.' She sighs. 'I'll tuck you in.'

Juno and I watch them walk out of the room, blowing kisses to our adored mini-me in her bare feet and slightly too small *Harry Potter* pyjamas.

Suddenly something crosses Juno's face. A memory. A realisation. 'Hey. Early on. Were you in my backyard?'

I nod. 'Sorry if I freaked you out.'

Something kinder crosses Juno's face then. She looks up at me, tracing her finger round the rim of her glass. 'You did all of that. For Ruby.'

'Mostly for Seren.'

'Did you regret it?' she says. 'I know what you're like and I imagine you decided to help her on a ridiculous bloody whim. But afterwards . . . Doing that for Ruby, when it meant your own life was so . . .' She glances towards the kitchen door. 'I know you wouldn't say it to her—'

But I am already shaking my head. 'I started to. I started to get really resentful, actually, even though it had been my choice. And terrified too, that I had made this, like, undoable catastrophic error and it had been typical me, exactly like you said, *done on a whim, on an impulse, typical Poppy, not thought out.*'

All the stuff everyone had said about me, my whole life.

'What changed?'

I think. 'I saw Ruby. I was back near home again. I saw her bump – she was getting big by then – and I remembered *why* I'd done it. And all the other stuff wasn't important. It was a reminder. After that, it was easy to stay away.' I bite my lip. 'Until I found out about the TV show.'

'And that's when it started? The sightings, the wildlife park . . .'

I dip my head low. 'Yeah.'

'All because of the TV show?'

'I was worried,' I say, nodding. 'I didn't think Ruby could cope with seeing that portrayal of me, and the guilt of it. I thought she might do something daft and confess. I wanted to tell her it was ok. I could live with that being the narrative. I was used to it, she wasn't. The last thing I wanted after everything we had done was for her to fuck it up now by handing herself in anyway. Seren being left without her, which was exactly what we had wanted to avoid in the first place.

'But I couldn't quite do it. I couldn't quite make contact. I was too worried that that would fuck everything up in a *different* way.'

Junie walks round to my side of the table, and holds me, tight. 'I'm still pissed off that you both lied to me. And I don't know how long that will take me to— But I do think you're an amazing person. I don't think I could have done it.'

'Hard disagree,' I say, muffled into her jumper. 'I think you'd have done it in a *shot* for either of us.'

'You know what I hated most when you were away,' she says, when we break away from each other. She is examining my face closely. Peering. She touches my cheek. 'The thought that you were unhappy. While you were away and alone. *Were* you?'

Ruby walks back in at that moment. Stands in the doorway and holds her breath, seeing us there, close, hearing the question and waiting for my answer.

I smile at her. Then at Juno. 'Not always, no. There were some fun times. Really *joyous* times, actually, in among it. I met some good people.'

That feeling, of being hunted, of looking over my shoulder, was exhausting. More terrifying at points than death. I have stood on bridges. I have walked too close to the platform edge.

But I also stood at summits. On the edge of lochs, soaked and buzzing. A lot of the time, I was happy. I didn't take drugs any more. That temper that had raged when I took coke had gone.

Once the identity was sorted, I cut contact with Lewis. He couldn't find me. It was simple and I was free, in the oddest of ways.

And then, all these years later, Eliza stepped in, like that bread-knife was a relay baton and it was her turn to take it, to slip it up the sleeve of her silk blouse and walk with her immaculately pedicured toes, into the path of that security camera.

In my head, as I read the note that she had slipped under that cocoa tin, written in her beautiful handwriting, she was saying it gently: *No more. It's my turn now, my darling. Rest.*

ACKNOWLEDGEMENTS

Firstly, thanks to the readers. I am so grateful that you've picked up my book, and I hope that you enjoyed it, fell into it and that it made you get into bed early and get lost in a story because that is my own favourite thing in the world to do. It's why I write.

Thanks to the team at DHH and particularly my agent Diana Beaumont, as ever, for the holy trinity of career/financial solvency/sanity. And for being so in the know that you get us tables at the best lunch spots in town. And for schlepping up to Chester mid-week to eat chorizo and drink champagne with me. And mostly, for being my friend.

To Hannah Shaw, the kindest, gentlest editor of all time. Hannah, I knew very early on that you got me, which as a writer/super emotional, sensitive human is so important and valued. Thank you. To the rest of the team at Thomas and Mercer, a huge thanks for everything, with special mention to mega fixer Nicole Wagner (apologies for my eight thousand emails) and to my OG editor Vic Haslam – you are missed and we can't wait to have you back.

Next, to my Development Editor Russel McLean, who I don't ever want to write a book without to be honest. Is that ok? Can we sign something re that? Thank you for everything Russel, especially for the in-depth chats about my third-person phobia, how to acquire a fake identity (book characters, not me) and how levels of twattishess vary across geographical regions north of the border. Thank you for gently guiding the book to where it needed to be, with so many LOLs along the way. I'm sorry again that it didn't have any Lululemon.

To my copy-editor, Anna Paterson and proofreader, Ian Howe. Thanks for paying attention to detail when my easily distracted brain has long since left dates, timings and detail behind and sailed excitedly onto the next chapter/book/what I'm going to have for dinner.

Thanks to all the Caribbean and Cairngorms locals who answered my questions. Pretty much everyone I spoke to in Scotland recommended Nan Shepherd's beautiful book *The Living Mountain* and they were right, it was invaluable (FYI, I did my own research on two trips to the Cairngorms with my family, but it was tricky because I was mostly not allowed to do anything but push sledges down hills – love you, boys).

Thank you to David Mellor (not that one), who styled Eliza, and to Hayley Doyle – a beautiful writer whose debut came out at the same time as mine – who told me everything I needed to know about the acting profession AKA how my life could have gone if I'd run with that Theatre Studies A level. Zoe McGurnaghan and Susie Dunham – there's still time . . .

Thanks to the RLF, who have been such a support to me as a writer, and to the magical book community, especially our little corner of it in the North West. Special note to my ADORED local indie Linghams (I have had it confirmed: I am an unofficial staff member), to Waterstones Liverpool, to The Mold Bookshop and Cheshire West Libraries.

The last year has been, for me, about finding pockets of bookish community to fend off the writing isolation (wri-solation? Sorry), so thank you to our Wirral Writers' group and to the

Chester Society of Authors crew, as well as the iconic Storyhouse for hosting us.

More widely, thanks to the writer pals who have supported with endorsements and social media posts, especially to Andrea Mara and John Marrs for the cover quotes for *The Next Woman*.

As ever, Lucy Vine, Daisy Buchanan and Harriet Johnson, AKA Diana's Dames: you are the nearest thing I've had to colleagues since I last worked in an office in 2013 – and as a bonus you don't bring pungent lunches in and cook them in the work microwave. Legends.

Thanks to Mum and Dad, for everything but particularly for instilling a love of reading that has been the most constant comfort of my life. There is permanently a pile of books next to my front door that I am passing on to my super-reader mum, and my dad is front row and centre at as many of my events as he can get to. As a parent, I'm paying it forward: just ask our local library (we'll return those eighty-seven books soon, Steph, I promise).

On, then, to my boys, who inform so much of the colour of my books. From *Dog Man* to *Gladiators* to a sneaky six-seven reference, these books double as a record of a moment in time, and are filled to the brim with you (side note: the parts where Junie and Ruby are navigating the scree and fearing for their lives are entirely for you though, my lovely friend, Jo Robotham).

Simon! It was very handy having an outdoorsy, hardy husband for this book. Especially when I personally take on more of a Maria-Winter-in-the-eighties role; lounging on the sofa under a blanket and leaving lipstick marks on my glass of Shiraz. Thanks for your wisdom on walking kit and more widely, for being the voice of reason and calm in the face of my emotive publishing rollercoaster whirlwind.

Lastly, and most importantly in a book that is at its core about sisters, thank you to Gem, who is the best and kindest sister in the world. You will never know how much I appreciate everything you have done for me in life, but especially for that three-week window in 2018/2019. There's no-one with a heart as big as yours. Just so you know, if you did happen to go on the run for a murder you didn't commit, I would find you and clear your name. If you could head to the Caribbean and not the Cairngorms though, that would be preferable.

ABOUT THE AUTHOR

Photo © 2022 Dan Bentley

A former journalist across magazines including *Grazia*, *Marie Claire*, *Stylist* and several of the UK's national newspapers, Caroline is now a *Sunday Times* bestselling author. Her work has been translated into multiple languages and sold around the world.

Her novels, often described as psychological thrillers, are also very much books about the female experience, tackling themes such as infertility, domestic violence, motherhood, sexual assault and mental health.

When not writing, Caroline is usually reading, going to book club, or interviewing fellow authors at her local bookshops. Some people might say she needs more varied hobbies.

You can follow Caroline Corcoran on Instagram at @carolinecorcoranwriter.

Follow the Author on Amazon

If you enjoyed this book, follow Caroline Corcoran on Amazon to be notified when the author releases a new book!
To do this, please follow these instructions:

Desktop:

1) Search for the author's name on Amazon or in the Amazon App.
2) Click on the author's name to arrive on their Amazon page.
3) Click the 'Follow' button.

Mobile and Tablet:

1) Search for the author's name on Amazon or in the Amazon App.
2) Click on one of the author's books.
3) Click on the author's name to arrive on their Amazon page.
4) Click the 'Follow' button.

Kindle eReader and Kindle App:

If you enjoyed this book on a Kindle eReader or in the Kindle App, you will find the author 'Follow' button after the last page.
Follow the Author on Amazon
Cipit restium ex excerat ibusci inciditatet rem idebis vitium quodis sant remquid elitatestios simperi tatusciist harum facient volupta simagnam, ut ulpari te moluptameni que liquos cus accullaborem voluptios estem sam faceperum aut abo. Nem aut et velita cum, officienti dolente prestrum si omnistium cullabo rrovit aboratem faccum, occus.